Double Dealing: A Detective Sergeant Catherine Bishop Novel

This book is a work of fiction and any resemblance to persons either living or dead or to actual events or circumstances is entirely coincidental.

Authors note: Northolme, its residents and its police officers do not exist and although some of the locations used do, they are used here in a purely fictional context. Although Lincolnshire Police is obviously a real organisation, it has no affiliation with this book.

MYS
Pbk

Cover art designed by paperandsage.com

For Tracy

1

Midnight. She was cold, her shivering uncontrollable. She hunched on the filthy carpet, her arms wrapped around her knees, nausea rising in her throat. The two men who had collected her were somewhere in the house, though she hadn't seen them for a while. They'd given her water and food but had left her alone now in this awful room after showing her where the toilet was, the bowl lined with plastic sheeting. She knew only too well what they were waiting for. Blinking tears from her eyes, she wished she had never agreed to this. It had been terrifying, from the moment she'd said she would do it to arriving here, grubby, humiliated and longing to be at home. Her stomach was bloated and felt enormous. She shifted her weight, trying to find a position that was a little more comfortable but it was impossible. Sniffing again, she wiped the tears away with the back of her hand. It would be worth it. She was so nearly there now, and then it would be okay. It would be over and she could go home. Trying to relax, to allow nature to take its course, she stretched out her legs. There was a buzzing sound in her head, louder and louder, and she raised a trembling hand, trying to swat the noise away as if it were an annoying house fly. It didn't work. The sound grew louder. She moaned a little, swiping at her ears with her hands.

There was a sudden explosion of colour behind her eyes, a kaleidoscope of reds, greens and blues; every shade she'd seen before and some she'd never dreamed of. She felt ill and disorientated, her mind reeling, every sense overwhelmed in a second. Glancing around, she blinked, trying to make sense of what she saw. There were faces, thousands of them, screaming, taunting and mocking. White light blinded her as she tried in vain to stay still. She knew she was falling forward but couldn't stop herself. She didn't want her face to make contact with the carpet but there was no way to prevent it happening. The light faded to black and she vomited. Her limbs twitched a few times and then there was nothing.

2

They climbed aboard the bus that would take them over to where the plane stood waiting. Thousands of stars danced in the dark skies above them, the moon bright and the air still warm at ten fifteen in the evening. Catherine Bishop turned to her companion as the driver started the engine and the packed bus began to move.

'I think we should come back as soon as we can.'

Thomas laughed.

'How do you think I'm going to be able to afford that? It'd be great, I just need a spare grand or so.'

As they settled into their seats, Catherine sighed in contentment.

'I love sitting by the window.'

'I know you do, you big kid. It's going to be a long flight home in the dark though.'

'You'll be all right, you'll sleep.' Catherine wriggled until she was comfortable, then adjusted her seatbelt and fastened it. Thomas stowed their rucksacks in the overhead compartment before taking his own seat.

'I'm so glad we came,' he said.

'Egypt is top of my list of favourite holidays.'

'I'll have to see how it goes, but I'd love to come back. Maybe in the summer? It would be good to have another holiday to look forward to, time to relax.'

Catherine settled back as the safety video began to play on the monitors.

Catherine's eyes opened when Thomas nudged her arm. The lights in the cabin were dimmed and the only sound was the noise of the plane's engines.

'Look,' he whispered, pointing towards the window.

Catherine sat up straighter, squinting. As she watched, there was a second's flash of white, lighting the sky below them.

'What is it?'

'Lightning. We're flying above a storm.' Thomas leant closer, angling his mobile phone towards the window to capture a photograph of the display, like fireworks that were being lit just for them. Catherine watched in awe as the blackness below was illuminated every few seconds. Thomas was right. The holiday had been a great idea.

She awoke with a jolt as the main lights came back on and the cabin crew manager began her final announcement: 'Welcome to East Midlands Airport, where the outside temperature is three degrees . . .'

'Ugh, no,' Catherine groaned. She stood up and collected her phone and book from the seat pocket in front of her. 'I'd just got used to it being at least twenty every day.'

'Back to the real world now,' Thomas said, leading the way down the aisle.

A world without Claire, Catherine thought as she followed her brother.

3

Footsteps on the floorboards outside, though she couldn't hear them. A cough.

'You all right in there?'

There was a pause, then a head appeared around the door, baseball cap pulled low over the brow.

'Oh shit.' He stepped over to her, bending closer, then raising his voice. 'You need to come in here.'

The other man stomped up the stairs.

'What's wrong with you? You want everyone in town to hear?'

He caught sight of the lifeless body slumped on the filthy floor. Middle-aged and wiry, he wrinkled his nose at the smell that filled the room. The younger man was almost wringing his hands.

'What are we going to do? She's dead, how can she be? The boss is going to kill us, you know how much that stuff is worth? Not to mention we've now got a dead body to sort out. God, she's been a nightmare from the start, whinging and whining, then we had to rearrange getting her home . . . '

'You can't blame her for that, it was just bad timing. Look, calm down, will you? Are you sure she's dead?'

'I'm not touching her, it looks like she is to me.'

Squatting over the woman on the floor, the older man felt for a pulse in her neck.

'She's gone all right.'

'So what do we do?'

'I'll show you.'

Taking a closed knife from his pocket, he exposed the blade and brandished it at his companion, who backed away, shuddering.

'You're not seriously going to . . .'

'No. You are.'

4

Opening his eyes, Mark Cook felt the enormity of his hangover, groaned and closed them again. As he swallowed, the lingering taste of alcohol and kebab meat almost made him retch. He reached out, fumbling on the bedside table to see if he'd remembered to bring a glass of water to bed with him. No such luck. His mouth was parched and his head pounded. Groaning again, he managed to sit up as rain began pattering the window. The room was dull, the half-drawn curtains blocking what little light there was outside. He leant over the bed, his stomach protesting, a vague memory of dropping his phone on the carpet flitting through his mind. Blinking at the screen, he checked the time: eight thirty-seven am. Lauren would have gone to work. Then he blinked, his stomach tightening as he remembered.

His wife wouldn't be at work today.

He stood, head still thumping, and made his way downstairs, downing half a pint of water as soon as he reached the kitchen. He hadn't wanted to come into the room, not with the smell and the lingering accusations, but he had to. He couldn't put it off any longer. As he turned to put the empty glass into the sink, it slipped from his grasp, shattering as it hit the tiled floor. With a curse, he bent to pick up the bigger pieces, swearing again when one dug into his thumb. Sucking the droplets of blood from it, he picked his way across the room, avoiding the spatter and mess, to retrieve the dustpan and brush. Wouldn't do for the cat to get a shard in her paw. He wrapped the fragments in several sheets of newspaper and shoved the lot in the bin. As he turned back, he caught sight of a few droplets of blood on the cupboard handle, more on the floor. Swallowing deeply, nausea climbing his throat, he moved to the sink, took a bucket out from beneath it. He squirted a good measure of bleach inside and turned on the hot tap. Bleach would do the trick. Better not let the cat in.

He mopped the floor and wiped down the cupboards, then washed the table top and legs and the wooden chairs and work surfaces with a spray cleaner that also contained bleach.

Adding to the sweet, sickly smell in the room was the cat litter tray, standing in the corner, needing attention. Sighing, he took the roll of black plastic bin bags from under the sink and emptied the mess into it, his stomach heaving again in protest as he did so. He also removed the head of the mop and dropped it into the bag with the mess from the tray. Nose wrinkling in disgust, he unlocked the back door and dropped the bag onto the path outside, planning to take it as far as the wheeled bin when he was wearing more than a pair of boxer shorts. Another black bin bag that contained his ruined clothes, stained and stinking, sat accusingly beside the back door.

The cat herself sidled up as he was closing the door and he bent to pick her up before she stood on the bleached floor, then turned to find her sachets of food in the cupboard. He set her down outside with her bowl, closed the door and filled the kettle and stood scrolling through Facebook on his phone while he waited for it to boil. Lauren's last status was a cheery sentence about how much she was looking forward to the weekend. He set the phone on the worktop, his hand trembling.

The house was silent, Lauren's absence echoing through every room. Mark took his mug of coffee through to the living room, avoiding Lauren's spot in the middle of the sofa and settling in an armchair. He glanced up at the framed wedding photograph on the wall and Lauren stared back at him, her eyes bright with joy and love. His lips tightened as he thought about the last time he'd seen her, her expression disgusted, accusations falling from her lips. His defensiveness, her disbelief.

His fury.

Mark went back into the kitchen and picked up his phone. He rang his wife's number, knowing there was no chance of a reply. Blinking back tears, he typed out a text instead: R U OK? Worried xx

She wouldn't answer, but he had to try, to show that he loved her, was thinking of her. It was all he could do now. He had ruined everything. They had been married just three years, having met at school.

How long should he leave it before he contacted the police?

5

With some swearing, Catherine Bishop managed to persuade her car into a tiny space between a liveried white van and a moped. She slid out of the driver's seat, then wriggled through the door in undignified fashion, hoping no one was watching her through the tinted windows. Northolme's police station was an unattractive building, two storeys of scruffy red bricks and peeling paintwork. It faced the main road through town with the grammar school sprawling opposite. On the patchy grass in front of the building, an elderly man was whistling as his Jack Russell emptied its bowels, a copy of one of the more provocative tabloids nestling under his beige rain-coated arm. Catherine gave him a pointed look as the dog straightened. He tutted, taking an age to remove a small plastic bag from his pocket and start bending towards whatever his dog had left behind. The terrier, no doubt feeling lighter, energetically kicked two tufts of grass into the air and one hit its owner square in the face as he neared the ground. Catherine hid a smile and hurried towards the main entrance, a cascade of swearing from the dog owner following her. She took a deep breath. *This is it then. Come on, you're absolutely fine,* she told herself.

The desk sergeant, Rich Smithies, tapped his watch.

'What time do you call this?'

'Half twelve, what time do you call it? We only got home in the early hours,' Catherine replied. She leant over and helped herself to a sherbet lemon from the bag Smithies was trying to conceal behind a pen pot on the front desk.

'Oi,' he protested as Catherine flicked the wrapper in the general direction of his bin.

'You need to find a better hiding place than that, Rich,' she called over her shoulder. 'Bunch of criminals in here, you know.'

Through the battered double doors and up the stairs, the worn carpet almost trodden through in places. A landing at the top where a hot drinks machine hummed away to itself. Next to that, another machine selling crisps and sweets and one filled with cold drinks jostled for space.

There was a canteen down in the bowels of the station, but these machines were quicker for a snack. That the hot drinks machine produced the same mid brown slurry whichever button you pressed was a minor point. Through another set of double doors and into the CID office. Whiteboards, filing cabinets, desks, all looking as if they belonged in a skip rather than a busy police station.

'Afternoon, Sarge.' Detective Constable Chris Rogers grinned as she walked through the door. 'Did you miss us?'

'Constantly. Every second was a nightmare.' She pulled a face at him. 'Yeah, about as much as you missed me.'

His laughter followed her to her desk. She sat down, the threadbare blue seat creaking in protest. Detective Constable Anna Varcoe appeared in front of her.

'Was that your chair? All-inclusive food for a week . . . ?'

'Funny. You should have seen the cakes though.'

Anna nodded towards the square of work surface that served as their office kitchen. No one trusted the hot drinks machine; one taste of its interchangeable brown watery beverages was definitely enough.

'I bet it was amazing. Tea?'

Catherine switched on her computer and monitor, which took its time to start up, wheezing like an ailing asthmatic.

'Go on then, thanks. What's been happening?'

Before Anna could reply, the doors at the other end of the office were flung open and Detective Chief Inspector Keith Kendrick strode into the room. He was a big man, well over six feet tall, with a voice to match his stature.

'Detective Sergeant Bishop. We've been pining away without you.' He waggled shaggy eyebrows at her.

'How's it been here?' she asked.

Kendrick snorted.

'Let's go through to my office and I'll update you. It's been non-stop thrills, I'll tell you that much.'

'Really?' Catherine followed him across the room.

'No, not really. We've had Willy Moffatt in the cells for a start.'
Catherine groaned.

'Let me guess - flashing little Willy again?'
He screwed up his face.

'In a nutshell, as it were, yes. He even did a dance this time so it jiggled around a bit. Three old ladies at a bus stop. One had a camera phone that her grandson had given her and took a decent close-up, so he couldn't really argue.'
They reached Kendrick's office door and he gestured for Catherine to go inside.

'He never argues, I think he's quite proud of himself.'

'God knows why,' Kendrick sniffed, heaving himself into the chair behind his desk. 'Little Willy is right.'
Catherine smiled at the man who sat in the corner of the office, flicking through a notepad. 'There can't be anyone in town that hasn't seen it by now,' she said. 'Good afternoon, DI Knight.'
Detective Inspector Jonathan Knight smiled, not quite meeting her eyes. 'You're looking better, Catherine.'

'I feel it.'
Kendrick leant back in his chair, counting on his fingers as he spoke.

'Ongoing cases: Willy Moffatt – I've mentioned him, indecent exposure and generally being a mucky little so and so. The Paul Hughes murder – Jonathan can fill you in on that. A domestic in Harborough Street – husband and wife brawling in the house, took it out into the street and he ended up cracking his head on the pavement. It's a messy case and we're trying to charge them both, but he's still in hospital. The muggings – that started before you went away,' Catherine nodded. 'Well, there was another one, got away with a new iPhone and a wallet full of cash this time. Same crap description: slim bloke, hooded top, nasty-looking knife. We've got a picture from the CCTV, but it's useless at best. And the rest . . . well, as I say, ongoing cases.' He grinned. 'Bet you're delighted to be back.'

'Have I been away?'

Kendrick picked up a pen up from his desktop and tapped it against his teeth as he studied her.

'How are you feeling?' he asked eventually.

Catherine looked away, over at the bedraggled pot plant that sat on the top of a blue metal filing cabinet, then at the blind that was higher at one end than the other. Finally, her gaze to fell to her lap.

'I'm okay, thanks. Better.'

'The Super's been asking after you too, wanting to know how you've been.'

'That's . . . that's kind of her.'

Kendrick lowered his voice a little.

'There's been nothing in the press, by the way. The Pollard case is over, closed. I know you want to come back to work and just get on with it, and I think that's for the best. The Paul Hughes case is still ongoing, but . . . I told the Super I thought your leave would have done you the world of good.'

'And it has.' Her voice was firm.

'Good. Well, I'm sure you'll have a thousand and one lovely emails to catch up on . . .'

Catherine took the hint and got to her feet.

'No doubt. Thank you, sir, for the support when . . . you know.'

Kendrick waved her away, not quite able to hide his smile.

Catherine worked through her inbox, reading a few emails and deleting the rest. She didn't seem to have been missed too much. Picking up her mobile phone, she scrolled through the contacts until she reached 'Claire Weyton'. She stared at the screen, knowing she should delete it. Claire was gone. Sipping tea, she brooded. Two uniformed constables who were standing at the other end of the room chatting cast a few glances in her direction. Catherine fought the urge to march up and confront them, but she knew it was futile. She would have to accept the fact that, for a while at least, she would be the talk of the station.

When she'd finished her tea she dialled the number for the Force Headquarters on the outskirts of Lincoln and asked for DI Foster. After a few clicks, his voice, bluff and belligerent, echoed in her ear.

'DS Bishop? What do you want?'

She hesitated, taken aback by his aggressive tone.

'Good afternoon, sir. I'd like to talk to you about the case we were . . .'

He interrupted with a sound of contempt.

'Would you? Didn't you do enough damage the first time around?'

'Pardon?'

'You know what I mean. You arsed up months of surveillance.'

She laughed, not quite believing what she was hearing.

'Are you joking? Anyone who was in that house disappeared long before we arrived on the scene.'

'Not the only cock-up you've made recently, though that's not the right phrase to use where you're concerned, is it?' Foster gave a nasty laugh and Catherine could hear voices in the background joining in. Her cheeks flushed and she gripped the receiver.

'I just wanted to see if I could help.'

'We don't want or need your help, Sergeant. Leave it to those who actually know what they're doing. '

He slammed down the phone and Catherine was left still holding the receiver to her ear. The venom in Foster's voice had shocked her, causing a tiny chink in the armour she'd pulled on since Claire's death. They obviously all knew the full story over at Headquarters. Claire had worked there of course; she had only been in Northolme for a few short weeks as part of another assignment. Catherine felt shaken; Foster's knowing, mocking tone had uncovered old memories, thoughts and feelings she had thought long buried. Her first few months on the force, keeping her sexuality hidden. Confiding in another new recruit that she had thought she could trust, who had then blabbed to everyone. The comments, the sneers, the looks of pity, some of understanding. No one willing to stick their own neck out enough to sympathise or empathise though. She swallowed, feeling sick. Just when you thought change had happened, that acceptance and equal rights were the norm, a throwaway comment, or unguarded phrase revealed the truth – that some people's prejudices were still hidden away. Scratch lightly and they would be revealed, sickening and abhorrent, running through them as deeply as bedrock and as eternal as the colour of their eyes.

What could she do though? It was Foster's case. She had resolved to keep her head down as much as she could, do her job with a fixed smile, however much it might hurt. Was it worth disrupting that, sabotaging her career, damaging it even more than it had been already?

She thought back to what she had heard about the ordeal of the young girls in the brothel, the filth they had lived in, the men they had been forced to service week after week, month after month. Stories similar to many she had heard during her career, but still so affecting, so tragic. Girls in their teens, girls whose lives were blighted, ruined. Girls whose days were endured, not enjoyed. Was she betraying them as well? Foster and his team were on the case, she knew that. He was an experienced officer, and who was she to think she could do a better job than he could? She shook her head, furious with herself. Her feelings about the case, about the betrayal and exploitation of the young women involved wouldn't help them. She had been blinded and had allowed, for the first time in her career, her personal life to infringe on her working hours.

She had let them down.

Hating herself, she turned back to her emails.

'Catherine?' Jonathan Knight was standing in his office doorway, smiling. 'Could I have a word?' She got to her feet slowly. 'Did you speak to DI Foster?' he asked as she approached. Catherine blushed, her eyes on the grubby carpet tiles.

'I did, but he wasn't encouraging. It might be best if I leave them to it.'

From her expression Knight surmised that Foster had said a lot more than that, but he didn't want to push.

'I see.' He met her eyes for once, seeing the hurt there, the betrayal. It would take time for her to come to terms with what had happened, he knew that. Being the talk of the station, if not the whole force, couldn't be helping. Catherine cleared her throat.

'How's the Paul Hughes murder investigation going?' she asked. Knight shook his head. 'Honestly? It's not. Dead end after dead end. I'm expecting the case to be reassigned, in fact I'm surprised it hasn't been already. Paul Hughes was a career criminal just like his dad Malc, involved in organised crime and who knows what else. We're struggling and I don't think I'll be given much more time.'

'But you've had experience with the Hughes family, you know how they work.'

'That might be part of the problem.'

'How do you mean?'

Knight met her eyes and held them for a few seconds. Having come to a decision, he got up from his chair, stepped across to his office door and closed it. Catherine half-turned in her chair as the DI began to loosen his belt.

'Don't worry . . .' Knight's shirt was untucked now and he was unfastening buttons. He turned his back, pulled his shirt up as high as he could, and Catherine gasped as she saw it. A crude tattoo filled the upper right part of Knight's back; the rough outline of an eye and the initials 'MH'. For a moment, Catherine couldn't speak but eventually she managed to stammer, 'Malc Hughes did that?' Knight let his shirt fall back to his waist and Catherine looked away as he straightened his clothing before moving back behind his desk.

'Not personally,' Knight said, 'but it was down to him. You can see why I don't go swimming.'

Catherine managed a smile.

'But why? What does it mean?' she asked.

He shook his head.

'I told you I had some history with the Hughes family, with Malc in particular. His name cropped up in a few cases while I was with the Met and I got a bit obsessed, I admit it. I wanted to bring him down a peg or two and I was careless. This,' Knight gestured over his shoulder with his thumb, 'was his way of telling me he knew what I was up to, had seen me coming if you like, and wasn't going to stand for it.'

'But . . . assaulting a police officer?'

'I don't know who actually did it, I didn't see anyone. They grabbed me off the street, I'd just come out of a chippy.' Catherine had to smile at that, knowing Knight's fondness for fish and chips. 'They threw me into the back of a van and blindfolded me. I think I ended up in some garage or workshop. I could smell petrol fumes, oil, that sort of thing. I don't know how many there were and I couldn't identify anyone. They gave me a bit of a kicking, then when I was on the ground they did this. I thought they'd cut me at first, it seemed to go on forever. In the end they chucked me back in the van and dumped me at the side of the road.'

Catherine was appalled.

'So he got away with it?'

'I never reported it. What would be the point? No witnesses, no names or faces to identify and a million and one people with the initials MH. It wasn't part of an official investigation, so . . .'

'So you might have a motive for revenge on Malc Hughes yourself?' Catherine kept her tone light.

Knight met her gaze.

'He'll start a life sentence one day, that'll do for me. Anyway, while Paul Hughes was being tortured and killed, we were on our way to the hospital.'

Catherine closed her eyes for a second.

'Of course we were.' she whispered.

6

Two forty-five in the afternoon. Mark Cook raised a hand to his aching neck and rubbed it, wincing. He sat up straight, feeling slightly better than he had a few hours before.

Then he remembered. Lauren. He snatched his mobile from the coffee table, prodding the screen into life. Who could he call? He jumped to his feet, scrolling through his list of contacts.

'Mark?' A baby bawled in the background.

'Steph? Have you heard from Lauren?'

'What? Wait a minute.' A few seconds of muffled noise, then the sound of a door closing. Mark paced the living room. 'What did you say?' Steph asked.

'Has Lauren been in touch?'

'No, why? She's away, isn't she?'

'Yeah, but she should be back in the country at least by now. She's not answering her phone, I've had no texts, she hasn't rung . . .'

A silence.

'I'm sure she's fine, Mark. She'll just be hungover, she's probably asleep on the ferry or at a mate's house. You know what she's like. She'll be home soon, I'm sure,' Steph told him.

Mark sighed.

'Yeah, I suppose so. All right, thanks.'

He closed his eyes for a second, wondering who else he could phone.

7

'Please tell me you're not growing a beard?' Catherine asked as she wound a few strands of spaghetti around her fork. Thomas raised a hand to his face.

'What's wrong with it? Anyway, it's not a beard, I just haven't been arsed to shave for a few days. It wasn't a priority while we were away.'

She chewed and swallowed, then picked up her slice of garlic bread and gestured to her plate with it.

'I didn't realise you could cook, this is delicious.'

He flushed a little.

'Thanks. Anyone can chop up an onion though, chuck a few herbs in a pan.'

'I don't normally bother.'

'Louise was a good cook, wasn't she?'

Catherine gazed at him, chewing steadily.

'Careful, Thomas, you've just been nice about her.'

He laughed.

'It was an accident. Her moving out was the best thing that could have happened to you.'

'You never liked her, I don't know why.'

'Honestly?' He stood, picked up his plate and took it to the sink, then rinsed it under the tap and set it in the washing-up bowl. With his back to her, he mumbled, 'I just never thought she was good enough for you, that's all.'

She spluttered for a few seconds, surprised by his admission.

'Not good enough for me? How do you mean?'

Thomas shrugged and turned to face her, leaning against the worktop his with hands in his pockets.

'Always making snide remarks about your work and making you feel guilty.'

Her last mouthful of food finished, Catherine pushed back her chair.

'I wasn't always that considerate.'

'She knew about your job when you met, she shouldn't have blamed you for doing it.'

'Well, maybe.'

'Why are you standing up for her?'

Catherine squirted washing up water into the bowl and turned on the hot tap.

'Because I feel guilty.'

'You shouldn't. I'm guessing what happened between you and Claire was different?'

'Different? You can say that again,' Catherine snorted, the conversation with DI Foster still raw.

'I'm just saying that you deserve better.'

'I thought I'd found it.'

'You need to forget Claire too. Move on, Catherine.' She slammed a couple of forks onto the draining board.

'I *know*. I'm trying to.'

He grinned. 'You know what they say, best way to get over someone is to get under . . .'

Catherine gave him a shove and he laughed, brushing soap suds from his sleeve.

'Just because you've had more girlfriends than you can remember,' she retorted, returning to the washing-up. He pulled a sad face.

'How do you know I'm not heartbroken too?'

Her laugh was scornful.

'Come on, Thomas, this is you we're talking about.'

'It's true. Why do you think I came rushing over from Manchester? Why I fancied a week in Egypt completely out of the blue, even if it took every penny I had?'

Catherine raised an eyebrow.

'I thought out of concern for me, but it was because you've been dumped? I suppose it had to happen in the end.' She emptied the water out of the washing-up bowl and squeezed out the dishcloth, setting it on the draining board. 'So tell me more.'

Thomas picked up the tea towel and dried a plate half-heartedly.

'I met this woman at the gym, Gina. Little bit older than me, gorgeous . . .'

'Usual story so far.' Catherine smirked.

'Ha ha. Anyway, I thought things were going well, but one afternoon we were at her house, up in the bedroom and we heard the front door slam. She hadn't told me she was married.'

'No . . .'

'Oh yes. Turns out her husband is a soldier, bloody huge great big bloke.'

'So what did you do?'

'I got dressed while she rushed down to distract him, then climbed out of the bedroom window, onto the garage roof, and legged it.'

'Meanwhile, the neighbour was on the phone reporting you for burglary.'

'It was a bit of a shock to say the least. Anyway, it gave me a kick up the arse. I was getting sick of Manchester anyway; no job, sleeping on the sofas of anyone who'd have me … I'd had enough.'

'So here you are.'

'When you phoned and asked if I could come on holiday, it gave me a chance to get away.'

'Oh, thanks,' she shot back.

He shook his head. 'I was thinking of coming back to Northolme anyway. I need to find a job, get a place to live. Do you think I could stay with you until I get myself sorted? Please?'

'Of course you can, you know that. Why aren't you teaching? You're qualified, why don't you use it?'

'I've started looking, but I might have to wait a few months. I'll go down to the leisure centre in the meantime and see if they've got anything, maybe do some lifeguard shifts.'

Thomas had decided to train as a PE teacher when his promising football career had been ended by a knee injury. He dried the last knife and set the tea towel down. Catherine filled the kettle and flicked it on to boil.

'So what about you?'

'What about me?'

'I'm not daft, Catherine. You're thin, you weren't yourself on holiday and you won't tell me what happened with this Claire you'd met. What's going on? I couldn't get it out of you while we were in Egypt, but if I'm going to be living here for a while . . .'

Catherine sighed, taking two mugs out of the cupboard and dropping tea bags into them.

'I don't know what to say, Thomas. The last major case I was on was . . . difficult.'

'Well I know that, your face had been battered for a start.'

'All right. Well, it was a murder case. There were two victims actually, and a third man had been attacked.'

'In Northolme, the land that time forgot? Bloody hell, I'm surprised I didn't hear about it in the news.'

They took their mugs into the living room. Thomas headed for the armchair and Catherine settled on the sofa, where she grabbed a cushion and held it close.

'It was in the news, though we tried to keep it as quiet as we could. Anyway, we had no real suspects until Anna and I – you remember Anna Varcoe?'

'Oh yes, I remember Anna.' Thomas gave a lascivious grin.

'Stop that. We called at this house to interview a bloke and found him unconscious – an overdose. When he came to, he told us enough to make it possible for us to work out who we needed to arrest. While it was all going on, I'd . . . well, I'd met Claire. She'd been working with us at the station for a while.'

'Aye aye.'

'She was perfect, Thomas: funny, intelligent . . .'

'Sounds good to me.'

'Yeah. We'd spent some time together and it was going well. I hadn't felt like that for a long time, not since Louise and I first met, if ever. Oh, and I'd also spent a night with Louise before I'd got together with Claire. Louise was keen for us to try again.'

'Bad idea.'

'Well, I was thinking about it.'

'Until you met Claire?'

'Yeah. Then Louise found out I was seeing Claire and sent me a text telling me to never contact her again.'

'No great loss.'

'It was awful though. I didn't want to hurt her, but when I met Claire, it was just . . .'

'Spare me the details. You liked her, she liked you, you had butterflies in your stomach when you saw her, you spent every minute you could in bed . . .'

'Thomas!'

'I know how it is. So what went wrong?'

Catherine laughed a little. 'You might well ask.' She reached forward and took a tissue from the box on the coffee table. Thomas looked concerned.

'If it's going to upset you, Catherine, I'll mind my own business.'

'Claire's dead,' she told him, her voice choked.

Thomas stared at her

'I'm so sorry, I never would have . . .'

'It's okay.' She wiped her eyes, giving her brother a shaky smile. 'And that's all I'm going to say.'

'All right, fair enough.'

'You know the worst of it though?'

'What?'

'I liked her. I liked her a lot, and I thought she felt the same.'

'It sounds like she did.'

'Well, maybe. I think she used me.'

Thomas frowned, confused.

'Used you for what?'

'Enough, Thomas, please.'

There was a silence.

'God, Catherine, I thought my love life was a mess, but you . . . '
He shook his head in mock despair as she threw the cushion at
him.

They sat up until around eleven, when Thomas began to yawn.
Catherine knew she should try to sleep at least. Thomas led the
way up the stairs, pausing outside the bathroom.

'Thanks for letting me stay. I'll find some work, pay my way.'

'I know you will.'

Catherine turned to go into her own bedroom, then stopped.

'Thomas?' He stuck his head back out of the bathroom door. 'I'm
glad you're here.'

He grinned.

'I think you need a night out.'

8

The headache that had been knocking at his temples for hours was in danger of becoming a migraine. Jonathan Knight propped his forehead on his fist as the lines of text blurred before his eyes. His body needed sleep. As usual though, his brain had other ideas.

He picked up the report and flipped to the first page, then began reading again from the beginning. Within minutes though, the letters were swimming. Knight stood up and went into his kitchen. Holding a glass under the tap, he filled it with water and knocked back a couple of maximum strength pain killers. They might hold off the worst of the headache, if he were lucky.

He took the rest of the water back to the dining table and sat down again, shoving his feet into his battered old slippers. The heating had gone off hours before and the cold was beginning to bite. Casting a weary eye over the papers on the table, he sighed, rubbing his forehead, then picked up his laptop instead and headed up the stairs to his bedroom. Sitting with his back pressed against the headboard, he pulled the duvet around himself and turned on the laptop. It was even colder up here than it had been downstairs. As he waited for the machine to load up, he listened to the silence of the house. During their last case, Catherine Bishop had spent some nights in his guest room and though he found it difficult to admit, Knight had missed her presence. Though there would never be any possibility of a romance between them, he had found that he liked and respected her. Having her around had been an experience he had enjoyed far more than he had expected to. It was good to have her back at work too. He knew she had been missed in the CID office, though muttering and giggling had gone on amongst some of the uniformed officers. It might take a little time for Catherine to live down what some were seeing as a huge error of judgment. Knight didn't take that view himself. He knew how easy it was to be blinded by attraction, by the sheer force of wanting someone. Anyway, hadn't they all been fooled?

When the laptop was ready, he opened his personal emails. There was one from his brother, whose wife was due to give birth any day to their first child. Knight read the excited words with a smile. He hadn't told his family that there was the possibility that he would become a father himself in the spring. Until he knew for sure whether his ex-girlfriend carried his child, or whether the man she had had an affair with was the baby's father, it didn't seem worth mentioning. Far better to let his brother enjoy centre stage. If the baby was his, there would be plenty of time to share the news. He scrolled down the page to the email which contained the scan of the foetus that Caitlin had sent him. She kept in touch, sending him a text or an email every week or so to say she was fine and that the baby was developing as it should. There was little else to say at this stage. Knight replied politely, feeling most of the time as if he were talking to a stranger. He and Caitlin hadn't had much to say to each other even when they'd been together, and the enforced continuation of their relationship, albeit as friends, had done nothing to change that. Caitlin was confident and sociable, but Knight was neither. Maybe her new boyfriend would be a better match.

He typed out a quick reply to his brother's email, then set the computer on the floor and hoped he'd remember it was there in the morning before he trampled it. He turned onto his side and pulled the duvet high around his ears, hoping sleep would come.

9

He couldn't do it. He sat in the front of the van, his hands shaking. No doubt this vehicle had been stolen a couple of hours before.

He couldn't do it.

'Where are we going?' he asked, the tremor in his voice obvious. The older man cleared his throat and sniffed. 'You'll see.'

'Can't you just tell me?'

'We're almost there.'

He squinted at the windscreen but just saw the road stretching in front of them, narrow, more of a track. Tall hedgerows rushed by on either side as his stomach lurched. His companion was whistling. It had to be to calm his nerves; no one could be this relaxed with a job like they had to do. He glanced at the other man, but he didn't look nervous. If anything he seemed to be enjoying himself, as if they were out for a drive with a picnic in the boot. He was singing now under his breath, the words unintelligible, as he steered the van to the left, then slowed it to a halt. Unfastening his own seatbelt, the older man nudged him.

'Come on then, we don't want to hang around.'

He swallowed.

'Look, I . . .'

His companion wrenched the seatbelt off for him.

'Get your arse in gear.'

10

It felt as though Catherine had been asleep for just a few minutes when she woke, the images of the nightmare still vivid in her head. She had seen Claire lying in a coffin, shrouded and pale, her beautiful blue eyes closed. All at once, Claire had sat up, her eyes unfocused, her fingers curling into claws. Her mouth had opened to reveal a black swollen tongue, and she let out a scream of anguish. To Catherine's horror, Claire had begun to decompose before her as she lay back down, her flesh changing colour, sinking and disappearing, her face becoming skeletal within a few seconds.

Catherine rolled over, wiped the tears from her face with the sheet and attempted to control her breathing. She turned on her bedside lamp, hoping the images would begin to fade. Sitting on the edge of her bed, she reached for the white towelling robe that hung on the chair nearby. The house was silent and cold. Catherine staggered across the landing to the bathroom, turned on the light and stared at herself in the mirror. She'd suffered heartbreak before, of course she had, but nothing like this. The feelings of guilt and those of betrayal. The numbing realisation that she had lost a relationship that had never properly begun, one that could never have been. She knew, not that she would ever say it out loud, not even to Thomas, that she would have forgiven Claire anything. She closed her eyes for a second, then turned on the tap and scooped up some water, splashing it over her face. She needed to stop thinking like this.

Tying the robe around her waist, Catherine went downstairs to the kitchen and made herself a drink. Curled up on the settee, she wondered how much tea she must have drunk over the past few weeks: gallons. It wasn't making her feel any better.

Nine am. The police station must be open by now? Mark Cook had been awake most of the night, calling Lauren's phone over and over, pacing the floor of the living room and drinking endless cups of coffee. He walked down the grey concrete path that led to the police station's door, located at the far-right end of a building that was never going to win any design awards. Mark had been past it hundreds if not thousands of times, but he'd never been inside. He felt sick, still not sure if he was doing the right thing, but he squared his shoulders and pushed open the door.

It was quiet, which he hadn't expected. He had thought there would be shouts, threats, accusations. He should have known better. It wasn't a prison, not quite, not yet. Mark hesitated, glancing around him. He finally noticed a tall desk, built into the wall, with an officer about his own age behind it who glanced up with a smile.

'Can I help you, sir?'

His voice was pleasant. Mark stepped forward, almost falling over his own feet.

'Yes, yes, please. I'm worried about my wife, she's not come home and it's not like her.'

'Okay, I'm Sergeant Smithies. Can I just take a few details?'

'Yeah, of course.'

'Thank you. Your wife's full name, date of birth and address, please?'

Mark gave them, then cleared his throat. Smithies asked for her mobile and their landline number and Mark reeled them off.

'And when did you last see her?'

Mark swallowed. 'Friday. She was getting the ferry over to Amsterdam to meet some mates there for a hen weekend. I expected her home yesterday, but she didn't arrive and none of her friends have heard from her.'

'She was travelling alone?'

'From Hull to Amsterdam, yes. The woman who's getting married is called Sarah. We met her and her boyfriend on holiday, they don't live around here. That's why Lauren was meeting them there.'

'And when did you last hear from her?'

'I had a text to say she was on the ferry. I thought it was weird that she hadn't been in touch since then, hadn't answered my texts, but I thought with it being a hen weekend . . . Well, you know what they're like.'

The desk sergeant scribbled down a few more notes, then met Mark's eyes.

'What I'm going to do, Mr Cook, is ask another officer to come and have a chat with you. If you wouldn't mind waiting over there?'

He nodded towards a few battered-looking blue plastic chairs that had been set against the wall in the corridor. Mark nodded and turned away. Rich Smithies watched him for a few seconds, then picked up his desk phone.

Hearing footsteps approach him, Mark glanced up from his phone. The woman who strode down the corridor wore a dark grey trouser suit with a black top underneath. Mark watched her pull the embroidered silk neckline away from her skin for a second, grimacing as if it irritated her. She held a couple of sheets of paper in her left hand which rustled as she walked, the tapping of her shoes on the tiles echoing down the corridor. When she stopped, Mark got to his feet, towering above her. She met his gaze and her eyes seemed to be assessing him. He felt his cheeks grow hot.

'Mr Cook?' Mark nodded. Her voice was quiet, the accent local. She seemed familiar, though he couldn't remember seeing her before. 'I'm Detective Sergeant Bishop. My colleague tells me you're worried about your wife?'

Mark nodded a few times, licking his lips. A detective. He'd expected an ordinary PC Plod. He glanced over Bishop's head and down the corridor. Who knew what was going on behind those doors? Maybe they were looking into Lauren's disappearance already?

'Mr Cook?' She was waiting for him to speak and he was flustered.

'I'm sorry, yes, I'm so worried. I've not heard from Lauren and it's not like her, she's usually on her phone all the time.'

'Okay. Let's go and sit down and I'll take some more details.' She led him down the corridor, about halfway, then pushed open a blue painted door and gestured for him to go in first. The lights came on as he entered the room; some kind of energy saving idea, Mark assumed. It was cold, the window letting in a draught. One-way glass in the windows - not surprising in a police station. Mark could see an elderly couple making their way slowly down the pavement outside. The man leant on a walking stick and the woman clutched his arm protectively. Mark swallowed, images of Lauren helping him out of bed after he'd had his appendectomy vivid in his mind. On another occasion, they had both had heavy colds over Christmas and had spent most of the holiday snuggled up in bed together, watching films. He blinked. The memories were tainted now, spoiled. The tone in Lauren's voice, the disgust in her expression.

His lies.

Sergeant Bishop came into the room, closing the door behind her, and he forced himself to concentrate. Blue carpet tiles on the floor, a small square table with a fake wood top and black metal legs. More of the blue plastic chairs, the same as the ones in the corridor. A water cooler glugged in the corner. His leg was trembling, his knee bouncing. He rubbed the palm of his hand across his thigh and clenched his jaw, trying to relax.

'Can I get you a cup of water, Mr Cook?' she asked.

'No, thank you,' Mark replied. He just wanted to get on with it. She waved him into a chair and sat down herself in the seat nearest the door, then looked at him, her head tilted slightly to the right.

'So. You've not seen your wife for three days?'

'Yes, she left on Friday morning. She should have been home some time yesterday, but she never arrived. I've tried her mobile hundreds of times, she's not phoned, not sent any texts, not been on Facebook . . . it's just not her. Her phone's not even ringing anymore.'

'What happens when you call her number now?'

'Nothing. It doesn't even connect.'

Mark watched as she made a note, her left eyebrow lifting. He looked away, not wanting her to think he was staring.

'And she was going on a hen weekend?'

'That's right, meeting a friend we met on holiday last year once she was in Amsterdam. The last text I have from her says she was on her way, but I've had nothing after that.' Mark gulped. The sergeant radiated a calm that only served to make him even more nervous. He folded his arms, then uncrossed them again. She looked up, watching him as he fidgeted.

'The friend's details, please?'

'This is going to sound bad, but I can't remember her last name. Her first name's Sarah.' Another note. Another twitch of the eyebrow. 'I could check on Facebook, see if I can find her surname? I don't know why I didn't think of that before. To be honest, I just found her annoying, her and her boyfriend, but Lauren got on well with them.'

'That would be helpful, thank you. If I could just ask you a few more questions first?'

Mark dipped his head. 'Of course.'

'What about clothes? What was Lauren wearing the last time you saw her?'

He gawped, his mouth hanging open. Sergeant Bishop waited, pen poised.

'Jeans, I remember that. The thing is, I nipped out to get some milk and when I got back she'd gone, so she might have got changed in the meantime. She took a little wheeled case with her, you know, hand luggage size? She's had it for years, it's a bit battered . . .' Mark realised he was babbling and closed his mouth.

'Have you checked her wardrobe to see what clothes Lauren might have taken with her?'

'No. No, I'm sorry, I didn't think to.' He hung his head like a child after a telling-off.

She smiled.

'It's not a problem. Can you think of any reason why Lauren might have chosen to stay away from home, Mr Cook?' Again, her eyes were on his face. There was no accusation in her voice, but Mark shuffled in his chair, feeling more uncomfortable with each passing moment. She was friendly enough, polite and professional, but there was a stillness in her manner that he found unsettling.

'No, none at all. She's happy, we're happy. She'd been looking forward to going away, once we'd saved enough.' He swallowed again, wishing he had accepted the water she had offered him. 'I was made redundant a while ago, you see, and I've struggled to find work. Lauren's parents gave her some money for her birthday and we managed to find enough in the end. I wanted her to go, she deserves a weekend away.' He raised his eyes, anxious to make Sergeant Bishop understand. 'I've done my best to find a job, but it's not easy.'

She nodded. 'Have you spoken to Lauren's parents?'

'About her not being in touch?' He hesitated. 'To be honest, no. Her mum . . .'

'Perhaps Lauren's staying with them?' Catherine suggested.

'No, she wouldn't do that.' Mark's voice was firm. 'Her mum's not easy to live with. Their house is the last place Lauren would be. Now Lauren's dad has retired, she's even worse, going on and on at him. No, Lauren won't be there. Maybe she's been in an accident?'

She didn't reply, and after a few more questions, Mark found himself outside the station again, wondering just what he'd achieved by going there. Perhaps he should have stayed away.

'Do you think she's got a new boyfriend then, Sarge?' Detective Constable Dave Lancaster asked over the hubbub of the office. Catherine shook her head, her mouth full of chocolate digestive.

'I bet she's just sleeping off a hangover somewhere, but . . . Do me a favour, Dave, see if you can find out whether she's back in

53

the country at least. Maybe she's just missed the ferry or forgotten her phone charger. I've got her car registration number here too.' Lancaster nodded, his eyes bright.

'I'll do it now, ma'am.'

'And don't call me ma'am!' she bellowed after him as he trotted away from her desk. 'If you must call someone ma'am, make it the Super, she loves it,' she added in an undertone. 'Makes me feel like the Queen.' She practised a royal wave. 'No good, I haven't got the wrist action.'

Chris Rogers grinned at her. 'Wonder why that is?'

Catherine stood to mime a belly laugh, then chucked a pen at him before logging into her computer as she sat back down. Lauren Cook, age twenty-four. No criminal record, and neither had Mark. Well, there wasn't a lot they could do. Lauren Cook was a responsible adult with no history of mental or other health issues. If she'd decided to have an extra day or two in Amsterdam without telling her husband, then that was up to her.

Back at home, Mark Cook was on the phone again. Lauren's parents need to know that he had reported her missing, though he knew she wasn't at their house. He steeled himself, ready for the inevitable onslaught of questions.

'So you've not heard a thing from her and the police won't help?' Celia Chantry was outraged. Mark closed his eyes for a second, willing himself to stay calm.

'I saw a detective. She said to give it another day or so and to contact her again if Lauren hadn't shown up by then,' he told her.

'Fat lot of good that is, she might be dead in a ditch somewhere,' Celia snapped. 'It's not like Lauren, did you tell them that?'

'Yes, I . . .'

'Did you, Mark? Because I know you, you're a lovely lad but you're too soft. You need to be firm.'

'I was, I told her.'

He could hear Celia having a mumbled conversation, no doubt with Lauren's dad Geoff. You had to feel sorry for the poor sod; it must be like being married to a whirlwind. Still, they'd been together a long time. There was no harm in Celia, Mark acknowledged, she was just overwhelming.

'Right.' She was back on the line, loud and clear. 'Geoff and I are getting in the car now. We'll be with you soon, then we'll all go down to the police station and give them what for. Fobbing you off like that, honestly, it's disgusting. What do we pay our taxes for, that's what I want to know.'

Mark made a feeble attempt at protesting, but reasoning with Celia in full flow was like trying to stop an express train by shouting at it. No chance.

'We'll see you soon then. Have the kettle on. Bye now.'

Resignedly, Mark slipped his phone back into his jeans pocket. He should have known. At least he'd tidied up.

11

Catherine sat alone, sipping orange juice and nibbling at the corner of a cheese sandwich that she didn't want. It was late for lunch, but she'd been trying to avoid the canteen. She should have brought a snack in from home but then she'd have had to come down here in the end, she couldn't avoid it forever.

The double doors opened, but Catherine didn't look up. Anna Varcoe came in, crossed to the counter and selected a couple of items. As she waited to pay, she glanced over at her sergeant. Catherine looked exhausted, and though she was as smart and groomed as ever, she seemed to have lost weight. Her face was drawn, her eyes almost shuttered, no clues as to how she felt or what she must be going through. Anna wondered whether Catherine had been away from the station long enough, but then what would be the point of her being at home brooding?

Anna thought back to the time she'd spent with her just after Claire's death, with Catherine struggling to say a word and Anna herself stunned, attempting to take in what it all meant. She had gone home from the hospital feeling almost as if she were dreaming, sleepwalking into her own flat and taking the longest, hottest bath she could stand. The events surrounding Claire's death had affected them all, the whole town in a sense. Anna knew Catherine was experiencing terrible guilt because she hadn't realised what had happened, what was going to happen. She'd said as much. Anna frowned to herself and resolved to speak to DI Knight when she had a chance. She picked up her tray again and went over to where Catherine sat.

'Mind if I join you?' Anna asked.

'Of course not,' Catherine replied, blinking away an image of Claire standing in just the same spot, smiling down at her.

Anna settled into the chair opposite her sergeant, picked up her jam doughnut and sank her teeth into it as Catherine looked on in envy.

'Wish I'd got a doughnut now. I'm not sure how long these sandwiches have been there, but the sell-by date's written in Roman numerals.'

Anna started to laugh, then was overtaken by a coughing fit as she struggled to swallow the mouthful of doughnut.

'You see, they're not good for you.' Catherine grinned.

'Just go and get one, Sarge, you know you want to,' Anna replied when she was able to, wiping her eyes. Catherine shook her head in defeat and returned to the counter. Back at the table, she took a huge bite and closed her eyes with pleasure. Anna smiled, relieved. Catherine was still pale, the smile a little forced and brittle, but the overall the signs were good. Perhaps she wouldn't need to voice her concerns to DI Knight after all.

Back in the office, DC Lancaster was waiting.

'Sarge, the Lauren Cook thing – I think you better come and have a look.'

Catherine followed him over to his desk.

'What's wrong, Dave?'

He sat down and she stood beside him, leaning forward as he pointed to the familiar website displayed on his monitor.

'See? The only friend Lauren has on Facebook called Sarah hasn't been on her hen weekend, not according to this. She spent Saturday and Sunday at home in Huddersfield decorating, not getting drunk in Amsterdam.'

Catherine squinted at the screen.

'And there's no other Sarah at all?'

'No, Sarge.'

'And none of her other Facebook friends have been on a hen night? Maybe Mr Cook got the name wrong.'

'There's no mention of anything like that.'

'Hmm. Did you find out if Lauren is back in the country?'

'That's the weirdest part – I can't find any record of her travelling abroad at all, not since the summer before last.'

'Oh, so she's been fibbing? You're sure?'

'Positive, Sarge. She went to Gran Canaria about fifteen months ago, but that's all.'

'I'll have a word with the DCI. It worries me that she hasn't been in touch with her husband, but then I bet she has a new bloke.'

'Maybe, but it that case you'd have thought she'd have thought up a better lie than that. Maybe Mr Cook isn't telling us the truth.' Catherine puffed out her cheeks. 'All right. I'll go and speak to DCI Kendrick now. Looks like you and I might be having a ride into town after all, Dave.'

Keith Kendrick watched her as she sat down, taking in the dark smudges under her eyes and the slow, careful movements. He'd need to keep an eye on her.

'How are you, Catherine? Really I mean, don't give me any flannel.'

She laughed.

'I wouldn't dream of it. I'm fine.'

'You only had three weeks off, it's not long.'

'I want to be here, this is what I'm paid for.'

'What does that lass of yours say?'

'Lass? Do you mean Louise?'

'Aye, that's the one. Mousy hair and a sour look on her face.'
Kendrick grinned, not sure if he was pushing his luck. Catherine
shook her head.

'No idea, I've not heard from her. Don't expect to either.'

'Very bloody supportive.'

Catherine took a deep breath. She didn't want to think about
Louise; there was only so much guilt she could handle.

'I need to talk to you about a missing person.'
She explained what Mark Cook had told her and what DC
Lancaster had dug up so far. Kendrick listened, pinching his lower
lip between his thumb and forefinger.

'Well, I think we need to talk to the husband again at least,' he
said. 'You'd think the bride-to-be would have been putting photos
and God knows what else on Facebook - who's been sick where,
how many times they've fallen over and all that. Have you ever
been on a hen night?'

'Not for a few years.'

'They sound worse than a stag do, and they're bad enough.' He
shuddered.

'It could just be that Lauren was spending the weekend with
someone she didn't want her husband to know about, of course, but
then why tell him a lie that was so easy to disprove?'

'A boyfriend you mean? Could be. So what are you suggesting,
we talk to a friend first, someone she could have confided in?'

'It might be best. It shouldn't take any time. DC Lancaster's been looking into it so far.'

'Good idea, give him some experience. Let me know what you find out and we'll take it from there.'

He held the mug of hot chocolate between shaking hands, blew across the top of the sickly-looking liquid and took a sip. It wasn't so bad. He hadn't wanted it but his colleague had insisted, saying it would do him good, that it was too cold to be just drinking the squash he would have preferred. He took another reluctant sip, the churning in his stomach not helping. He'd received a text early that morning, short and to the point as always: **Pint tonight? Collect you at 7**. They wouldn't be going for a pint, of course. He screwed up his face. He didn't know what to do and there was no one he could ask for advice. He'd been stupid; so very stupid. He might have more cash than before, but was it worth it? No. No way. He couldn't eat, couldn't sleep, and who knew what he'd have to do tonight. It couldn't be as bad as what they'd done already. He closed his eyes, the image of the knife blade sinking into the soft, pale flesh unbearable. Chewing on the inside of his lips, he pressed them together, willing himself not to be sick.

The memory of what he had done afterwards was even worse.

He gave up on the last mouthful of hot chocolate and turned to rinse his mug in the sink. He needed to think.

12

There was a tap on Kendrick's office door and the desk sergeant, Rich Smithies, stuck his head into the room.

'Sorry, Guv. I wondered if I could have a quick word with DS Bishop?'

'Can't it wait, Rich? We've almost finished.'

'Not really, I'm afraid. The woman who was reported missing earlier, Lauren Cook? I've got her husband back downstairs, as well as her mum and dad. The mum's causing a proper scene.'

'Bloody Norah,' Kendrick complained. 'We've already told the husband that there's nothing we can do.'

'I know, that's the bit she has a problem with.' Smithies shrugged. Catherine heaved a sigh and got to her feet.

'It's all right, I'll come down. I wanted another word with Mark Cook anyway.'

Kendrick waved a dismissive hand. 'Fine.'

Catherine reached the door and followed Rich down the corridor, smoothing her hair as they walked.

'Is she really kicking off?' she asked in an undertone.

Rich snorted. 'I'm surprised you can't hear her yet.'

'Great. I can understand it, but . . .'

'I know. She's insistent, she was going on about phoning the papers, the Chief Constable, her MP and I don't know who else. The Queen and the Prime Minister, I expect.'

Catherine stopped walking and looked at him, making as if to turn back.

'You're not selling this to me, Rich.'

He gave a tired smile as she caught him up.

'She'll be fine with a bit of reassurance.'

'Couldn't you have reassured her?'

'I'm not the detective who spoke to her son-in-law.'

Catherine groaned.

'No, lucky me.'

They had arrived at the bottom of the stairs. Rich put out a hand and stopped Catherine.

'Wait a minute. I'll go first and tell her you're coming. Then you can rush in as if you were in the middle of a meeting and look like you're doing her a real favour.'

'I *was* in a meeting.' She hesitated. 'I think there might be a bit more to this than meets the eye.'

Rich stepped forward before she had time to explain that Lauren hadn't left the country.

'Let's hope not,' he said as he went through the double doors, allowing them to swing closed behind him. Catherine took a deep breath. *Fingers crossed,* she thought.

Mark Cook and his in-laws were waiting in the room in which she had spoken to Cook earlier. As Catherine approached the door, she could hear a female voice raised in complaint. She could sympathise with Lauren Cook's family, but at this point there was little more she could do. After a second's pause, she pushed open the door.

A woman, tall and slim with short black hair, jumped out of her chair as soon as she saw Catherine and demanded, 'Is this the person you spoke to, Mark?'

Mark Cook was nodding, but Catherine held up a hand.

'Please, Mrs . . .'

The other woman pounced on her hesitation.

'You see? She doesn't even know our name, Geoff, that's how many details she took. Doesn't even know Lauren's maiden name. It's Chantry. Do you want me to spell it for you as well?'

Catherine felt her eyes narrowing, but when she spoke her voice was calm.

'Mrs Chantry, I apologise for the delay. I understand you have concerns about your daughter. Could we sit down and discuss them, please?'

Thrown for a second, Celia Chantry glanced at her husband, who had a weather-beaten face, thick grey hair and a beard. He reached out a hand to his wife and took her arm.

'Come on, love, sit down.' His voice was quiet, soothing. 'Let's hear what she has to say.'

Catherine shot him a grateful smile as Celia sank back into her chair.

'Thank you. I think Sergeant Smithies told you my name.' Celia folded her arms.

'*He* didn't tell us anything, Mark remembered – somebody Bishop. Good for you. Can you explain why you've done nothing to find our daughter?'

'Mrs Chantry, as I explained to Mr Cook this morning, we have certain procedures . . .'

'I don't want to hear about your procedures, I want to know where my daughter is.'

'Why don't we let the officer speak?' her husband said in that same soft, calming tone. Celia Chantry looked mutinous, but she was quiet.

'As I said, we have procedures we have to follow. As it stands, Lauren is considered at low risk. There's no reason to believe that she's a danger to herself or anyone else. I'm sorry to sound blunt, but we just don't have the resources to launch a full-scale operation every time an adult doesn't come home when they're expected.'

Catherine knew she sounded like a manual or handbook, but what she was saying was true. However much she wanted to help, she was in no position to be able to do so. There was a pause while Lauren's family digested what Catherine had said. She prepared herself for another onslaught from Celia Chantry, but when the other woman spoke her voice was quiet, almost reflective.

'So we've just got to wait for her to get in touch or come home? Assuming she ever does?'

Catherine nodded.

'At the moment, yes. I'm sorry, I know it's frustrating. There was a point that I wanted to check though. Mr Cook, we couldn't find any mention of a hen weekend on the Facebook pages of any of Lauren's friends and from what we can see, Lauren hasn't left the country at all.'

Catherine's voice was gentle, but there was no kind way of suggesting that Mark's wife had lied to him. Mark himself seemed stunned, his mouth open. Catherine kept her eyes on his face, but his bewilderment seemed genuine.

'But Lauren said . . . She told me . . . I don't understand, she said she was going to Amsterdam.'

'What's this, Mark?' Celia demanded.

'You mean there's no hen weekend?' Mark whispered, his eyes wide like those of a bemused child.

Catherine pushed back her chair a little. 'It could be someone who's not on Facebook, but obviously I don't know.'

Mark Cook looked close to tears. 'But Lauren said they'd arranged it through Facebook.'

Geoff Chantry looked at Catherine, his blue eyes entreating. She blinked. They were the same shade as Claire's had been.

'Is there nothing you can do, Sergeant? It's not like Lauren at all.'

'I believe you, Mr Chantry, but as I know you'll understand, people don't always behave in the way we expect them to. I am sorry.'

'Of course. It's just that Lauren . . . Well, she's always been so steady . . .' His voice trailed off.

With another apologetic smile, Catherine got to her feet.

'Please contact us again if you've still not heard from Lauren in another day or so. There's no doubt a simple explanation for why she hasn't been in touch.' Another platitude. She hated spouting this stuff. Her instinct was to make Mark Cook and the Chantrys a cup of tea, then crack on with finding Lauren, but she couldn't do that.

Celia stood, her expression pensive. When she'd heard that her daughter had lied to her husband, the fight seemed to have gone out of her. The glance she gave Mark was scornful.

'Well, thank you for seeing us. We'll be back though if she doesn't come home, whatever she's been up to.'

Catherine stepped backwards, opening the door as the two men also stood, their expressions unreadable. Standing back to let them pass her, Catherine met Geoff Chantry's eyes again. He nodded a goodbye.

After following them out into the corridor, Catherine waited until they'd left by the main doors, then went over to Rich Smithies on the desk.

'You managed to persuade her that we know what we're doing then?'

'She's just worried about her daughter, Rich.' Catherine frowned. 'What's wrong?'

'I don't know, it just seems odd. Lauren hasn't even left the country. Why would she lie, a lie that's easy to disprove as well?'

'Really? It's obvious then - new bloke. It's her way of letting her husband down gently.'

'Maybe so.'

'Suppose you'll be after another sherbet lemon now?' She grinned, holding out her hand and blinking the gnawing doubt away.

'Suppose so.'

Back upstairs, she sat behind her desk with a quick glance at the clock on the wall.

'Catherine.' She started. Jonathan Knight was smiling down at her. 'Sorry. You know we were discussing the Paul Hughes murder yesterday?' She nodded. 'Well, the Superintendent left me a voicemail saying she was coming over from Lincoln to see me. Anyway, she's just rung to say she's running late, but to expect her soon. It'll be about the Hughes case, no doubt.'

Detective Superintendent Jane Stringer had an office at Northolme police station but she spent most of her time at headquarters. Catherine pursed her lips.

'I might nip off now before she gets here then, in case she wants to see me too. What do you think she's going to say?'

With a sigh, Knight shrugged.

'I'm not sure. She may just want a progress report, but I think it's likely that she'll tell me the case is being reassigned.'

Catherine tipped her head to the side, trying to gauge Knight's mood.

'Do you think so?'

'I wouldn't be surprised. She needs results.'

'Oh yes, she loves her facts and figures.'

'I've had three weeks and I've made no progress whatsoever. It's not unexpected.'

His tone was impossible to read and there was a silence, broken only when Catherine's phone beeped to announce the arrival of a text message and she pulled it out of her jacket pocket. It was from

Thomas: **Managed to find a few hours' work at the leisure centre. Shall we go out for a curry to celebrate? Invite some of your workmates.** Catherine rolled her eyes. She could imagine who Thomas would want her to ask: Anna Varcoe. He'd met Anna once at a meal Louise had organised for Catherine's birthday one year and hadn't been able to stop going on about her. It looked like nothing had changed. She glanced over at Knight, who was studying his computer screen. Why not?

'Are you doing anything tonight?' Knight looked up, surprised. 'It's just that my brother's staying with me and he's suggested a few of us go out for a curry. I'm going to ask Anna and Dave, Simon will probably want to get straight home to the baby, but Chris might come. Maybe a couple of the uniforms, depending who's on shift tonight. I could phone Dr Webber . . .?'

13

Her face looked thinner than ever, but there was strength in the bony hand that gripped his own. The veins were clearly visible, dark blue, almost purple, lying flat under the thin, pale skin. Dan Raynor frowned and bent closer, tracing their path with a gentle fingertip.

'You're not drinking enough, Nan.'

Her hand fluttered back down onto the embroidered blanket, worrying a loose thread that she soon coiled around her thumb.

'Rubbish.' Her voice was the only part of her that was unchanged. She looked up at him, her green eyes dulled by pain. 'They make tea constantly here, not very well most of the time. Too milky.'

He laughed. 'I'm surprised you haven't complained.'

She arched a silvery eyebrow. 'They never listen, they just smile and pat your hand as if you're an idiot, then dole out more bloody tablets.'

He sat in the armchair next to hers, her skinny legs sheltered by the blanket, her swollen feet stuffed into fluffy navy blue slippers.

'You need your tablets,' Dan pointed out. She snorted.

'Says who? They do no good whatsoever.'

She shifted in her chair, her face creasing. Dan leant forward, concerned.

'Nan? Are you okay?'

She batted him away and adjusted her blanket.

'I'm fine, just a twinge. Have you been at work today?'

He hesitated, wondering if she was confused. 'Of course.'

Pressing her lips together, she sat up a little straighter.

'Don't look at me like that. I was making conversation.'

'Look at you like what?'

'I know what you were thinking. My body might be falling to pieces, but I've still got my marbles.'

'Don't say that.'

'It's true.' She folded her hands in her lap. 'When you get to my age, you have to face facts. You just don't know how long you've got.'

'None of us do.'

'There's a fair chance you have longer left than me though.'

'Well, try to hang on as long as you can, won't you?'

Her eyes brightened, dancing for a second. 'I'll do my best.'

14

As usual, Detective Superintendent Jane Stringer looked as if there was an unpleasant smell. After meeting her a few times, Knight had realised it was her natural expression and not a result of any offensive odour that might be lingering around Northolme police station. Stringer wore her usual outfit: a well-tailored jacket and skirt, smart blouse and understated make-up. She rested perfectly manicured hands on the polished surface of her desk and said, 'After speaking to the Assistant Chief Constable, I believe this is the right decision.'

Knight didn't respond. He was annoyed but not surprised; he'd been expecting this, after all. DCI Kendrick shuffled in the chair beside him, impatient as always at having to sit still for any length of time, then spoke up.

'With respect, ma'am, I'm not sure I understand. Why do yourself and the ACC think that another officer is going to have any more joy finding out who killed Paul Hughes than Jonathan has?'

Stringer inclined her head with a regal air, treating Kendrick to the sort of glance you might bestow on half a mauled mouse that the cat has dragged in.

'Fresh eyes, Keith. You know how it is. It's no reflection on the investigation you've been running here, of course.'

Oh, of course not, Knight thought.

'It's not been easy with the Hughes family in London, ma'am,' he said. 'If I could have gone down there, spoken to them myself . . .'

Stringer gave him a hard look.

'That wasn't an option, Jonathan. Malc Hughes was interviewed by our very capable colleagues in the Metropolitan Police, as was his wife and the rest of the family. Their alibis were verified and they were eliminated as suspects. We need to press on with discovering who killed Paul Hughes, but at the same time you have other cases piling up here.'

'I wouldn't say they're piling up . . .' Knight protested. Stringer's lips pinched and her nostrils flared.

'I'm afraid the matter is closed. Detective Inspector Shea will arrive tomorrow afternoon and I know you'll make him welcome as well as offering him any assistance you can. He'll be bringing a DS with him and they may need a couple of DCs to help out as necessary. He can use this office in my absence - I trust that won't be a problem?'

Kendrick folded his arms.

'None at all, ma'am,' he said. 'You do realise that he may never solve this case either, I suppose?'

She glared at him.

'And what does that mean?'

'Malc Hughes is the head of an organised gang of criminals. I know it, Jonathan knows it, the whole of the Met knows it, and yet we can't touch him. Of course he has a solid alibi, he always does when anything kicks off. He has lots of unscrupulous types ready and willing to do just about anything to get in his good books, so why would he dirty his own hands?'

Stringer tapped a fingernail on the desktop a few times. When she spoke, her voice was quiet.

'If Malc Hughes killed his son, either with his own hands or through someone else, we will prove it. Looking at the evidence though, I don't think he did. Do you?'

She gave Knight a pointed look and he shook his head with a sigh.

'No. No, I don't.'

'And so our priority, regardless of who Paul Hughes' family is, regardless of what he may or not have done, is to find the person or persons who killed him. Also regardless of any involvement he might have in any other case, including the one involving the people trafficking and prostitution ring. I don't think I need to remind either of you that that particular case is no longer your responsibility either.'

'So we just fob both investigations off onto someone else? Heaven forbid they sit around mucking up our stats.' Kendrick couldn't let it lie and Stringer looked at him with what almost seemed like pity.

'It's not like that and you know it.'

With a noise of exasperation Kendrick said, 'I have good officers here, officers who want to do their jobs.'

'Your officers' abilities aren't being questioned. It's time for a change, that's all, especially after what happened here during the Pollard case. You know how that would have reflected on the force had it become public knowledge. If there are any links between any of the cases, they'll be investigated too. I'm assured that DI Shea is a capable officer.'

'Good for him,' Kendrick muttered.

Stringer ignored the comment, allowing herself a tiny smile. 'I'm sure he'll fit in well here.'

He stood by his living room window, gazing down onto the street below. There had been a police car parked outside earlier, not that it was unusual to see one around here. His partner, if that was the right word for him, wouldn't come to the flat, he'd wait in the car. He had all sorts of tricks designed to avoid being noticed or followed. It was no doubt paranoia, but then if they were caught it would be the two of them serving the time in prison, not the man who gave them their orders. The boss would never be caught, they knew that much. It would be the likes of himself and other young lads, turning to this sort of life because they had little other choice who did the time. He sighed, knowing it wasn't true. There was always a choice, wasn't there? No one had forced him to miss his exams, to drop out of college, to smoke dope, to start dealing. No one had forced him to become a servant to a career criminal. His childhood hadn't been great, but then whose really was? There were still options, different paths. People from the most privileged backgrounds often had miserable lives while people from scruffy estates like the Meadowflower excelled. In the end, everyone made their own choices. He turned away from the window. He had made his.

It wasn't the car they usually used. This one was newer, sleeker, faster. Still anonymous, of course. He opened the door and slid into the passenger seat, hoping his reluctance wasn't visible in his face.

'Evening,' he said, yanking the seatbelt over his chest. 'New car?' The older man turned to face him and he froze for a second, hating the dead snake eyes that seemed to see right into his thoughts. He swallowed. They pulled away from the pavement and the silence stretched until he could bear it no longer.

'Why have we got a different vehicle?' he asked, not sure he wanted to know the answer.

'There's a problem,' came the terse reply.

15

'What are you drinking?' Thomas asked.

'Just an orange juice, please,' Catherine replied, running a hand through her hair, glad she'd had time to rush home for a quick shower and change of clothes. Both she and her brother were casual in jeans and t-shirts under their winter coats.

'Evening all.' Chris Rogers strolled up to the bar and joined them. 'Faye and her mate have gone to the loo.'

Catherine raised an eyebrow at him, instantly alert. 'Her mate?'

'Yeah, a woman she works with. I might have mentioned her before.' With a swift movement, Rogers turned away from Catherine and smiled at the barman. 'Pint and two halves of lager, please.'

Thomas handed Catherine her drink and she took a sip, annoyed and dismayed.

'Chris, please tell me you're joking?'

He held up his hands in mock surrender. 'It was Faye's idea.'

Catherine groaned.

'Shush, they're coming in. Be nice, Sarge . . .'

'Cheek, I'm always nice.' Catherine forced a smile. 'Hello, Faye.'

Faye took her drink from her husband and beamed.

'Lovely to see you again, Catherine. I'd like you to meet my friend, Ellie.'

Ellie gave a shy nod. Her dark blonde hair was quite long with a heavy fringe which emphasised her eyes. Catherine smiled back, ignoring the tiny pang in her chest. This was not what she needed.

'This is my brother Thomas.' She waved her hand towards him and he grinned.

'Pleased to meet you all.'

'Is DI Knight coming?' Chris asked.

'He said so.'

'Did you ask Dr Webber as well?'

'Ha, no, I was joking. I'm sure he fancies her though.'

'Who doesn't?' Chris winked at his wife, who laughed and gave him a playful push. Ellie caught Catherine's eye with a smile.

An hour and several drinks later, the table was filled with food. Faye had managed to orchestrate the seating so that Catherine and Ellie were next to each other. Thomas had grabbed a chair by Anna while Dave Lancaster sat between two constables from uniform, Emily Lawrence and Natalie Roberts. Lancaster was in his element, like a giddy puppy that you couldn't help patting. DI Knight had turned up at last, still wearing the crumpled suit he'd had on at work.

'Sorry, I was in a meeting with the Super,' he explained.
Catherine threw him a questioning glance and he nodded.

'Now, now, we're not talking about work tonight,' chided Chris.

'Wouldn't dream of it.' Knight's smile was awkward. He glanced around. 'Dr Webber not here then?' His colleagues smirked knowingly. 'Just wondered.' Hastily, he broke off a piece of garlic naan bread. Faye leant across to rescue him, leaving Catherine and Ellie sitting in silence.

'I'm sorry about this,' said Ellie in an undertone. 'I know you weren't expecting me. Faye was insistent and she's my boss, so . . .'

'You've had your arm twisted then?' Catherine grinned. Ellie looked horrified.

'I'm sorry, I didn't mean . . .' she backpedalled.

'I know, I'm joking.'

'It's not that I don't want to be here.'

Catherine gave her a sideways glance, then opened her eyes wide.

'Really?'

Laughing, Ellie lifted her glass.

'All right, I was dreading it. It's too much like a blind date and I've always hated the thought of them.'

'Me too.'

'Faye just presumed that I'd want to meet you because we're both single and . . .'

Catherine took a swallow of orange juice.

'And we're both gay.'

'She seems to think that's all it takes.' Ellie shrugged.

'She's not the only one,' Catherine said, giving Chris a hard look that he pretended not to notice.

'Faye told me you'd had a tough time and needed cheering up.'

'Did she?'

'I'm sorry, it's awkward. I know what it's like to have people think they can wave a magic wand and make it all better.'

'I'm sure they mean well.'

Ellie met Catherine's eyes. 'Faye told me your last girlfriend died.'

'Did she?' Catherine raised her glass again, aware of the coldness of her tone.

'It's just that . . . well, so did mine.' Ellie's gaze was on the table top.

Catherine looked at her properly for the first time. A dimple in her left cheek. Perfect teeth.

'I'm sorry. I didn't know.' Now she felt terrible.

'How could you have?'

'Anyway, Claire wasn't my girlfriend, not really. We'd only been together a few days.' She twisted the tablecloth in her fingers. 'Did Faye tell you what happened?'

'No, not the details. It's none of my business.'

Catherine didn't know how to respond to that and the awkwardness returned. They were quiet for a few minutes, mechanically shovelling rice and curry into their mouths, their thoughts far away. After a time, Ellie put down her fork.

'Your brother seems nice.'

Catherine looked at Thomas, his arm thrown across the back of Anna's chair.

'He is. The trouble is he's a bit of a flirt, always has been. I'm hoping Anna has enough sense to see that, but . . .'

They watched Anna laugh at some joke Thomas had made, her eyes never leaving his face.

'You think so?' Ellie laughed.

Catherine let out a groan.

'I have to work with her every day, which would make it awkward if he dumped her – and he would.'

'You never know, maybe he just hasn't met the right person.'

'I doubt it. He's lovely, he just needs to grow up a bit.'

Ellie swallowed the last of her lager.

'Good luck to them, I say.'

They said their goodbyes on the pavement outside the restaurant. Thomas and Anna were heading off for a 'nightcap' as he told his sister with a smile. A genuine, beaming smile Catherine couldn't help but notice, not borrowed from his collection of knowing grins or lascivious winks. Maybe Ellie would be proved right, but Catherine doubted it. Knight had already headed home, offering to drop off Dave Lancaster and the two female PCs on his way. Chris Rogers grinned at Ellie and Catherine.

'I've phoned for a taxi, he said five minutes, so you've not got long.' He gave a tipsy giggle and Faye nudged him, then took his arm.

'We'll give you some privacy,' she said, smiling as if she were doing them a huge favour.

Catherine rolled her eyes as Faye and Chris moved down the road a little.

'Subtle as a brick through your living room window, as always.' Ellie winced. 'I'm sorry about all this, Catherine.'

'It's okay, it's not your fault.' Catherine shuffled nervously. 'It's been good to meet you, however much you were forced into it.'

Ellie laughed. 'Thanks. I'm glad I came, believe it or not.'

They looked at each other, smiles uncertain.

Catherine said, 'It would be good to . . .' just as Ellie began, 'I'd like to . . .'

They laughed, the tension broken.

'It would be good to meet again, I was going to say.' Catherine made herself voice the words. 'If you want to, I mean. Maybe a coffee?'

'I'd like that. I don't have many friends in the area, so . . .'
Catherine nodded.

'Goodnight then.'

There was a second of confusion as they dithered over whether to hug or shake hands, then Catherine found herself pressed against Ellie for a second. Cold skin against her cheek, fruity shampoo, a tiny note of perfume. She walked away, raising a hand to Chris and Faye in farewell.

In her car, she shoved the keys into the ignition and gripped the steering wheel. Who was she trying to kid? Ellie wasn't Claire. She felt an irrational fury that Faye and Chris had forced herself and Ellie into the position they'd been in tonight. It had been a mistake to go, the whole evening seeming like an elaborate sham, a farce that she and Ellie had been caught up in. Just because they were both single, it had been assumed that they'd be irresistibly drawn to each other like magnets. She thumped the steering wheel, furious. It was all Thomas' fault; he'd only arranged the meal so he could see Anna again. Back in Northolme for a couple of days and he was already turning her life upside down. She felt as though she should phone Ellie to apologise, but then why should she? It wasn't her fault. She gave a bitter laugh. Ellie hadn't passed on her mobile number, so she couldn't have rung if she'd wanted to.

At home she slammed the door, tempted to leave the keys in the lock so Thomas wouldn't be able to get in. She didn't, of course. Thomas wouldn't change and both he and Anna were adults; what they did was up to them. A tiny voice asked her if her anger stemmed from a touch of jealousy, but she ignored it. That the person she'd thought she was falling in love with had deceived her was irrelevant.

Catherine climbed into bed, snapped off the light and glared out into the dark. The truth was that the person she was really angry with was Claire. She should have been there tonight, sitting beside her, laughing and joking, chatting - loving. Instead, Claire was dead and gone, buried without ceremony in the corner of the cemetery on the other side of town. Catherine and Jonathan Knight had been the only people at her funeral apart from the minister, who had said a few perfunctory words and then left them to it. She had stared down into the grave, unable to untangle the emotions she was feeling. Grief, yes, but more than that. Disbelief. Horror. Anger; a violent, white-hot fury. Knight had stood beside her, his face expressionless, skin almost as pale as the white shirt collar that just showed beneath his thick black overcoat.

She was grieving for a love that had almost been, a future that had been snatched away. Stronger still was the fury. She wouldn't live like this anymore. Claire wasn't coming back, and she didn't deserve Catherine's devotion. She had made her own choices and set herself on a path that could only have ended in disaster, then paid with her life.

Catherine reached for the bedside cabinet, picking up her mobile phone. She looked again at the name and closed her eyes for a second, remembering. Claire's smile, the delicate, thrilling touch of her hand . . . No. Edit. Delete contact. She replaced the phone and turned onto her side.

It was over. She was alone.

16

She hadn't heard Thomas come in, but he obviously had at some point as he was standing by her bed, wearing a t-shirt and some old jogging bottoms. Catherine rubbed bleary eyes.

'What's wrong?'

'Haven't you heard your phone? The landline's been ringing as well.' He held up her mobile.

She reached a reluctant hand from under the duvet and rolled onto her stomach.

'I'll put the kettle on,' Thomas said with a shiver. 'And the heating.'

She tucked her hair behind her ears and touched the phone's screen.

'Catherine Bishop.'

'Hi Catherine, it's Raj Dhirwan.'

A uniformed inspector calling her at home. It didn't bode well.

'Morning Raj, what's up?'

'I'm just going off duty, but I thought you'd want to know – we've had a call about a body.'

Catherine sat up, fully awake now.

'A body? Where? Who is it?'

'It's female, that's all I can tell you. You'd better get over here.'

Catherine thanked him and scrambled out of bed with one thought running through her mind: Lauren Cook.

DI Knight was waiting in his car when Catherine arrived at the station. She hurried across the car park, her unfastened coat blown straight back by the icy wind like black wings. Knight called to her over the noise of the idling engine.

'Catherine, there's no point going inside. The DCI told me to wait out for you. Get in, we may as well travel together.'

She nodded, climbing into the car. Knight had the heater going full blast but still had a black woollen beanie hat pulled low over his ears.

'Wasn't the bloke we arrested for the cash point muggings wearing that when we brought him in?' she asked, fastening her seatbelt.

He shook his head.

'Found it in the lost property box.'

'Just need a pair of tights over your face. So where are we going?'

Knight pulled out onto the main road.

'Somewhere called Moon Pond? The DCI said you'd know where it is. Popular with courting couples, he said.'

'Courting couples? Where did he wake up, the nineteen fifties?'

'You know it then?'

'Yeah, next left.'

'Have you been there as part of a courting couple?'

'Certainly not. Any fumbling and groping I did was somewhere a bit warmer than the back of a clapped-out old banger parked in a field of geese.'

Knight flicked the indicator on.

'Geese?' he queried.

'I'm assuming. Carry straight on for a couple of miles. What do we know about her?'

'Her?'

'Raj said the body is female, that's why he phoned me.'

'Because of Lauren Cook?'

'It's a bit of a coincidence, don't you think?'

'I don't have any details. It was called in at about six this morning.'

'Who'd be out at Moon Pond at that time of day, especially at the end of November?'

'I'm told the call came from a teenager who was parked up there last night with her boyfriend.'

'Ah.'

'Yes. He's older than her and she didn't want her parents to know about it. I don't think they were sure about what they saw, but she'd been awake all night worrying about it and finally rang in.'

'And some of our lucky uniforms went to see?'

'Yep. PC Lawrence and PC Roberts.'

'Good thing we didn't stay out too late last night then.' Knight hesitated, then asked, 'Did you have a good time?'

'Apart from Chris and Faye doing their Cilla Black act, you mean?'

'Ellie seemed nice.'

'I'm sure she is, but that doesn't mean I fancy her or that she fancies me. It's only a month since Claire died.'

'I know. They had good intentions.'

'I'd rather they didn't bother,' Catherine muttered, sounding like a spoilt brat even to her own ears. 'It's the next right.' They were out in the countryside now, the trees bare and the verges thick with frost, the road little more than a track. Catherine peered through the windscreen.

'It's here somewhere . . . Here, left here.' Knight slowed down and they turned into a gravelled area. There were a couple of small white vans parked close together and a squad car stood to one side. Knight pulled in beside it. As they crossed the car park, the tiny stones crunching beneath their shoes, PC Roberts appeared with a clipboard in her hand. The outer cordon had already been set up, the familiar 'POLICE LINE DO NOT CROSS' tape moving in the breeze.

'Good morning. She's by the pond, that way. Mick Caffery's just getting set up.' She gestured with her thumb. Catherine took the clipboard from her and signed her name, then handed it to Knight.

'Morning, Nat. Good thing you were on the mineral water last night then?'

Roberts shuddered.

'I'll say. She's not a pretty sight, I'm afraid, poor woman.'

'Is it Lauren Cook?' Catherine's voice was quiet. Her stomach, already tight, seemed to turn over and she swallowed.

'You'd better see for yourself, Sarge. To be honest, I'm not sure who she is and I don't think you will be, either. You can see her from the path, you won't need to get near enough to worry about contaminating the scene.'

'I thought the kids who called it in were in a car?' Knight asked, rubbing gloved hands together.

'The boyfriend got out for a pee and thought he saw a body. He couldn't believe his eyes and got his girlfriend to go and have a look.'

Roberts stamped her feet, the chill of the frozen ground finding its way through to her toes despite the uniform boots and her thickest thermal socks.

'That was considerate of him,' Catherine commented.

'Yeah, now they'll both be having nightmares. They couldn't tell if it was human or just a roll of carpet or a lump of wood. So they said.' She shrugged. 'It was dark, I suppose. Emily's staying by the body, I'll wait here. There are a couple of other paths leading to the pond but this is the only one with a car park. Mick says that because of the severe frost last night he's not expecting to find footprints, so we might never know which path she was brought down, if she was killed somewhere else and the body was dumped here. We've cordoned off all the possible routes anyway.'

After they had donned their white protective suits, shoe covers, face masks and gloves, Knight led the way down the narrow winding path towards the pond. Catherine followed close behind him, careful where she put her feet. Although the ground was frozen, it would have been easy to trip and fall over the many stones and pieces of tree branch that littered the ground. Caffery had placed footplates here and there and she took care to set her foot in the centre of each one.

The path soon opened out into a clearing with the pond itself beyond it. It was about the size of an average swimming pool, the water greenish-grey and still. The grass around the edge was short and trampled, but longer grass grew around the far side. Several trees surrounded the pond, a large fallen branch lying half in, half out of the water. Constable Lawrence stood about ten metres away, her hands tucked under her armpits, her breath visible in the

freezing air. Catherine couldn't see the body. The stocky figure of
Mick Caffery, easily recognisable despite the protective suit, stood
a few metres away talking to three members of his team.

'You okay, Emily?' Catherine called as they approached.
Emily Lawrence looked up and nodded a greeting. They were
silent as they moved closer, almost reverent. Emily realised she
was blocking their view and stepped away.

On the far bank, lying on her side, propped against the trunk of
another fallen tree was the dead woman. She was naked, her skin
mottled. Her long blonde hair, tangled with pond weed, tumbled
over her shoulder, covering her breasts. Her stomach gaped, a
terrible wound that looked like raw meat but colourless, anaemic.
And her face . . . Catherine swallowed, fighting the almost
irresistible urge to close her eyes. Knight took a shaky breath
beside her and Catherine reached out a hand and rested it on his
shoulder for a second, as much for her own comfort as for his.
Emily Lawrence was pale too, biting the inside of her lips, but
keeping her back straight and her chin up. Catherine wanted to go
to her, to tell her that this was the worst she would ever see, even
though it wouldn't be true. She knew only too well that there was
no limit to the horror people could inflict on each other.

The woman's face had been obliterated. The bones of her face
were pulverised, the flesh a churned mess of blood and tissue.

17

'I've asked them to set a tent up over her,' Mick Caffery said. He nodded towards two members of his team who were leaving the area. A third had started taking photographs of the body. 'I'm not hopeful of finding too much because of the conditions, but we'll do our best.'

'Do you think she was killed out here?' Catherine asked, though she had a good idea what Mick would say. His eyes twinkled at her for a second above the face mask he still wore.

'Do you, Sergeant?'

Catherine glanced over at the body again, before saying, 'No.'

'I'd be inclined to agree, but you know how it goes. We'll need to wait for the pathologist. Is she on her way?'

'I'll call her now,' Knight said, taking his phone from his pocket. 'I'll also request some uniforms so we can get a fingertip search started, okay, Mick?'

Caffery nodded, then carried on speaking as Knight moved away.

'If she wasn't killed here, she must have been dragged or carried. There's no way a vehicle could have been brought near. I've already established that the widest path leading from the car park to the pond here should be our common approach path. There's no way we could get our equipment down any other way, they're barely big enough for one person.'

With a frown Catherine asked, 'Doesn't that mean that the same path is the most likely way of whoever dumped her here getting in though?'

'It looks to me as if she's been dead for a couple of days,' Mick said. 'If that's so, we've no way of knowing yet when she was brought here. Any number of people could have walked down that path in the meantime. I'm not hopeful of finding much in the way of evidence out here, so it's important that we preserve the body as best we can and hope the post-mortem gives us more clues. I'm fairly confident that the path we're using wasn't used by whoever brought her; there are few snapped branches and signs of trampling on another of the paths which leads from a side road. Maybe they didn't want to leave their vehicle in the car park.'

Knight rejoined them. 'Doctor Webber is on her way. I presume we'll need to search the pond as well?'

Mick nodded. 'We should do. Who knows what might be down there.'

'I'll update the DCI.'

As Knight stepped away again with his phone, Mick lowered his voice. 'How are you getting on with him?'

Catherine frowned. 'With DI Knight?'

'He seems all right to me, but I've heard mutterings about him being a bit odd.'

'I like him.'

'That's good.' Mick glanced over to where the body lay, the tent now almost fully erected around it. 'I better get back over there. I've a bad feeling about this one, Catherine. Her face . . .'

'And her stomach.'

'Well, I have an idea about that, but we'll wait for the pathologist.'

Catherine watched him walk away. She had a bad feeling herself. Worse, she had no idea if the dead woman was Lauren Cook. The corpse's battered face made comparisons with the photographs she'd seen of Lauren impossible. The hair was the same colour and looked to be a similar length, but they would need much more than that.

As soon as Mark opened his eyes, he wrapped the duvet around himself, reached over to the other side of the bed for Lauren's pillow and held it close. The scent of her perfume lingered on the pillowcase and he pressed it to his face, breathing it in. He could hear Celia's voice; she and Geoff must be up already. They had insisted on staying the night, or at least Celia had. Geoff would no doubt rather have gone home to his own bed. It sounded as if they were in the kitchen, probably drinking some of the milky tea that they preferred and Mark hated. Celia had never asked how he liked his tea, or coffee, or anything else. It would never have occurred to her that other people might have different preferences to herself. Though she was generous in her own way, she wasn't a considerate woman. He'd better get up; it wasn't polite to leave them down there on their own, though it was what he felt like doing. At least he could be sure that the kitchen was spotlessly clean.

'Did you sleep, Mark? I didn't get a wink,' Celia started bleating at him straight away. Mark didn't think it wise to mention that Celia's snoring had practically rattled the windows, so he just shook his head and went over to refill the kettle. Celia swooped on him.

'You sit down, let me do that. I want to keep myself busy. Now, Geoff and I have been talking about what we can do.'
Mark silently corrected her: *You mean you've been telling Geoff what he's going to do.*
He sat at the small table in the corner of the kitchen, opposite his father-in-law. Geoff was drinking from Lauren's favourite mug, which was oversized and decorated with a beach scene. They'd brought it back from a holiday they'd taken before they were married. Corfu, he thought. His hands clenched into fists beneath the tabletop. Mark wasn't sure why Geoff using the cup was

bothering him so much, but he wanted to rip it out of the other man's hand. He didn't, of course; Mark never lost control.

Almost never.

Celia set a mug of tea in front of him. Pale, weak and unappealing. He picked up the cup and sipped anyway.

'I think we should go back to the police station today,' Celia went on. 'That Sergeant Bishop had no intention of helping us. Well, we'll see about that. I'll insist on seeing her boss if we're not satisfied. Geoff will have to go out for his walk first, the doctor's insisting he gets more exercise since he retired. At least three miles a day, isn't it, love?' Geoff nodded, winking at Mark as he did so. Mark gave Geoff a tiny smile. More like three pints a day. Celia bustled back over to the worktop. 'I'll do you some toast, Mark.' Mark tuned her out. He didn't want any toast, but it was pointless saying so. Celia had toast for breakfast, therefore so did everyone else. Geoff still hadn't spoken.

As Mark stood to take his plate to the sink, having managed to force most of the toast down his throat, there was a knock at the front door. Celia looked at him.

'Do you want me to go?' she demanded. Geoff sighed, lifting his gaze to the ceiling.

'It's their house, Celia, not ours. I'm sure Mark can manage.'

'I'm only trying to help. He's got enough on his mind,' Celia tutted.

Mark ignored them both and turned away. He felt sick, his stomach lurching. It could be anyone, of course: someone wanting to read the gas meter, a delivery driver or lost motorist. It wouldn't be though, he knew it.

Sure enough, as he approached the front door he could see two hazy figures silhouetted through the privacy glass panel, one tall, one shorter. Dark clothes. He gulped and all at once seemed to be floating, not walking, down the hallway with his breath coming in uneven gasps. The door felt heavy when he pulled it open.

'Good morning, Mr Cook. I wonder if we could come in?'

Mark knew he was staring, but he couldn't help it. He gazed at them, his mouth working. Then he was aware of movement behind him and Geoff pushing him aside, his hands gentle.

'Sergeant Bishop. Good morning.'

'Hello, Mr Chantry. This is my colleague, Detective Constable Lancaster. Could we come in, please?'

Celia shouted from the kitchen. 'Let them in, Geoff. I hope she's got some good news for us.'

Geoff winced. 'I'm sorry about my wife,' he said in an undertone. 'She's very worried.'

Catherine inclined her head. 'I understand.'

Celia also appeared in the hallway, the five of them cramped together uncomfortably. Mark recovered himself a little and suggested, 'Shall we go into the living room?' They all trooped after him and he waved a listless hand towards the three-piece suite. 'Please sit down.'

Sergeant Bishop unbuttoned her woollen coat. Today's suit was black, Mark saw, with a pale lilac shirt beneath it. He had no idea why he'd taken note of her clothes; he never usually saw such details. Lauren had moaned at him countless times for not noticing her new dress or haircut. He could hear the clock on the dresser ticking too, as if his senses were somehow heightened. The male police officer was silent. He took a small black notebook from his coat pocket and looked expectantly at Catherine Bishop, who shuffled forward a little.

'Mr Cook, we're here because there's been a development.' Her voice was formal, precise.

'Have you found her?' Celia demanded. Mark's mouth was suddenly dry. He fought the urge to bolt from the room.

'I'm afraid not. However,' DS Bishop glanced at her colleague. 'With your permission, Mr Cook, we'd like to take some items belonging to Lauren with us, so that we can carry out some tests.'

'Of course he doesn't mind, do you, Mark? Anything to find her,' Celia butted in again.

'It's Mr Cook's permission we need, Mrs Chantry.' Catherine set her jaw, attempting to keep the bite from her tone. Celia's eyes narrowed.

'If you want me to shut up, Sergeant, just say so.'
DC Lancaster's lips twitched, but he said nothing. Geoff Chantry exclaimed, 'Celia!'

'Take anything you like,' Mark croaked. 'What do you need?'

'If it's okay, I'll need access to your bathroom and your wife's clothes and other possessions. We'll give you receipts for anything we take away, of course.'

'Will I get them back? When Lauren comes home, she'll need them.' Mark's voice disappeared and Geoff Chantry cleared his throat.

'Can I just ask what's changed, Sergeant Bishop? Yesterday, and we do understand why, but you said you couldn't help us.'
Catherine hesitated, but only for a second. She hadn't wanted them to know but better to hear it from her now than on the television later on.

'I'm afraid that a body was discovered this morning.'
Celia gasped, one hand covering her mouth. Mark sat as if turned to stone, his hands on his knees, his mouth open, while Geoff stood and went to the window, staggering slightly. He gazed out onto the tiny front garden.

'Do you think it's Lauren?' he asked.

Celia whispered, 'No. No, it can't be.'

'At this stage, we just don't know. I'm sorry.' Catherine's voice was gentle.

'There she is, her picture's on the wall, I've got hundreds more on my phone.' Mark exploded. 'How can you not know? Is it Lauren or not?' He got up, strode across to the opposite wall, yanked down a wedding photo and shoved it under Catherine Bishop's nose. 'Here she is, look. Is it her? Tell me!' She looked up at him, perfectly calm.

'Mr Cook, please sit down.'

He paced restlessly. 'You've eyes in your head, just tell me. Is my wife dead?'

Geoff Chantry said, 'Mark, please. Let them do their job.'

Mark rounded on him. 'Come on, Geoff, how hard can it be? Is it Lauren or isn't it?'

Catherine was on her feet now. 'Mr Cook, please sit down. If you'll listen to me I'll explain as much as I can. I'm sorry to say, there is a possibility that the woman we've found is Lauren. We need some of her possessions so that we can either confirm her identity, or rule the possibility out.'

Mark stumbled over to the armchair and sank into it. 'You mean you can't tell by looking? What sort of state is she in?' His head span, and he knew he had to be careful.

Catherine shook her head as Celia began to sob.

'Please, Mr Cook. The sooner you give me your permission, the sooner we can answer your questions.'

He slumped forward, his head in his hands. 'I've already said, take anything you want.'

'Thank you. It shouldn't take long. Could you tell me if Lauren has any tattoos or other distinguishing marks please? And her blood group, if you know it?'

'She doesn't have tattoos, she doesn't like them.' Mark's voice was almost a whisper. 'No scars or anything like that. I don't know her blood group.'

'It's A positive,' Celia told them, her voice choked. Lancaster noted it down.

'Thank you. I'm going to go upstairs now if that's okay – I'll just be a few minutes.'

Mark Cook gave a listless nod and Catherine turned away, just wanting to be out of there now. Lancaster followed her out of the room.

Back in the hallway, Catherine closed her eyes for a second, running a hand across her mouth.

'I'll nip up to the bathroom and see if she's left her toothbrush, or there might be a hairbrush,' she whispered. 'You stay here and make sure none of them leave the room.'

Lancaster nodded and Catherine turned to go up the stairs. She trod lightly, trying to make her presence as unobtrusive as possible.

Marching into people's lives and turning them upside down wasn't part of the job she enjoyed, but it was unavoidable. They'd usually been turned upside down already.

Slipping on a pair of blue nitrile gloves, she glanced around. Four doors opened off the landing. One was ajar and she poked her head around it. It was the bathroom, painted in a light blue with sparkling white tiles, very clean with a lemony scent slightly masking the stronger smell of bleach. She stepped over to the wash basin, also white and set into a wooden unit. Squatting down, she opened the cupboard doors. There was only one toothbrush, standing in a small glass - a green one. Catherine wrinkled her nose. It had to be Mark's but she needed to be sure. She went to the top of the stairs and called, 'Dave?' Lancaster appeared. 'Can you check with Mr Cook if this green toothbrush is his, please?'

'Will do.'

There was a murmur of voices and then Lancaster called, 'It is. Lauren's is grey but she took it with her.'

'Thank you.'

She glanced in the cupboard again. Shower gel, shampoo and various cold and flu remedies. She left the bathroom and opened the next door along. A double bed just fitted inside, and there was a wheeled suitcase parked in the corner. Spare bedroom. She closed the door. The next one opened to reveal an airing cupboard. Catherine had a quick poke through the stacks of towels and sheets, but there was nothing of interest. She turned to the final door.

The master bedroom was tidy, not even any clothes hanging on the back of the chair that stood in front of the dressing table. Catherine couldn't see a hairbrush, though she supposed Lauren would have taken that too. She opened the drawer in the nearest bedside cabinet. A couple of battered paperbacks, a box of tissues. She opened the cupboard underneath. A hot water bottle. A tiny teddy bear. She moved around to the other side of the bed. In the drawer: a packet of paracetamol capsules and a box of contraceptive pills with one month missing. Again, Lauren would have packed those. The cupboard contained a few more books and some old birthday cards. Pulling back the duvet, she examined the pillows. Sure enough, there was a long blonde hair on the one nearest to her. Picking it up, she held it to the light. It looked like the root was attached. She slipped an evidence bag from her jacket pocket and placed the hair inside, then sealed it. There were two wardrobes, his and hers. There didn't seem to be too many clothes missing from Lauren's, but it was hard to tell. Catherine hesitated for a moment before moving over to the chest of drawers. Underwear in the top one. Socks and t-shirts in the next. She opened the bottom drawer. A pile of letters, documents, certificates. Mark's passport. No sign of Lauren's though. Interesting. Catherine sat back on her heels. She needed a personal item which might help them obtain Lauren's fingerprints, but what? The hair would be fine for DNA, but fingerprints would be quicker. Back to the bathroom then. A deodorant? She bagged one, then a bottle of fruity shower gel, hoping that would give them enough.

She took her hoard downstairs, where Lancaster was waiting to write the receipts. Then Catherine went back into the living room while Dave took the items out to the car. The Chantrys and Mark Cook were just as she'd left them, all three looking like they had been punched in the stomach.

'So what happens now?' asked Mark.

'As soon as we have news we'll be back to inform you.'

'More of your procedures?' Celia Chantry spat.

'I'm sorry. I know this is incredibly difficult . . .'

'You know nothing.'

Catherine fastened her coat. She wasn't going to allow the other woman's hostility to get to her, knowing it wasn't personal.

'I understand you're distressed, Mrs Chantry.'

'How can you?'

Geoff Chantry went to his wife, sat beside her and drew her close. He looked up at Catherine.

'As soon as you know . . . Please?'

She nodded, feeling a little choked though she'd been in similar situations countless times.

'I can promise you that.'

'Thank you.'

Mark Cook stood as if in a daze. Catherine touched his arm.

'I'll see myself out, Mr Cook.'

Back in the car, Dave started the engine.

'How do you do that?' he asked as he pulled away from the kerb.

'What?'

'Stay so calm, keep your temper.'

Catherine glanced at him.

'Come on, Dave, how long were you in uniform? You do it too.'

'It's not the same though, is it? It's not like ignoring some drunk who's giving you a mouthful because you've just chucked his mate in the back of a van on a Saturday night. It's a different kind of control.'

'Is it?' She'd never thought about it. 'I just remember that the people we're dealing with are victims, one way or another. It's also about how I'd want to be spoken to if I was in their place.'

'Even if they're winding you up?'

'Like Mrs Chantry, you mean? She's worried, scared. If having a go at me helps her deal with all that, then fair enough.'

'It doesn't bother you?'

'Yeah, it does, but she's just hitting out because you're there. You're representing police involvement, meaning that what's happened is out of her control, out of her experience.'

Dave was quiet, thinking about it.

'My grandparents were burgled once,' he said after a while, his voice reflective. 'This copper came, few years off retirement. He was rude, made them feel like they were wasting his time. He more or less told them that it was hopeless, that there wasn't much he could do and they might as well get used to the fact that they'd never get their stuff back. They took jewellery that my great-grandma had brought into the country as a refugee, my great-grandad's medals – sentimental value, but it hurt them. It hurt a lot.' Catherine nodded, not wanting to interrupt. 'My grandad died soon after. I'm not saying that it was because of the burglary, but . . . Anyway, when I told my grandma I wanted to join the force, she reminded me of that copper, not that I'd ever forgotten him.' He swallowed a couple of times. 'I just don't want to be like that, you know?'

Catherine looked at him again; his slim hands with the big knuckles bunched on the steering wheel, the slightly raw skin along his jawline.

'It's up to you, Dave,' she told him. 'You can climb the ladder, scramble over people, or just do enough. Then again, you can go another way. Your decision.'

He nodded, wrestling with the gearbox as they slowed to approach a junction.

'I don't want to look back in fifty years and know I could have done more to help people.'

'You also don't want to be burnt out before you're thirty. You have to know when to let things go as well, close your eyes at night and not see their faces.'

He thought about it. 'Can you do that?'

Catherine hesitated. 'No. No, not completely. But you have to try, you have to have a life away from all the crap. A family, a partner. Not let it take you over. You can't help everyone.'

He was silent, brow furrowed. The ringing of Catherine's mobile broke through the quiet, a number she didn't recognise displayed on the screen.

'Is that DS Bishop, please?' A male voice, quiet with a hint of an accent originating far away from Lincolnshire.

'It is.'

'My name's Owen Howell, Trevor Foster's my DI.'

'Okay.' Catherine wondered where this was going.

'It's just that . . . Well, I know what Foster said to you, how he spoke. I know how he can be and I wondered . . . Look, could we meet?'

'Meet? Why?'

'Just to talk. I'm on the Ron Woffenden case, you see.'

Catherine frowned. 'I've been told to stay away, to leave you to it.'

'I know you have. I just thought, if it was me I'd want to know what was going on.'

'And you'll tell me?'

'Can we meet?' he asked again. She hesitated, knowing she should keep her distance and yet unable to all the same.

'Look, I've got to go. I'll text you.'

Catherine slid her phone back into her pocket.

'All right, Sarge?' Dave asked.

She nodded. So much for not letting the job take you over.

18

At Moon Pond, Jo Webber listened as Knight explained what little they knew so far.

'Okay, let's go and see her,' the pathologist said.

When they approached, a couple of crime scene investigators moved away. Under the shelter of the tent, the body seemed safer somehow, protected. Knight forced himself to look at the ruined face. Beside him, Jo Webber made a sound in her throat that Knight couldn't identify. Pity? Anger? It might have been either. Mick Caffery came to stand beside them and they were silent for a few seconds. Knight couldn't have said what passed through the minds of the others, but he guessed it would be similar to the silent promise he made to the dead woman. It was the same as he had to every victim he'd met since the day he first put on his police uniform: *We will find the person that did this to you.* It didn't always happen, but that wasn't for the want of trying, on his part at least.

Jo Webber squatted and bent closer to the body.

'What can you tell us about the stomach wound?' Knight asked her.

'It's more an incision,' Webber replied, peering closer. 'I'll examine it during the post-mortem of course, but at the moment I'd say she was cut after she died. That raises some interesting questions.'

'Such as?' Mick asked, though he had his own ideas.

'Well, I'm not seeing an obvious cause of death. No trauma to her head, no signs of strangulation. She could have drowned, but . . . I'll take the swabs and other samples now, then I want to get her to the mortuary as we soon as can.'

Mick Caffery nodded. 'She's been out here long enough.'

'Can you give us any idea as to the time of death?' Knight asked. In his experience, it wasn't a question on which pathologists were too keen this early, but they needed to get the investigation moving. Jo Webber looked up at him. Although he had only met her a few times before, Knight knew she had a very good reputation in her field.

'Inspector, you know it's going to be difficult for me to even give you an estimate. I'd say more than forty-eight hours, but you can appreciate it's impossible to be more precise at the moment. She didn't die here, I can tell you that much, and I don't think she's been in the pond.'

'She hasn't?' Knight was surprised. 'But I've just asked the DCI to arrange an underwater search.'

Jo shrugged. 'I'm not saying that you won't find anything in there, just that she hasn't been in it. Not submerged for any length of time anyway.'

Mick nodded in agreement. 'I didn't think so either but I wanted to wait for you to say so. We'd better still search the pond. Maybe her clothes will be in there.'

There was a rustle as another protective suit joined them. Catherine Bishop stood and watched as Dr Webber swabbed, combed and plucked the samples she needed from the body. Catherine had phoned DI Knight from the car on the way back from the Cook's house to tell him what she had found out from Lauren's family, which didn't amount to much, she had to admit. She gazed down at the dead woman's blonde hair. Was it the same shade as Lauren's? It looked it, though it was damp and dirty, the length of weed threaded through it seeming obscene. Blinking, she turned away. She couldn't tell for sure, and there was no room for guessing. Behind the face mask she swallowed, wishing she had thought to grab a bottle of water from somewhere. Knight turned to her.

'I think we ought to head back to the station.'

She nodded. DCI Kendrick would have started the wheels in motion but he would want them there too. Dr Webber stood up straight, holding the small of her back for a second.

'I'll say two o'clock for the post-mortem,' she said. 'That should give us all time to do what we need to in the meantime. Mick?'

'Yep, fine with me,' he agreed.

'I'll see you then.' Knight nodded. Catherine flashed a quick smile at Jo and Mick before following Knight, who was making his way back to the outer perimeter where they removed their protective clothing and bagged it. There was a car parked out in the lane and Catherine nodded towards it.

'Looks like the press have arrived.'

'Let's hope they stay out there. Any thoughts?' Knight asked.

'I just wish we knew if it was Lauren.'

'How are her family?'

'I had to tell them about the body,' she admitted.

'Difficult to remove the items we needed otherwise, I'd have thought.'

'The wound to her stomach's odd.'

'It's an incision, I'm told. Not confirmed until the post-mortem of course, but that was Dr Webber's first impression.'
Catherine was horrified.

'It was deliberate? I thought maybe she'd been caught by a rock in the pond.'

'Jo Webber says that she doesn't think the body has been in the water. I'll see you back at the station.'

Catherine nodded and started to walk away, then stopped and turned back.

'Jonathan? If the body was never in the water, how did she get the weed in her hair?'

As Catherine and Knight went in through the back door of the station, Rich Smithies appeared in the corridor. He beckoned to them.

'What's up, Rich? Someone nicked your last sweet?'

Smithies shook his head.

'No, thankfully. Just a word of warning: Guess who's turned up early?'

Knight cleared his throat. 'DI Shea?'

'That's the one. Settling into the Super's office as we speak. He's been looking for you, boss.'

'Right. Thanks, Rich.' Knight passed his hands over his face.

'I don't see what he's going to achieve that we can't,' Catherine muttered under her breath as they climbed the stairs.

'We'll see,' Knight replied.

'Do you know anything about him?'

'No. You?'

'Never heard of him. I'd have said if I had.'

'No doubt.' Knight lifted his eyebrows as he pushed open the door at the top of the stairs. Catherine grinned at him.

'Have you heard from Caitlin?' Only a month previously, she would never have asked him such a personal question, but the time she'd spent at Knight's house during their last major case, coupled with his visits to her house while she'd been on sick leave, had brought them closer. He was still looked on as an oddity by most of the station, but people were beginning to warm to him a little, Catherine could see that.

'I've had a couple of emails.' Knight shrugged, following Catherine across the office. 'She's fine, the baby's fine. That's about it.'

'How long until it's due?'

'Four months. Towards the end of March, I think.' *The twentieth,* Knight said to himself. *The twentieth of March.* His ex-girlfriend's pregnancy was occupying his thoughts more and more. As much as he'd tried, he couldn't fight the attachment he was developing to the child. As Catherine dropped into her chair, Knight headed for the DCI's office. He tapped on the door, but there was no reply. He turned, frowning. The Superintendent's office door was also closed, but Knight could hear voices inside. He knocked and the door opened to reveal Detective Inspector Patrick Shea, who strode straight past him, followed by a woman in her early thirties. Shea glanced around the main office with a slight frown as Knight took a step towards him. He had to look up to meet the other man's gaze; Shea was tall and broad, his belly straining the buttons of his black pinstriped suit. His fairish hair was thinning and his plump cheeks were flushed.

'You're DI Knight? Come in, come in.' He clapped a meaty hand onto Knight's shoulder and ushered him and the young woman inside the Super's office, thumping the door closed behind him.

On the other side of the room, Catherine Bishop was making tea. 'Anyone else?' she called, knowing she would be met with a volley of responses. She handed out the mugs, leaving Anna Varcoe's until last. As she approached her desk, Anna glanced up from her computer screen, her cheeks red. Catherine set the cup on her desk.

'Thanks, Sarge.' Anna kept her eyes on the monitor in front of her.

'All right, Anna?' Catherine sipped from her own mug. Anna nodded and Catherine decided to take pity on her. 'Anna. What you do outside of work and who you do it with is none of my business. Okay?'

Anna's cheeks grew even redder as she stammered, 'Okay, Sarge.'

'I'm the last person to say anything about who's going out with who, as you know.' Catherine's voice was quiet and Anna met her eyes.

'I'm sorry about what happened with Claire. We all are.'

Catherine's smile was an effort. 'Thank you.' She walked away a few paces, then turned back. 'Oh, and Anna?'

'Sarge?'

'Don't give him an inch.'

'So the car that Paul Hughes was driving was found abandoned in Leicestershire?' Patrick Shea asked, his protuberant pale blue eyes flickering from Knight to the screen of the laptop he had set on the Superintendent's desk. Knight noticed that Shea had shoved all of the Super's belongings, including her silver framed photographs and crystal water glass to one side of the desk. He didn't think Stringer would be too impressed, especially since Shea had obviously eaten a pasty or sausage roll in here at some point since his arrival. There were pastry crumbs on his shirt front, on the desktop and no doubt on the floor too.

The DS Shea had brought with him, Melissa Allan, sat to one side with a notebook propped on her lap. Her hair had been pulled back into a neat ponytail and her eyes were alert. She wore a grey jacket with a matching skirt and shoes with heels that seemed precarious for someone whose job was anything but predictable. Knight realised Shea was still waiting for him to speak, his eyes wide and his plump lips open.

'Oh,' Knight said, trying to remember what Shea had asked him. 'The car was found at Leicester Forest East services. He was heading back to London, from what we could piece together about his journey. The number plate was recognised at several points between Lincoln and the services.'

'And you've evidence that Hughes was in Northolme on the day we think he was murdered.'

Knight nodded. 'I saw him myself.'

Shea sat back, threading his stubby fingers together. Knight was quiet, waiting.

Eventually, Shea said, 'I find it strange that Hughes should be brought back up to Lincolnshire to be killed, don't you, DI Knight?'

Knight shrugged. 'It must have been planned beforehand, with the barn where we found his body marked as a suitable place to bring him.'

'But why here? Why draw attention to Northolme? If we're presuming, and I think you have been, that the killer or killers of Paul Hughes live in this area, why soil their own patch?'

'Because they felt more comfortable bringing him onto their own territory? I don't know. We met a brick wall with pretty much every line of investigation.' Knight raised a hand to his face, rubbing his eyes. Shea pursed his lips and raised almost invisible eyebrows. His eyelashes were pale too and Knight was reminded of an earnest-looking pig, then had to blink a few times to try to remove the image.

'Yes, I can see that you had difficulties.' Shea nodded. 'DS Allan and I were just discussing how we can best attack this investigation.'

Knight glanced at Allan who sat up even straighter, a hint of a smile playing across her face.

'Attack?'

Shea waved a plump hand. 'Address it, approach it. You're a capable investigator and yet you seem to have struggled.'

'It's been challenging, yes.' Knight kept his voice neutral.

'How did you come to see Paul Hughes the day he died, Inspector?' Allan spoke for the first time. Knight turned to look at her again.

'It's all been documented. I'd noticed the car a few times that day and thought it might be following me. When I saw it parked in the road out there,' he nodded towards the window, 'I went out and took the number plate, then found that it had been hired by one of the companies Malc Hughes owns down in London.'

'Malc Hughes being the father of Paul?' Shea waited for confirmation, as if he didn't know. Knight frowned, feeling uneasy. He didn't like the way this was going. 'And what did you do then?' Shea frowned, pleading ignorance.

'As I've said, you can read it for yourself; no doubt you already have. I approached the car. Paul Hughes recognised me and drove away. The next time I saw him he was dead.' Knight took a few deep breaths, trying to calm himself. The image of Hughes in that place was one he would never forget.

'And you didn't see Paul Hughes again until you were called to the scene where his body had been discovered?' Shea's voice was polite, as if he were offering Knight a cup of tea.

'I've already said so. Just what are you implying?' Knight asked. Shea looked horrified.

'Nothing, nothing at all. I'm establishing the facts.'

'The facts have already *been* established. Cameras picked Hughes up leaving Lincoln. He stopped for petrol near Newark, then joined the M1 somewhere between Nottingham and Leicester, where he stopped again. As you know, that's where we think he met his murderer, or was abducted by him. Most likely there were at least two people - Paul Hughes was quite a big man.'

'So I believe,' Shea said, his eyes taking in Knight's average physique. 'And you weren't able to identify a vehicle that might have been following Hughes, or obtain any CCTV footage from the services that was helpful?'

'There was nothing. No witnesses, no suspicious vehicles. If they followed him from Lincoln, they could have changed cars. You *know* all this if you've read the reports,' Knight sighed, frustrated.

This was a waste of his time, and there was an undercurrent to the whole meeting that was making him defensive. He'd done nothing wrong and had run the investigation to the best of his ability, as always. What was going on here?

Shea shuffled in the Superintendent's chair and folded his hands across his belly.

'I think that's all for now, Inspector.'

Knight's teeth itched at his condescending tone – they were the same rank, however important Shea seemed to think he was. He got to his feet, eager to be far away from the pair of them as soon as possible. 'No doubt we'll bump into each other around the station.' Shea flashed Knight a false smile and lumbered to his feet. Allan also stood, smoothing her skirt over her thighs. Knight saw Shea's piggy little eyes feasting on Allan's backside as she stepped across to open the door and clenched his teeth.

'Have a good afternoon.' Allan smiled as he passed her. He nodded, not trusting himself to speak.

19

Knight went across to Catherine's desk, where she was dunking another chocolate biscuit into a mug of tea.

'Burnt my fingers now,' she said, rummaging on her desk for a spoon.

'Did you see them?' he asked in an undertone. Catherine raised an eyebrow.

'Pinky and Perky?'

He laughed, the tension broken.

'That's perfect.'

'I caught a quick glimpse of them coming out of the Super's office. What did they want?'

'To accuse me of killing Paul Hughes.' He waited as she choked on her tea.

'They what?' she coughed.

'Do you know where the DCI is?'

'His office. I think he's avoiding them,' she said, twirling a strand of hair around her finger.

'I don't blame him. I better go and have a word.'

'They didn't say that, did they?'

'Not in so many words, but I didn't like some of the questions.'

'I've never heard anything so stupid.' The image of the tattoo on Knight's back crossed Catherine's mind but she refused to dwell on it. 'What about the post-mortem?' she said instead.

'Plenty of time. I want you to come with me.'

'Well, okay.' She didn't look too thrilled at the prospect, but Knight knew that if the body was Lauren Cook, and there seemed a fair chance it was, the more information Catherine had first-hand the better. Lauren's husband had spoken to Catherine first and she deserved a chance to prove herself again. Not, Knight thought as he crossed the room to Kendrick's office, that she had anything to prove in his opinion, but he knew only too well how soon a good reputation could be destroyed. He hoped it wasn't about to happen to him again here.

'I'm not sure where they're from,' Kendrick said in a low voice. Knight had to lean forward to hear him, which was a new experience. Usually every sentence the DCI uttered was loud and clear, more often than not to people in the next county.

'You're not?'

'I presumed they were from HQ in Lincoln, but the Super didn't say that, did she?'

Knight thought back to the meeting the previous evening. 'No. No, I don't think she did.'

What had Stringer said? *If there are any links, they'll be investigated too.* What had she meant by that? After the questions he'd just sat through, he had to wonder.

'They can't think you're involved, it's just . . . ludicrous. Anyway, you wouldn't still be here if that's the way their minds were working.'

'I'm not sure how much of an alibi they need. I was here at the station all day, then at the hospital most of the night.'

'You're looking at no less than an hour's drive each way to get to Leicester.'

'Plus all the time needed to inflict the sort of injuries Hughes suffered. It wasn't a rush job, that's for sure.'

Kendrick was pinching his lower lip again. 'I don't like it,' he said. 'I'm sure they can't think you have anything to do with it, but why even give you that impression?'

'No idea. Do you know anything about Shea, or DS Allan?'

'Never heard of either of them. I should have realised when I didn't recognise his name that he wasn't from around here, and the same goes for her.' He raised a hand to his face and scratched his cheek. 'If I were you, I'd keep my head down and hope they either find who did it and sod off, or give up and sod off anyway.'

Knight glanced at his watch.

'I thought I'd take Catherine to the post-mortem.'

'Good idea. If this is how they're playing it with you, I dread to think what they'd say to her.'

As Catherine drove, she glanced at Knight, wondering what he was thinking. It had to hurt, another detective, especially an officer of the same rank, being sent in to mop up your mess. Knight was quiet, his face turned to the window most of the time. The sky was a heavy grey with ominous clouds hovering. Speeding along the lanes, Catherine flicked on the headlights, the flat Lincolnshire fields bleak and unimposing as the countryside turned in on itself before winter took hold.

The turreted entrance to Lincoln Prison, which stood opposite the hospital, always reminded Catherine of the castle itself, down towards the city centre. Locking the car, she glanced across at the tall walls and panelled wooden gate. How many of the men inside were there as a result of operations she had been involved with? She turned to Knight, who was buttoning his jacket.

'Which would you rather spend a night in?' she asked. Knight followed her gaze.

'Hospital. At least you can sign yourself out of there if you want to.'

They set off, wincing as a shrieking ambulance flew past them towards the waiting doors of the emergency entrance.

'They both sound grim to me,' she said, glancing up at the main hospital building and thinking back to the night she'd spent here as a patient a few weeks earlier. She shook her head as she hurried to catch up with Knight.

In the corridor, Doctor Jo Webber was chatting to a couple of technicians. When Knight and Bishop approached they fell silent, Webber's perfect features relaxing into a welcoming smile. Catherine grinned back and Knight gave a nervous nod.

'I didn't expect to see both of you.'

'We thought it would be useful,' Knight croaked. Webber raised her eyebrows but didn't pursue it. They all looked up as footsteps approached and Mick Caffery joined them.

Catherine emerged from the changing room first, adjusting the mask over her face as she entered the mortuary itself. Although it was an essential process and vital to any investigation into a suspicious death, being present at a post-mortem was not a pleasant experience. She had attended a few now, but the strange mixture of dread and wonder had never changed. As difficult as it was to stand as an observer as the pathologist went through each gruesome step, it was also intriguing.

Early in her CID career, a DI had told Catherine that she should look at a post-mortem as a unique opportunity, not a horror show. However difficult it was to stand there, however intrusive the procedure was, it offered an unparalleled chance to pick up all sorts of information about the victim about what, and more importantly who, killed them. To Catherine, the stomach-churning sounds and smells were to be endured as stoically as possible, because in the end the only chance a victim had to tell their story was during the post-mortem, and if you couldn't bear to listen, then could you do investigating their death justice? If you focused on the process and tried to forget, just for a few hours, that the subject had been a real person with hopes and dreams and wishes, then it was endurable.

Endurable, but still terrible.

Knight and Caffery shuffled into the room, as did the mortuary technician. The victim was on a trolley, still encased in a body bag. Catherine turned away. It was time to begin closing her mind, to focus on the body as an 'it' rather than a 'her'. For the next few hours, the victim would cease to be a person and would just be a subject. It was the only way. Jo Webber strode in.

'Are we ready to start?' she asked. There was a general murmur of agreement.

Webber bent over the body and removed more samples with swabs and tweezers. She also took the victim's fingerprints, carefully setting the woman's hands back on the stainless steel table beside her once the process was complete. Catherine took in a deep breath, then blew it out through pursed lips. The fingerprints could be vital in confirming the dead woman's identity. Her stomach tightened as Webber bent towards the woman's face, but the doctor just studied the ruined expanse of flesh. After a minute or so, she turned towards the wound in the woman's midriff, studying it without touching. Then she turned away.

Once the body had been photographed and washed, Jo Webber began to examine it in detail. She worked methodically from the top of the victim's head over every inch of her body, recording a few small scars and any other unusual features she saw. She spent a long time examining and photographing the injuries the woman had sustained to her face, and then again focused on the stomach wound. Catherine was silent, standing beside Jonathan Knight. This part wasn't so bad. The woman was still recognisably human. That she was naked and exposed to the eyes of five strangers plus a camera and video equipment was the only indignity so far. Catherine kept her gaze away from the woman's face; the ruined flesh a constant reminder that she needed them, that they were the ones who had to provide answers. Catherine was not a religious person and she did not believe in an afterlife, but sometimes, in the presence of a victim of violent, unnatural death, there was a connection, almost a whisper, a promise or pact. Though she didn't think to 'rest in peace' was an actual state of being, Catherine had to acknowledge that dead victims seemed to need an explanation, and their living relatives certainly did. They had no answer yet as to how this woman had died, but in any case, Catherine didn't think for a second that she'd hacked her own stomach open. Someone, somewhere knew what had happened and Catherine intended to find them. She gave the woman on the table a tiny nod. It was a promise.

They waited in Jo Webber's office for the pathologist to reappear. She hadn't said much during the autopsy apart from the observations she had to make, and both detectives were keen to hear her thoughts. The cloudy afternoon had darkened into a miserable evening, rain hammering on the murky window of the room. Knight had phoned Keith Kendrick for an update on the team's activity that afternoon but it didn't sound like much progress had been made. With no witnesses except the two teenagers who had found the body and no name as yet for their victim, progress was slow at best.

'Has Jo Webber come up with any ideas about that gash to her stomach?' Kendrick's voice reverberated in Knight's ear and he held the handset away from his face with a grimace.

'Not yet. She's getting cleaned up.'

'Bloody hell. Your mates have left for the evening, by the way.'

'Mates?'

'Shea and Allan. Sound like a country and western act, don't they?' Knight waited while Kendrick had a chuckle at his own wit. Eventually the DCI said, 'I'll tell this lot to get off home then if you don't have anything for us yet, then they can be in early for a full briefing. I'll see you and Catherine in the morning.'

Knight slid the phone back into his pocket just as Catherine received a text from her brother: Going out with Anna. Don't wait up x

'They haven't wasted any time,' she muttered.

'Sorry?' Knight asked.

'Doesn't matter.' There was another text too that must have been received when she'd left her phone and other belongings in a locker outside the mortuary. It was from Chris Rogers; he'd sent her Ellie's mobile number: Faye asked me to pass this on. Don't kill the messenger Sarge. She smiled to herself and typed: Does Ellie know about this?

In the chair beside her, Mick Caffery was scrolling through his emails. They all looked up as the office door opened and Jo Webber stuck her head inside.

'Can I get anyone a drink before we start?' she offered. Knight and Caffery both asked for coffee and Catherine got to her feet.

'I'll come and give you a hand.'

She wanted to ask Jo about another post-mortem she might have performed, this one a few weeks earlier, but she didn't quite dare. Anyway, what good would it do her? The pathologist would never share any details, and she knew how Claire had died.

A small staff room was located a few doors down from Jo Webber's office. Its ancient-looking cupboards held the usual assortment of battered crockery and ill-matched cutlery. Webber filled the kettle from a dripping tap and flicked it on to boil as Catherine attempted to select the least grotty mugs from a motley collection. The walls were painted a sickly green and the beige carpet tiles needed replacing. Jo Webber, now dressed in a grey suit and a crisp white shirt, ran her hands through her hair.

'Long day,' Catherine observed, leaning against the wall.

'Aren't they all?' Webber's smile was tired.

There was a pause, the only sound in the room the kettle building up steam. Webber dropped tea bags into two of the mugs and took a jar of instant coffee out of a cupboard, then turned to Catherine.

'So what's the story with your DI?' she asked.

Catherine stared at her in surprise.

'Jonathan?'

'How come he's washed up in Lincolnshire?'

'He told me he'd had enough of London.'

Jo pulled her hair back into a ponytail and then let it fall again.

'I can understand that. I love visiting the place, but I wouldn't want to work there. Is he married?'

Catherine hid a smile. Jo Webber was nothing if not direct.

'No. He had a girlfriend, but they split up before he transferred up here.'

Jo nodded

'He's so quiet.'

'Shy, I think.'

'You can say that again,' the pathologist laughed.

The kettle boiled and Webber poured water in the cups, then hauled a litre of milk out of the fridge and added a splash to each one.

Back in her office, Jo sipped from her mug before setting it on her desk.

'Okay,' she said. 'I think I can give you a cause of death, though I'll need to wait for confirmation from the toxicology samples.'

Catherine frowned and Knight sat forward in his seat, cradling his cup against his chest.

'Toxicology? You mean she didn't drown?'

Jo Webber shook her head. 'No. The incision in her stomach gave me a clue, but the samples I've taken should confirm it.'

'I thought you said the cut was made after she was dead?' Knight was bemused.

'It was. Look,' Jo said, exchanging a glance with Mick Caffery. 'Why would you cut open a dead body? Unless you're a pathologist there's no reason to, is there? We do see mutilation of corpses sometimes, but I think this was done for a specific reason. Most people can't wait to get away from a body.'

'I'm sorry to sound thick, but . . . you mean someone wanted to take some sort of evidence out of her stomach?' Catherine puzzled. Jo took pity on them.

'In a way, yes. I'm pretty sure the toxicology report will confirm that this woman died of a drug overdose.'

Knight stared at her as she picked up her cup again.

'So . . . wait a minute. You don't mean . . .?'

Jo Webber drank the last of her tea and nodded.

'I think this woman was a drug mule.'

There was a silence. Mick didn't seem surprised, but to Catherine and Knight it was a shock. Catherine recovered first.

'I can't believe we didn't think of it when we first saw her – obviously you two had an idea though?'

'I thought it made sense, but there was no point in having a guess when the post-mortem would tell us for sure,' Mick admitted.

'So you're saying that this woman had a belly full of . . . what? Heroin?' Knight asked.

'I'm expecting cocaine. It won't take us long to find out,' Jo replied.

'So she would have been carrying a number of packets of the drug, one or more of which burst?' Catherine was trying to make sense of it. 'And rather than get her to a hospital, some heartless bastard let her die, then sliced her open rather than lose their merchandise and run the risk of being caught?'

Jo sighed.

'That's what I'm assuming happened, yes. Along those lines anyway.'

There was another silence as they digested the inhumanity of it.

'Just when you think you've seen it all . . .' Mick mumbled.

'What else can you tell us, Jo?' Catherine asked. 'I'm still wondering if this is Lauren Cook.'

'How old is Lauren?'

'Twenty-four.'

'The ages fits then,' Jo sighed.

'Lauren has green eyes – sort of hazel.'

'Then the colour matches too, though there's been some deterioration of our victim's eyes, of course.'

'It's supposition until we have some confirmation from fingerprints or DNA, but it's not looking great for Lauren,' Catherine said, the faces of Lauren's husband and parents filling her mind.

'What about the damage to her face?' Knight asked. Jo Webber shook her head, her nose wrinkling.

'Savage is the best way to describe it. Post-mortem, thankfully.'

'To delay identification or done in a fit of anger?'

Jo shrugged. 'Either of those, or it could be neither. I'm not going to speculate on the reason behind it, Inspector, you know that. Not my department.' She smiled at him as he cleared his throat.

'Her hands were left alone though,' Mick pointed out. 'He wasn't worried about her being identified from fingerprints.'

'Maybe he knows she doesn't have a record,' Catherine suggested. 'If you were hiring a drug mule, wouldn't you want one that hadn't been in contact with the police before?'

Mick nodded agreement.

'The damage to her face was caused by several heavy blows with a flat weapon; a shovel perhaps,' Jo went on. Catherine took a breath, trying not to allow the images of the impact enter her mind. 'The incision in her stomach was clumsy – our man is no surgeon. There were a couple of small nicks at one end of the wound as if he made a few false starts before really going for it.' Jo Webber paused for a second. 'I'd say the blade used was around nine or ten centimetres long.'

'Not a scalpel then?' Catherine checked.

'No. As I say, the cutting was done with no care at all – he seems to have just hacked away until he found what he was looking for. I'm surprised he didn't slice any of the packets open, or at least I didn't find any evidence that he did.'

Catherine swallowed. 'As you said, Mick – just when you think nothing will surprise you . . .'

He nodded. 'Talk about plumbing the depths.'

Pushing back his chair, Knight got to his feet. 'I better phone the DCI again.'

'Just a second.' Jo Webber held up a hand and Knight waited. 'I think this will be useful. In the stomach incision, I found an eyelash. Now, since we've established that our victim was already dead when the cut was made, I'd be surprised if it belongs to her as she wouldn't have been leaning over to have a look at what had been done.'

Mick let out a low whistle as Catherine asked, 'You're thinking it could be from whoever did the cutting?'

'It could be.' Jo nodded. 'Whoever it belongs to though, they must have been near her body after death. I doubt it got into the incision from the floor or another surface, but I can't say for sure.'

'Either way, they're a person of interest.' Jonathan Knight had sat back down.

'You said she didn't die by the pond,' Catherine said. 'Was there anything else on her body that might help us find where she was when she died or when she was cut?'

'I doubt it.' Webber's tone was regretful. 'I think the body had been washed.'

'Washed in what?' Catherine asked.

'Again, I'm not sure yet, I'm afraid. Some kind of cleaning fluid though. Diluted bleach is a possibility.'

'Someone who knew what they were doing then,' Caffery observed.

'They missed the eyelash though,' Jo pointed out.

'Let's hope that's a stroke of luck for us,' Knight said, on his feet again. He left the room, phone pressed to his ear.

'Use the staff kitchen,' Jo Webber called after him.

Out in the corridor, he sidestepped a trolley that was being wheeled along at speed by a porter, and ducked into the dingy little room. As he waited for Keith Kendrick to pick up the phone, he gazed out of the window. The rain was still being driven against the glass, the night blustery. He could see a ward in the next building where a middle-aged man and woman were sitting by the bed of an elderly patient who appeared to be asleep. A nurse approached them and Knight turned away.

'Jonathan?' Kendrick's voiced boomed in his ear at last. Knight filled him in on Webber's preliminary report.

'Finding the eyelash is a stroke of luck then,' Kendrick said. 'I'm glad Jo Webber did the PM.' He sighed. 'Right. I'm still at the station; is it worth me trying to find someone with a brain in their head who can start looking at missing person reports?'

'It's hard to say. We can't confirm that the victim is Lauren Cook, but the PM didn't rule the possibility out either. It seems a huge coincidence that a body should turn up matching her description within hours of her being reported missing.'

'But then there are any number of blonde-haired, hazel-eyed young women wandering around the place,' Kendrick pointed out. 'Wasn't there anything unusual about the body that we can check with her husband or parents? A tattoo? I thought everyone had one now.'

Knight's hand sought out his shoulder blade. 'Not quite everyone. Our victim didn't and neither has Lauren Cook.'

Kendrick sucked air in over his teeth and Knight cringed at the sound.

'Typical. No scars, no blemishes, no birthmarks?'

'No.'

'Bugger.' Kendrick paused, then said, 'I suppose it'll be classed as murder.'

'I don't know.'

'Hmm. I'd better speak to the Super. I'll see you tomorrow.'

Knight put his phone away, feeling a sudden chill. If it wasn't murder, what was it?

20

The wind howled, buffeting the car each time there was a gap in the hedge. The rain had become icy hail that bounced off the windscreen as the wipers struggled to cope.

'What a night,' Catherine's eyes were fixed on the road ahead. When Knight didn't reply, she said, 'I can guess what you're thinking.'

He glanced at her, surprised. 'Can you?'

'The Hughes family.'

'I wasn't actually,' he retorted.

'I thought this was just the kind of thing you'd have their card marked for.'

'If we were in London, maybe. It's too messy for Hughes anyway.'

'Messy?' Catherine braked as they approached a sharp corner.

'Too amateurish then. Hughes would have had some dodgy doctor around to make sure the woman survived as well as the drugs. Disposing of a dead body isn't easy, as we know.'

'It's weird, isn't it? Why go to the trouble of destroying her face if you're going to dump her somewhere she'll be found quickly?

They must have realised she would be. Why not weigh her down and put her in the pond? Jo seems to think the weed was threaded through her hair deliberately, since she hadn't been in the water. Why would you?'

Knight heard a beep and pulled his phone out of his pocket. 'I don't know.' He opened the text: **This is my personal mobile number. I thought you might want to use it some time. Jo.** He stared for a second, then a grin spread across his face as he took in what she meant. Catherine glanced at him and smiled to herself.

They arrived at the station and Knight ran across to his own vehicle. Catherine drove away, giving him a helpful wave when he struggled to open his car door against the wind. As she accelerated away from the station, she tried to put the post-mortem out of her mind and focus on tonight's meeting. She still didn't know whether what she was doing was wise, but it was too late now.

The pub where they had agreed to meet was in a tiny village, no more than ten houses and a church squatting against the gusting wind. Catherine ran inside, her hair whipping around her face, her shoes and the bottoms of her trousers splattered with muddy water from the potholed car park. She shoved open the heavy wooden door and stumbled into a corridor, taking a few seconds to run her fingers through her hair. There wasn't much she could do about her wet, grubby clothes though. Another door displayed a sign which said 'Public Bar' and she pushed through it.

Inside, the floor was black slate tiles, the bar set in the corner of the room. Dark wood tables and chairs stood along one wall and comfortable-looking booths upholstered in navy blue made up the rest of the seating. The walls were painted white, swirls of plaster giving them texture, with horse brasses hung along them at intervals. Framed photographs decorated the rest of the wall space, some black and white and some colour, all of them of landscapes, both local and further afield. Catherine took in the scene, liking what she saw, feeling herself begin to relax. The pub was quiet with a couple studying menus at a table and an elderly chap reading a newspaper at the bar with a glass of whiskey at his elbow. A young man sat alone in a booth, sipping from a pint of bitter. When he saw her come in, he smiled and raised a hand. His hair was thick, cut close to his head. He got to his feet as she approached and she saw he was quite short, an inch or so taller than her with broad shoulders and an appealing grin. He was casually dressed in dark jeans and a white polo shirt.

'Sergeant Bishop?' He held out a hand and she shook it. 'Can I get you a drink?'

'Call me Catherine. Just a lemonade, thanks, I'm driving.'

'That's part of the reason I asked if we could meet here,' he admitted, flashing her another smile and pointing at his pint. 'It's my local. Well, it is now.'

As he set her drink on the table, she said, 'You're Welsh?'

He nodded and took a mouthful of beer. 'I grew up in Powys, in a village not too far from Shrewsbury.'

'Isn't that in England?'

'Shrewsbury is.' Owen nodded again. 'My village is in Wales, but it's close to the border.'

'Sounds like that matters.'

'To some people. My dad's Welsh and my mum's English. Doesn't matter to me where people are from or,' he met Catherine's eyes, 'who they sleep with.'

She smiled, acknowledging the point. 'Pity your boss doesn't feel the same.'

He screwed his face into an expression of disgust. 'Tell me about it. If it makes you feel any better, he's not too keen on me either. He thinks it's funny to leave inflatable sheep on my desk.'

'You're joking.'

'No. And when England play Wales at rugby . . . Well, you can imagine. Bloke's a dinosaur.'

Catherine leaned forward, lifted her glass of lemonade and said, 'You're working on the Woffenden case?'

'Have been for months now. We almost had them.'

'What happened?'

'I don't know. We knew they were using the house as a brothel, suspected that they were keeping the women there against their will. One night the surveillance was called off and the next thing we know, the house is empty, just when we were going to go in there.'

Catherine frowned. 'Wait a minute. Your DI blamed us for that, said me and my colleague turning up at the house blew your cover.'

'He would do, anything to cover his own arse. No, they knew they were being watched well before you got there, but we don't know how.'

'My boss said you've found Ron Woffenden though?'

Owen drank more beer. 'Yeah, at least we thought we had. We know they'll have set up somewhere else by now, they won't want to miss out on the money.'

'Any idea where?'

'Ron's back in Lincoln.'

Catherine coughed as her lemonade threatened to choke her. 'Seriously?'

'I know, last place you'd think of. That's what he'll be banking on.'

'Have you brought him in?'

'Not yet. Forensics ties him to the house that we know was being used as a brothel, but DI Foster wants to catch him in the act.' Owen drank deeply, frustration clear on his face. 'The DI won't bring Woffenden in. We know where he is, we know what he was doing, what he's still involved in. Foster says we don't have enough to charge him with yet.'

'He's probably right.' Catherine sighed. She nodded at Owen's empty glass. 'Can I get you another?'

'Thank you.' He pushed his glass across the table. Catherine approached the bar, where a woman sat flicking through a magazine.

'Lemonade and a pint of whatever he's drinking please.' She jerked her head in Owen's direction. The woman stood up, smiling. 'Gorgeous, isn't he? That accent . . . I keep pointing him out to my daughter but she doesn't seem interested.' Catherine smiled as the barmaid set a clean pint glass under the beer pump. 'He's never met a woman in here before.'

Her eyes were curious and Catherine felt compelled to admit, 'We're just colleagues.'

'Oh right. So he's single then?'

'I'm not sure.'

Catherine took the drinks back to where Owen sat, now frowning at his phone.

'Cheers,' he said as she sat back down. 'You know, it is strange that Woffenden and his gang knew we were watching. And why would he come back to Lincoln so soon after being found out?'

'I don't know. Is he still under surveillance?'

'Yeah, but he's keeping his nose clean, stays in all the time.'

'He has a house?'

'Renting a flat in the city centre. Short-term lease, one bedroom. No visitors, nothing dodgy going on.'

'So either Woffenden's turned over a new leaf - which doesn't seem likely -, or . . .'

'Or he's lying low.'

'There is another possibility.' Catherine drank some lemonade, not wanting to put the words in Owen's mouth.

'That he knows he's safe?' he added at last.

'It all comes back to how they knew you were going to raid the place.'

'A tip-off?'

'It's possible, isn't it?' She watched his eyes darken as he thought about it.

'Someone feeding Woffenden information?' He hated the thought of it just as much as she did, she could see it in his face.

'I don't know, not necessarily. They could still have just seen you watching and cleared out as a precaution.'

'Still means someone messed up though, and I don't mean you.' He drank a third of his bitter, then wiped a hand across his mouth.

'Did you find any trace of the girls who were working in the brothel?' Catherine asked. It was them she was most worried about. Who knew where they were now, or what they were suffering. Owen shook his head.

'Nothing. We got loads of forensic evidence as you can imagine, but they'd done a pretty thorough job of cleaning up. They'd had a bonfire in the garden, burnt sheets and bed clothes, but the house was empty otherwise. I'm sorry I don't have much to tell you, but I'll keep you updated.'

'Are you sure? Your DI won't like it.'

Owen made a sound of disgust. 'What he doesn't know won't hurt him. Anyway, after the way he spoke to you with the whole team listening, he deserves it.' He drank again, then set the glass on the table. 'You want to know the problem he really has with you?'

'I'm gay? I've no doubt got a Welsh ancestor somewhere on my family tree?''

He smiled. 'Both of those, but the real reason is he fancied Claire himself.'

'You're kidding?' Catherine shuddered.

'No. He asked her out soon after she started and she turned him down. Then, when the news broke about her and what had happened, I think he felt a bit daft, so he's taking it out on you.'

She drained the last of her lemonade. 'Thanks for meeting me and telling me all this. Will you keep me informed? I want to know what happens to those girls.'

He nodded, raising his pint to her as she picked up her bag and got to her feet. 'Hopefully we'll soon have some news.'

At home, Catherine made a huge mug of tea, set her phone on the coffee table and threw herself onto the sofa. She rubbed her eyes, propped her head on her hand and listened to the silence. She'd lived alone for seven months now and had been surprised that she had enjoyed the experience. There was a freedom in knowing that there was no one waiting up for you, getting more and more annoyed as the meal they'd prepared congealed slowly in the oven. Louise had also been especially good at "tidying" items away and then having no idea where they were. It was just one of the details of her character that had driven Catherine to distraction. Still, Louise was part of her past, just as Claire was. She wished Thomas was around though; it had been a long day and although she couldn't share any of the details of it with him, it would have been good to have had the company. She sighed, knowing she couldn't begin to rely on him. That wouldn't be fair. She had managed alone this far. When she and Louise had been together, they'd had a group of friends that they went out with sometimes, but thanks to her job and the break-up with Louise she hadn't stayed in touch with them. She picked up her phone again hesitantly. Ellie had said she didn't have many friends in the area, and Chris Rogers had confirmed she didn't mind Catherine having her number. There was no chance of a romance, Catherine knew that, but a friendship – why not?

First though, she should be a dutiful daughter. Listening to the phone at the other end, Catherine pictured her parents looking at each other in surprise as their evening television viewing schedule was interrupted. It rang a few more times and she knew they would be having a disagreement about who should pick it up.

'Please answer before I die of old age,' she muttered, stretching her legs out and resting her feet on the coffee table.

'Hello?' Her mum. That meant her dad would have shuffled off to put the kettle on.

'You are in then?'

Her mum tutted. 'Where do you think we'd be, Catherine?'

'Oh, I don't know. A nightclub? A swinger's party?'

'A what?'

'Never mind. Are you okay?'

'Of course we are. What have you been up to?'

Catherine screwed up her face. 'You don't want to know.'

Her mother sighed. 'I was talking to Pat Goodwin today.'

'Who?'

'Her daughter was in your year at school.'

'Gemma?'

'She's a solicitor now. You could have been a solicitor.'

Catherine rolled her eyes. 'Not with my A levels, Mum.'

'You've got a degree.'

'In English, not law.'

'Then Pat told me her nephew's in the police force as well, but he's being fast-tracked. Are you being fast-tracked, Catherine?'

'No, Mum.'

Her mother sighed. 'They don't appreciate you. I hear Thomas is staying with you?'

'For now, yes.'

'He's another one. A qualified teacher who never teaches.'

'I'd put him on for a chat but he's not in.'

'Out with some woman no doubt.'

'I don't know.' She picked up her tea and took a swig.

'What's that you're drinking? It's not vodka is it?'

'Vodka?' Catherine laughed. 'It's tea, Mum.'

'Your Auntie Sandra was telling me about a programme she watched. They said more than half of police officers have a drink problem.'

'More than half? Doesn't sound enough to me.' She set her mug back on the table and waited.

'You can laugh, just make sure you stick to the tea. Here's your dad.'

There was a muffled fumbling noise as the handset was passed between them.

'Catherine?'

'Hello Dad. Move the phone away from your mouth, you're heavy breathing again.'

He gave a few more pants and then asked, 'Arrested anyone today?'

She smiled. 'Not today, no.'

'Hit anyone with your baton?'

'Going to have to disappoint you again, I'm afraid, Dad.'

He clicked his tongue. 'I'm out going for a pint in a minute, thought you might have a new story for me.'

'Sorry. I did fit a whole chocolate digestive in my mouth this morning.'

He laughed. 'That's hardly news, Catherine, you've been doing that since you were eight years old.'

21

The incident room the next morning was busy, filled with the energetic buzz of the first full day of an investigation. Presiding over the room was DS Robin Cuthbert - rotund, balding and better known as 'Monk'. Catherine leant against a desk, hands in her trouser pockets, while Monk coaxed an electronic smart board into life.

'It's brilliant, it's going to make a huge difference,' Monk enthused. 'I've been waiting for another major investigation, especially since the last one . . . Well, you know.'
Catherine tutted as he fiddled with his new toy. 'Come on, I haven't got all day.'

'Stop whinging.' The board flickered for a second before displaying a photograph of Moon Pond. 'Right. So here's where our victim was found.' He pointed and Catherine shook her head.

'Monk, I know where she was found, I saw her lying there. Have we heard anything from Mick Caffery this morning?'
Cuthbert leant over a computer keyboard. 'Not yet, I said so in the briefing.'

'That was an hour ago. Until we get an ID on the body, we're stuck. We've got no witnesses, no properties near where the body was found, so we can't do house to house. I've got people standing around with their hands in their pockets.'

Cuthbert looked at her. 'People like you, you mean?'

Catherine glanced down at herself, then straightened up and pulled her hands free. 'Ha ha. I'm going to give Mick a call.'

Cuthbert shrugged. 'Do it, but I bet he tells you to sod off. Give them a chance.'

'We need to get moving, we've a missing woman and her family to think about.' She'd spoken to Mark Cook earlier, who had confirmed that his wife still hadn't come home. Cuthbert gave her a pitying glance.

'You mean you don't think it's her lying in a drawer in Jo Webber's big fridge? Come on, Catherine. I'm surprised you're not sniffing around Lauren Cook's husband yet.' When she didn't answer, Cuthbert asked, 'Where's Inspector Wallpaper this morning?'

'DI Knight? He was at the briefing.'

'But where is he now?' Cuthbert looked smug and Catherine narrowed her eyes. Monk was a good office manager, but he was also the most irritating officer in the place.

'Does it matter?' she asked.

'He was dragged into the Super's office again by that Inspector Shea and his glamourous assistant.'

'"Glamourous assistant"? Monk, even for you . . .'

'Don't tell me you haven't noticed.' Monk actually winked. Catherine walked away before her irritation turned violent. Kicking Robin Cuthbert up the arse was a much more attractive prospect than talking to him for any length of time.

In a corner of the room, Keith Kendrick was standing over DCs Rogers and Sullivan, who were sitting at computer terminals. As Catherine approached, Chris Rogers made a "Help us!" face.

'It seems Chris may have located Lauren Cook's car,' Kendrick said to Catherine.

'Really? Where is it?'

Rogers turned to the screen on his monitor, which was displaying some CCTV footage.

'Decent quality for a change,' Catherine commented.

'Yep.' Chris pointed at the screen. 'This is her car, heading into town. She turns left,' he waited while the images caught up with his commentary, 'and arrives at the multi-storey. We'll need to request their footage next – I've already spoken to a PCSO who's in the town centre and she's confirmed that the car's still there, she's just been to have a look.'

'Good stuff.' Kendrick clapped a huge hand down on Sullivan's shoulder, making him wince. 'Right, Simon, you get onto that while Chris keeps trying to track Lauren in town.'

He turned away and started to walk away. Catherine scurried along with him, taking two steps to each one of the DCI's.

'It all feels a bit pointless at the moment,' he said, eventually coming to a halt with his back against the wall, gazing out at the activity in the room. 'Until we have an ID on our dead woman . . . We've got Lauren Cook and three other women who it might be, according to our missing persons reports. Wherever Lauren went, she obviously didn't go there in her own car.'

'I was going to give Mick Caffery a ring, see where they're at with the fingerprints.'

'It can't hurt.' Kendrick nodded.

Rather than make the call in the hubbub of the incident room, Catherine went out and into the relative calm of the CID office. As she hurried across the room towards her desk in the corner, the door of the Superintendent's office opened and DS Allan appeared. Catherine glanced at her but carried on walking.

'Sergeant Bishop?'

Catherine stopped, annoyed. 'Can I help you?'

Melissa Allan smiled, perfect white teeth gleaming under the fluorescent strip lights. Today's outfit was a smart black dress with a bright red jacket. Catherine straightened her shirt. Allan was one of those people who would look perfect in a rainstorm.

'Inspector Shea would like a word,' Allan simpered.

'I'm busy at the moment, I'm afraid.'

'It won't take long.' It was a command. Catherine bristled, but knew she may as well get it over with. She took her time walking back towards Allan. The other woman looked her up and down with a hint of a sneer before opening the Super's door fully.

'Do come in.'

Catherine bit back a smart reply as she went inside.

'So you're DS Bishop?' The man behind the desk sat back in his chair and smirked at her. 'Detective Sergeant Catherine Bishop.' He rolled the name around his mouth as if tasting it.

Catherine watched him as Allan settled in the seat next to Shea's.

'That's right. Do you want to see my warrant card, just to be sure?' Shea gave a little titter, setting his jowls wobbling. 'That won't be necessary, thank you. We've been looking forward to meeting you, you're quite famous in the force at the moment, aren't you?' She ignored Shea's insinuation as he gave a condescending smile. 'And you're fully recovered from the injuries you sustained a few weeks ago?'

'I wouldn't be here if I wasn't.'

'I suppose not. It must have been a difficult time for you.'

She said nothing, alarm bells not so much ringing as almost deafening her.

Allan cocked her head to the side, licked her lips and blinked. 'You're obviously dedicated to your job. We're impressed.'

Again, Catherine kept quiet. What was going on? Was Allan actually trying to flirt with her? Shea cleared his throat and straightened his tie.

'Superintendent Stringer is also impressed,' he said. His fleshy cheeks looked slightly damp. Allan tapped red painted fingernails on the arms of her chair and treated Catherine to a beaming smile.

'She is. How long have you been a sergeant now, DS Bishop?'

'A couple of years.' *Which you no doubt know,* she thought, bemused.

'Hm,' said Shea, pretending to think about it. 'Any thoughts about taking the next step up the ladder? If a DI's job were to become vacant, I mean. Inspector's exam?'

'I'm not sure.' Catherine was determined to give them nothing.

'What do you think of DI Knight?' Allan asked, her tone friendly. 'Capable, would you say? Trustworthy?'

'Absolutely, yes. Look,' Catherine said, not liking the way this was going. 'I don't mean to be rude, but I was just on my way to make an important phone call. Could we get to the point?'

Shea's demeanour changed at once. He narrowed his pale, watery eyes and replied, 'Certainly. Why don't we discuss the Paul Hughes murder case?'

'Why don't we?' Catherine folded her hands in her lap. 'Though you understand I've not really been involved? I've just come back from three weeks' sick leave.'

'Ah yes.' Shea raised his pale eyebrows and nudged Allan, who gave a nasty smile. 'Your "sick leave."' He made quotation marks in the air with fingers - further proof in Catherine's eyes that he was a complete dickhead. 'Three whole weeks to get over a bit of a bump to the face, I'm told.'

'Including a week in Egypt,' Allan put in. 'Lovely.'

'Is that a crime now?' Catherine asked mildly.

'Not at all. An expensive way to run away and hide to get over your embarrassment though, eh, Sergeant?'

Catherine shook her head, unable to believe what she was hearing. Shea laughed, realising they were going to get nothing from her. He reached into a beige cardboard folder that lay on the desk between them, took a couple of photographs from it and threw them in front of Catherine, face down. She glanced at them.

'What are they?' she asked, pleased that her discomfort wasn't showing in her voice.

Shea shrugged podgy shoulders. 'Have a look.'

She reached out and turned them over. The first image was a close-up of a man, his eyes wide and panicked, obviously terrified, screaming into the camera. He was sitting in some sort of outbuilding. The second photograph showed the same man, clearly tied to a chair. His head had fallen forward towards his lap and blood pooled around his feet, which were purple, hideously swollen and damaged. More blood streaked the man's limbs and stomach. Several large petrol cans stood ominously next to him. Catherine's breath caught in her throat but she wasn't going to let these two idiots know that she was the least bit rattled.

'Are you trying to shock me?' Her voice was neutral.

Shea shook his head, the flesh around his throat wobbling again. 'Not at all. You're an experienced officer; it would take more than a few sick photographs to disturb you. What might be more of a surprise though is where these pictures came from.'

'Or *who* they came from.' Allan's tone was loaded. Catherine stared from her to Shea and back in confusion.

Suddenly Shea sat forward, grabbed the photographs and tucked them back in the folder. He smiled at Catherine, his face friendly again.

'Thank you for your time,' he said. Allan got up and moved over to the door. Catherine, entirely bemused now, stood and looked down at Shea.

'So what's your point?' she asked. He continued to tidy his papers as if she hadn't spoken. Catherine shook her head contemptuously and marched out.

Knight was in his office, his eyes fixed on his computer screen. Catherine knocked sharply on his door before walking straight in. He looked up in surprise.

'Are you going to tell me what's going on?' Catherine demanded. She closed the door behind her but remained standing.

'What are you talking about?' Knight was totally calm, which only served to make her angrier.

'I've just had Shea and Allan showing me photos of Paul Hughes.'

He stared at her. 'What?'

She pulled the chair that stood in front of his desk nearer and sat in it, running her hands through her hair. 'Pictures of Paul Hughes screaming his head off and then dead in a chair, covered in blood.'

Knight was shaking his head, bemused. 'I've no idea what you're talking about. There were no photographs like that. I mean, obviously we took some once the fire had been put out, but . . .'

'That's it.'

'What?'

'These were taken before the fire had even been lit. There were petrol cans next to Hughes but no fire damage at all. Shit, they must have been taken by whoever killed him.'

Knight's mouth was open. 'But where have they come from?'

'Haven't you seen them?'

'I told you, we only had photos taken after the fire brigade had finished and they realised there was a dead body.'

'Then how have Pinky and Perky got hold of them?'

'You'll have to ask them that.' His lips were pressed together and he looked as angry as Catherine had ever seen him. There was a tap on the door and the grinning face of Patrick Shea appeared.

'Could we have another word, Jonathan?'

Down in the canteen, Catherine grabbed a piece of chocolate cake and a cappuccino, her mind still reeling. As she sat down, she heard the foghorn voice of Keith Kendrick chatting to Sally, who was operating the till. He clumped over, set a mug of coffee and a huge fruit scone on the table and slumped into a chair.

'Don't often see you down here.' Catherine took a bite of cake as Kendrick scowled.

'Don't often have a jumped-up DI taking over my station either.'

'What are they doing here?'

'You tell me. Fresh eyes on the Hughes case.' He widened his eyes. 'Apparently.'

'I've just escaped from their lair.'

'What did they want? You haven't even been at work. Jonathan's in there again with them now.'

He chomped on the scone as Catherine took a sip of coffee.

'They seem to be implying that Jonathan wasn't thorough when he investigated Paul Hughes' death.'

Kendrick swallowed a lump of scone.

'Wasn't thorough by accident or by design?'

'They didn't actually say.'

'He does have a bit of a Hughes obsession but he did all he could, I'd stake my pension on it.'

Catherine remembered the tattoo that scarred Knight's back and wished he hadn't shown it to her.

'Me too,' she said, hoping her unease wasn't evident in her voice. 'They seem to have their knives out for him though. They've somehow got hold of two photographs . . .' Her voice trailed off as she thought about the pictures of herself that had caused her so much anguish during their last major case.

'Photos taken by whoever killed Hughes?' Kendrick asked.

'It looks like it. They said Jonathan didn't have them, or that they weren't in the reports at least. He doesn't seem to know about them at all; I've just asked him.'

'He won't do. They were sent to Malc Hughes on the day of Paul's funeral, and he kept hold of them. It was only when our intrepid pair went down to London to speak to him that he gave them up. They showed me the photos earlier today – bloody grim.' Catherine gawped at him.

'So they were just winding me up?'

'Who knows what they were doing? I think they're just rattling a few cages and seeing what falls out. I wish they'd bugger off though.'

'You're not the only one.'

Taking a slurp of coffee, Kendrick lowered his voice to what he obviously thought was a whisper, the volume of most people's normal speaking voice.

'You and I know there can be nothing in it. I haven't known Jonathan long but I've seen nothing while he's been here to worry me at all, have you?'

She swallowed, banishing the image of that tattoo from her mind. 'No.'

'Well then.' Kendrick finished the scone and pushed back his chair, coffee mug still in his hand. 'The best thing we can do is forget about them and concentrate on finding which of our charming local drug dealing friends sat by and watched the lass we found yesterday die, then cut her open like a Sunday joint.'

Catherine headed back up to the incident room, still fuming over Shea and Allan's lies. Whatever game they were playing, she didn't like it. Kendrick had seemed to know all about the photos and no doubt the Super did too, so either Pinky and Perky were being crafty about how much they revealed and to whom, or . . . what? They were investigating Knight's handling of the Hughes case with the blessing of his superior officers? She couldn't imagine Kendrick standing for that, but what could he do if the Super had given it her approval?

She shoved open the door of the incident room, instantly hit by the mixed noise of several phones ringing, the tapping of computer keys and a cacophony of voices.

Chris Rogers waved her over.

'This CCTV footage is getting interesting, Sarge.'

She went over to him, rested an arm on the back of the shabby blue desk chair he was perched on and leaned in to focus on the images on the screen.

'What am I looking at then?'

'Lauren Cook got out of her car in the multi-storey, yeah? We saw that earlier.'

'And?'

'Well, she goes off and gets a ticket. Then she returns to her car, takes out her little pink suitcase, locks the vehicle and disappears.'

'I know that, Chris. So what?'

'Guess who was driving the next vehicle that came in and parked up?'

She blew out her cheeks.

'Father Christmas?'

'Bit early for him yet. It's Mark Cook.'

Her eyes widened.

'No way.'

Rogers nodded at the screen.

'Here he comes now.'

Sure enough, a small white van appeared. Mark Cook climbed out, trotted over to buy a ticket and stuck it to the vehicle's windscreen, then went off in the same direction his wife had taken.

'Whose is the van?' Catherine wanted to know. 'The Cooks only own the car that Lauren was driving.'

'Belongs to a Peter Davis who lives fairly near the Cooks. I'm still waiting on the footage from the street outside the car park, but it shouldn't be much longer.'

'Cook didn't mention this when I spoke to him.'

Chris opened his eyes wide. 'Funny that. We'll soon see if he was following her anyway. By the way, Sarge, I hear you spoke to Ellie last night.'

She straightened up.

'So what if I did?'

He grinned. 'Faye said you'd get on. So when are you taking her out?'

'We might meet for a coffee sometime, not that it's any of your business.'

'A coffee? Bloody hell, Sarge, you're losing your touch,' he laughed. She couldn't help smiling.

As she walked away, a young uniformed officer who was manning the phones waved at her from across the room.

'Mick Caffery's on the line, ma'am. He asked for Inspector Wallpaper, but I told him you were here.'

Catherine fixed him with a stern look as he smirked at the officers around him. 'Thank you Ryan, I'll pick it up at my desk.' She turned to walk away, then span back. 'And Ryan?'

He half-stood, looking sheepish. 'Ma'am?'

'You can stay in at playtime.'

At her desk, she flung herself into the chair and snatched up the receiver.

'Mick?'

'Good morning, Catherine. Are you well?'

'Fine thanks,' she said, making a "get on with it" gesture with her hand. 'How are you?'

'Keeping busy. Now, we're still waiting on most of the results, as you'd expect.'

'Of course.'

'We were able to get decent prints from the deodorant bottle you provided us with, as well as some that weren't quite as good quality from the shower gel.'

'Okay . . .'

'Anyway, we've completed our initial fingerprint analysis, based on the prints of Lauren Cook from the bottle and from those taken from the subject of yesterday's post-mortem.'

'And?' Catherine bit back a scream.

'There's no match.'

There was a second's pause as she digested this.

'Really?'

'Yes. The two sets of prints are totally different. The DNA test confirms it - the woman we found by the pond yesterday isn't Lauren Cook.'

22

'So who is she?' Kendrick asked.

'We still don't know.' Knight loosened his tie.

'So we've got a missing woman but no body and a body but no missing woman,' Catherine said. They were in Kendrick's office with the door firmly closed.

'We need to keep liaising with the UK Missing Persons Bureau. Let's get this woman identified.'

'What about Mark Cook?' She'd already explained what Chris Rogers had discovered. 'If the body isn't his wife and as far as we can see, Lauren hasn't left the country, then . . .'

'Then Mark Cook following Lauren and not telling us about it starts to look a little bit sinister,' Kendrick agreed. 'Why don't we bring him in for a chat?'

'You don't want me to go back to the house?' Catherine frowned.

'We'd better send someone to break the news, as well as bring Cook in. He might be more talkative here, especially without his mother-in-law listening over his shoulder – you said she was the domineering type?'

'Just a bit.' Catherine rolled her eyes.

'Okay. A cosy heart-to-heart it is then.' Kendrick turned to Knight and whispered, 'What did our friends want?' He nodded towards the wall that separated his office from the Superintendent's next door.

'To show me the photographs Catherine mentioned. Told me in no uncertain terms that they were having the originals analysed for fingerprints, DNA, moon dust . . .'

Kendrick gave him a hard look.

'They've got a bee in their bonnet about you.'

'I've no idea why.'

'Catherine and I have agreed on that too, but if you've been doing your mystery man act . . .'

Knight looked bemused. 'Mystery man act?'

Kendrick waved his arms. 'You know: giving one-word answers, never really saying what you're thinking, disappearing into the background . . .'

'Like wallpaper?' Knight grinned.

'Exactly like wallpaper.' Kendrick nodded. 'I just don't want them to come in, get no further on with finding out who killed Hughes than we did but damage your reputation while they're at it. Shea's a spiteful sod, we've seen that already.'

'All right,' Knight agreed. 'I'll keep it in mind.'

'Who do you want to interview Cook?' Catherine asked.

Kendrick pondered.

'Get Simon and Dave to do it,' he said. 'I want Chris to keep going with the CCTV stuff. And Catherine, you observe. You've spoken to Mark Cook before, so let's see how he reacts to being brought in.'

Mark looked ill as he followed Dave Lancaster into the interview room. It wasn't the grimmest one in the station, but it wasn't far off and it certainly made the room in which Catherine had spoken to him seem luxurious by comparison. Cook shuffled along, then sat down and stared around him. Simon Sullivan followed them in and closed the door, setting a manila folder on the table as he took his seat.

'Mr Cook, thank you for coming in today,' Dave began. 'You understand that we need to talk to you again about your wife?' Mark nodded. 'I'll do anything I can to help you find her.' His voice was deadened, a monotone. Catherine felt slightly guilty about dragging him here, but they needed an explanation. Dave and Simon exchanged a glance. 'Excellent,' Dave said. 'Now, when you spoke to Detective Sergeant Bishop, you told her that you hadn't seen your wife since she left the house to travel to Amsterdam, didn't you?'

'That's right.'

'And that was the truth?'

Mark was indignant, a spark of emotion breaking out of his gloom. 'Of course it was.'

Dave opened the folder and took out a sheet of paper, then turned it over and slid it towards Mark Cook, who stared at it. It was a still from the CCTV footage, clearly showing Cook locking the white van.

'Can you explain this, Mr Cook?' Simon asked.

'When . . . when is it from?' he gulped.

'The day you told us your wife went away,' Dave told him, tapping a finger on the date and time printed on the corner of the page.

'I'm not sure what this has to do with Lauren?' Mark sat up straight. 'I borrowed a mate's van and nipped into town. I had to go to the job centre, if you must know.'

'Do you often borrow the van?'

'No, but Pete had a day off and offered it to me, knowing Lauren had taken the car.'

Dave shook his head and pointed again at the image on the table.

'Take another look, Mr Cook. Recognise anything?'

He glanced down, then did a double take.

'But that's our car! I don't . . . What's it doing parked there?'

Simon took out a second sheet.

'It doesn't take much to work it out, Mark.'

This image showed Lauren climbing out of the car. The time stamp showed that it was only a matter of minutes before Cook himself had arrived at the car park.

'Well, Mark? What do you have to say to that?' Dave asked. Cook shook his head, his bewilderment seeming genuine.

'I didn't know. I swear, I didn't know she was there. She told me she was driving to Hull to get the ferry. I really don't understand.' Mark Cook looked wretched, his face pale and his eyes filling with tears. Catherine shifted in her chair. Cook's discomfort seemed genuine, but it was too much of a coincidence.

'You expect us to believe that you walked past your own car and didn't recognise it?' Simon scoffed. 'Come on, Mark.'

'I'm telling you, I didn't see it. Why would I? There are millions of silver cars around and it wasn't like I was expecting it to be there.'

'So you got out of the van, walked past your own car, didn't see it. You went . . . where?'

'Out of the multi-storey, turned right and cut through the bus station to the job centre. I signed on, then came straight back to the van.'

'Taking the same route through the bus station?'

'Yes. I dropped the van back at Pete's, then I walked home. I didn't see Lauren at all.'

Dave touched a finger to his lips, his brow furrowed. 'Tell me, Mark.' His voice was gentle. 'When did you first suspect that Lauren was lying to you?'

Cook stared at him. 'What? What are you talking about?'

With a shrug, Dave said, 'Just wondering. If it was my missus, I wouldn't have been happy about it.'

Catherine had to smile – Dave Lancaster was resolutely single. Mark looked from Dave to Simon, his eyes panicked.

'I only found out she hadn't gone to Amsterdam when you told me, I'd no idea. Look, yesterday that sergeant came and told us you'd found a body. Today you tell me it isn't Lauren, and now you seem to be accusing me of killing her?'

'That's a bit of leap, isn't it?' Dave asked.

Simon cleared his throat. 'No one's mentioned you killing anyone, Mark.'

'Unless you have information that we don't?' Dave's face was stern now.

Cook laid both hands on the surface of the table in front of him. 'I don't know where my wife is. You have to believe me.' Catherine could barely hear him, his voice cracking as he pleaded with them. 'I've no reason to believe that she was cheating on me. We're happy.'

'And she'd say the same?'

'Of course she would.'

'Lauren passes this camera in Melrose Road, outside the multi-storey, then I can't find her anywhere,' Chris Rogers said. 'Mark's glimpsed by the camera, turning right out of the car park just as he says he did, and we've also picked him up doing the return journey forty minutes later.'

'But Lauren went left, not right as Mark did?' Catherine asked.

'Yep. The only thing I can think of is that she got into a vehicle near the car park.'

'But we've no evidence of that?'

'No.'

'What about her mobile phone records?'

'The request has been put in, but we've not heard anything back as far as I know.'

'Not even where it was last used?'

'Not yet.'

Catherine sighed in frustration.

'Okay. Thanks, Chris.'

Rogers turned back to his screen. With a glance at the clock on the wall, Catherine headed back to the CID office. As she sat at her desk, she pulled her phone from her pocket and opened a text: **Good to talk last night.** It was from Ellie. She put her mobile down, not knowing what to say in reply. There was no rush. She picked up her desk phone instead.

'Boss, I was wondering if it would be worth us having a word with Helen Bridges?' she said when Kendrick answered. Bridges was a senior journalist on the local newspaper and had been both a help and a hindrance in the past. Catherine hoped she was in a good mood.

'Helen Bridges? About the body you mean?' Kendrick didn't sound convinced.

'It might help us identify her. We could mention Lauren Cook's disappearance too.'

Kendrick thought about it. Catherine pictured him mulling it over, frowning and pursing his lips.

'Go on then,' he said finally.

'Lauren as well?'

'Not yet. I still think she's shacked up with her boyfriend somewhere.'

'All right. I'll tell Helen to be subtle.'

Kendrick snorted. 'I doubt she knows what the word means.' There was a clunk in her ear as he replaced the receiver. She picked up her mobile to call Bridges but jumped when it began to ring in her hand.

'Jo?'

'I've had a result from the eyelash I found. Jonathan's phone went to voicemail, but I thought you'd want to know right away.'

Catherine sat up straight.

'Already?'

'I know, it's the quickest turnaround we've had for a while. You'll see why when I tell you who the eyelash belongs to.'

'You have a name?'

'Certainly do.'

'So it's a known offender?'

'Not exactly. It's Lauren Cook.'

Catherine blinked a couple of times.

'Wait a minute, Jo – the eyelash belongs to Lauren?'

'It does.'

'But . . . how?'

'Like I said after the post-mortem, she was either present when the woman was cut open or she was near the body afterwards. It's possible it was put there deliberately to throw us off the scent, I suppose, or that the woman died in a location Lauren had visited. I don't know, all I can say for sure is that the eyelash belongs to Lauren Cook.'

Whatever Catherine had been expecting, it wasn't this. There was always going to be the possibility that Lauren was somehow involved with the woman they'd found at the pond, but this was a surprise.

'Well, that raises lots of questions.'

'You'll have my full report as soon as I can get it over. Oh, and the drug was cocaine, that's also been confirmed.'

'Okay. Thanks, Jo.'

Catherine stood up, wondering what this meant. She needed to speak to Knight and Kendrick.

23

He scrolled down the page to the local news, his throat tight. They'd found her then. It was no surprise; the boss had wanted the body to be discovered quickly, a message to show the others that they meant business and were in control. The quick departure of the Hughes family had left a gap that the boss was keen to fill quickly. There was always a market for coke, it was easy money. If you could bring it into the country yourself and cut out the middle man, so much the better. Less mess, less hassle and fewer people involved. They still had their small-time dealers pedalling weed to anyone who wanted it, but the coke market was different.

Still, the police would be involved now and the thought terrified him. The boss might think it a good idea to give a public display of what they were capable of, but it seemed to him a stupidly risky boast. He didn't like it and wished he had never got involved. The day job kept the wolves from the door, but he'd been greedy. When the opportunity had been offered, he'd jumped at it.

Her face came into his mind again, the paleness of her skin, the yellowy fat that he'd had to slice through. He shuddered, remembering the relief he'd felt when the packets – treasure to them, but the reason she was dead - finally appeared. He'd not spoken to her much before she'd died, but she'd seemed nice enough. Desperate for the money, of course. Why else would you do it? Even swallowing the packets in the first place had to be a nightmare.

He remembered her heavy limbs as they'd washed her naked body, the other man making comments about what he would have liked to do to her had she lived. Laughing, he'd said it would have earned her a few quid more. He'd stayed silent. Running the cloth over her unresisting skin had reminded him of caring for his mother. His brow creased as he thought back to those days in the flat with his mother comatose. He had done his best to persuade her to eat, to go out and feel the sun on her face, but it had been futile in the end.

The succession of men. The needles. Her death. He blinked, wiping a hand over his eyes. It was a common enough story.

They'd carried her to the pond wrapped in plastic sheeting, then rubbed her down again with antibacterial wipes as she lay on the ground. Lots of precautions. People knowing they were now top dog was one thing, but the police being able to trace her back to them was another.

There was the other problem to think about too. The boss didn't like loose ends.

24

In the incident room, Catherine updated her team on the information provided by Jo Webber.

'I'm meeting with Helen Bridges shortly to discuss an appeal in the press,' she said. 'Chris, you need to keep trying to find out who our mystery woman is. Until we have an ID, we're struggling. Simon, go back to Mark Cook and Lauren's parents and ask them if Lauren had any involvement with drugs. We have to start considering the possibility that Lauren's disappearance is linked to our mule and start digging. The eyelash proves that Lauren has been in close proximity to our body at some point.'

'I'll chase up her mobile phone records again,' Anna Varcoe said. 'Maybe there'll be a text or voicemail that can help us.'
Catherine nodded. 'You never know. I want you to come with me to Lauren's workplace as well, Anna, after I've seen the lovely Ms Bridges. Maybe she'll have confided in a colleague there. Dave, get onto Lauren's best friend - Steph Goacher? I know she said she couldn't help us, but we need to talk to her again. Make the point that Lauren could be in danger and see if she knows more than she's been admitting, please. Also, have a chat with Pete Davis

about lending Mark Cook his van. Make sure he got it back in one piece, that there were no unidentified women in the back or blood stains on the seat.'

He grinned at her. 'You still think Mark knows more than he's telling us, Sarge?'

'It's a huge coincidence that he happened to arrive at the car park just after his wife, but maybe he's genuine.' She shrugged. 'Anyway, our priorities are to find Lauren and to identify our dead woman. I'll see you back here at five.'

Dave raised his hand as if he were at primary school. 'What about talking to some of the local drug users?' he asked. Catherine looked at him and he smiled, his eyes bright.

'I was hoping Anna and I would have a chance to do that on our way over to Lauren's workplace. Then again, there are quite a few people to talk to there. All right, Dave, see what you can dig up. Be subtle,' she cautioned. 'You might not get the warmest of welcomes.'

He gave an enthusiastic nod, grabbed his notepad from the desk in front of him and rushed towards the door, tripping over the legs of a chair in his haste to be out and getting on with his task.

'Daft bugger.' Chris Rogers shook his head.

'Anna, just give me half an hour to talk to Helen and then we'll go.' Catherine pushed back her chair.

'Good luck with that one.' Chris smirked, heading over to a spare computer.

As the door closed behind their sergeant, Chris turned to Anna, who was gathering a pile of reports together, preparing to go back to her own desk. 'So what do you think?'

'About what?'

'Catherine. She seems a bit brighter since our night out, don't you think?'

'Hard to tell.'

'She phoned Ellie.'

'You didn't leave her much choice.' Anna laughed. Chris opened his mouth, then closed it again, looking hurt.

'We were only trying to help,' he said. Anna came over and patted his shoulder.

'I know you were, but don't push her, that's all I'm saying. Thomas says she's struggling, having nightmares and stuff.'

'God. That doesn't sound like Catherine, she's always been so . . .'

'Solid?'

'Yeah, steady.'

'I think the thing with Claire really hit her hard. Imagine it though, Chris. Talk about a betrayal of trust.'

'Yeah, I know. Ellie would be good for her.'

'Chris!'

He held up his hands. 'All right, all right. I'll not mention it again. Anyway, you're a dark horse.'

'What do you mean?'

'You and the Sarge's brother?' He looked up at her, fluttering his eyelashes, and she shoved his arm playfully.

'Mind your own business.'

Helen Bridges was sitting at a corner table when Catherine entered the café.

'Full English please, Sergeant, and another coffee,' the journalist called. Rolling her eyes, Catherine made her way to the counter. The place was quiet, just an elderly couple sipping tea in one corner and a young woman frowning at a tablet computer in the other.

'And for yourself?' the man behind the counter asked, his hand poised over an order pad. Catherine screwed up her face.

'Just toast thanks.'

'Only toast? You're sure?'

'Maybe some scrambled egg,' she relented. The man beamed and Catherine couldn't help smiling back at him. 'And I'll have a pot of tea, please.'

'That's more like it. I'll bring it over.'

Helen Bridges was waiting, her long tan-coloured coat slung over the back of the chair beside her. She had her notebook ready, sitting on the red and white checked tablecloth, with a pen lying beside it. As Catherine pulled out the chair opposite her and sat down, Bridges smoothed her already immaculate hair and leant forward.

'How are you, Sergeant Bishop?'

'Never better, thanks.'

'Really? Well, if you say so.' Bridges looked doubtful, her eyebrows climbing towards her hairline. 'What can I do for you?' Catherine didn't wait to consider what Bridges had meant by her comment and ploughed on.

'You know that a woman's body was found yesterday?'

'I wouldn't be much of a reporter if I didn't, it doesn't happen every day after all. I was down by the pond most of the day, but no one had the decency to come out and tell us anything. The constable who spoke to me was quite abrupt.' Bridges pouted as Catherine hid a grin.

'We need some help from the public to identify her.'

Bridges nodded, a knowing smile flitting over her lips. 'I thought you might say that. What's in it for me?'

'I can tell you she died from a drug overdose.'

'That's not front page news, Sergeant.' Bridges shook her head. 'There must be more to it. All that activity at the pond yesterday, you and that new DI down there? I'm not stupid.'

Catherine sighed. Bridges was right. She was a lot of things, but stupid certainly wasn't first on the list.

'All right. As I say, the woman died of an overdose.'

'And that was enough to warrant all this interest?' Bridges probed.

'Off the record, there was a substantial amount of cocaine involved. Her body was . . . mutilated.'

'Mutilated in what way?'

'Well, we're not going to be able to provide you with a photograph of her face to use, put it that way.'

'Nasty.' Bridges grimaced.

'We need to find out who she is, Helen. Some bastard let her die so they could get hold of the drugs she was carrying.'

Helen Bridges stared, her mind working.

'A drug mule? Are you serious?'

Catherine folded her arms. 'We need to speak to anyone who can help us.'

'I bet you do.' The journalist whistled.

Their food arrived and Bridges tucked in with enthusiasm. Catherine enjoyed her scrambled egg more than she had expected to.

'I'll email the description we have of her over. Don't mention the amount of drugs or the fact she was carrying them,' Catherine told Bridges.

'I'll keep it quiet for now, but if anything comes of the story . . .'

'You'll be the first to know.'

'There's no chance at all of a photo?'

Catherine allowed the woman's ruined face into her mind for just a second, then shut it away again, out of sight.

'None, at least until we can identify her.'

'A facial reconstruction then?'

'Not at the moment. Maybe in time, if we need one.'

Bridges drank the last of her coffee and wiped her mouth on a red paper napkin, shrugged on her coat, then collected her notepad and bag.

'The story will run in tomorrow's paper and I'll get it up on the website as soon as I can. Thanks for the food.'

'You're welcome.' Catherine poured out the last of her tea.

'Oh, and Sergeant?' Bridges was by the door now, a smile hovering around her lips. Catherine glanced up. 'It's such a shame you didn't have a chance to introduce me to that gorgeous Claire Weyton.'

Catherine cradled her tea cup between both hands. What did Helen Bridges know? She was no fool. DCI Kendrick had said there had been nothing in the papers about herself and Claire, and if Bridges hadn't written about it there must be a reason. It certainly wouldn't be because she was afraid of hurting Catherine's feelings. Perhaps the Superintendent had had a word? Catherine sipped her tea. No. Bridges would have taken no notice if she thought she had a story, and it would have been quite a scoop. Claire Weyton had murdered two men and badly injured another. She had been working on the investigation with Catherine and her colleagues as part of their civilian support staff, all the time knowing that the person they were seeking, the vicious killer, the monster, was herself.

Catherine closed her eyes, remembering her conversations with Claire, the intimacy, the excitement. All of it a lie, a fabrication, on Claire's part at least. Catherine had been in no doubt of her own feelings; she had believed that she and Claire were beginning a relationship, that Claire's feelings mirrored her own. She had thought they were falling in love. Catherine screwed up her face. It was a cliché, a clumsy attempt to attribute words to emotions that went beyond description. Still, it was true. Her shock, her disbelief and the pain that followed choked her, even now. The deceit still took her breath away. There had been no sign, no indication that Claire was anything other than what she appeared to be – clever, confident and dedicated to her job. The circumstances that had driven her to kill, the persona she kept so well hidden, had only emerged when it had become absolutely necessary. Even then, Catherine knew, it had been a monumental struggle for both herself and Claire to play out their story. Catherine had a duty, an obligation to bring those responsible for crime to justice. That kind of justice wasn't enough for Claire. She had pursued her victims as a victim herself, a person driven to kill by circumstances beyond her control. Claire had paid for her own brand of justice with her life and Catherine was left to pick up the pieces of the life she had thought she was building. She wore the guilt like a skin, wrapped in shame, in regret. There were questions she hadn't answered – if she had known the truth about Claire, what would she have done? She had confronted her, it was true, had attempted to do her duty as a police officer. If she had realised before though, what then? If Claire had escaped exposure, had escaped capture? Would they have built a life together? Catherine set her cup on the table, fighting tears. No. She could have forgiven Claire, tried to understand her, but that would have been too much.

She couldn't believe that Kendrick would have lied about Bridges not exposing her and Claire's relationship, so the only other explanation was that the journalist had withheld what she knew for reasons of her own. That she'd just dropped the scoop into conversation could be seen as a warning. It wouldn't be as crude as blackmail; perhaps "leverage" was a better word. Either way, it meant Bridges had ammunition.

25

DC Anna Varcoe guided the vehicle over a well-used car park. As they got out, Catherine gazed at the premises of John Worthy and Son, her hands on her hips.

'Could do with a lick of paint,' she noted. 'Reception must be around the other side.'

Anna glanced left and right.

'Looks like it. Seems a strange place to put it.'

'Come on then.'

They had to walk about halfway around the building before they saw it, a tiny door, its blue paint as dull and flaking as that on the rest of the building. Catherine pushed open the door to reveal a well-maintained reception area, quite a contrast to the run-down appearance of the exterior of the building. A woman in her fifties glanced up from her computer monitor with a polished smile.

'Good afternoon. Do you have an appointment?' Her expression said she knew they didn't.

'No, I'm afraid. I'm Detective Sergeant Bishop, this is Detective Constable Varcoe. We're here to see the owner, please.'

The receptionist flapped a little.

'Oh, the police? I'm not aware of anyone calling you, is there a problem?'

'We need to speak to Mr Worthy.' Catherine was firm. 'Is he in today?'

'Yes, he is, but he's in an important meeting, I never usually disturb him . . .'

'I'm afraid today you'll have to.' Catherine's tone made it clear the woman had no choice and she backed away, still muttering. Catherine wandered over to sniff at the vibrant flowers that were arranged in a cut glass vase on a low wooden table.

'Real,' she said to Anna, who nodded.

They both turned when a loud voice and clumping footsteps heralded the arrival of John Worthy. He burst through the wooden door by the reception desk and strode towards them.

'Are you the policemen?' he demanded. Catherine met his eyes before looking down at herself and then at Anna. Worthy held up his hands. 'Sorry, sorry, police officers. Didn't think what I was saying, my wife tells me I'm always doing it. So what's so important you have to interrupt my board meeting?'

'Is there somewhere we can talk privately, Mr Worthy?' Anna asked.

Worthy loosened his tie.

'Privately? Well, yes. I can assure you that Margaret here is trustworthy though.'

The receptionist, who had followed Worthy in and retaken her seat, blushed and bent closer to her monitor.

'I'm sure she is. Please, sir.' Catherine made it clear that the subject wasn't open for discussion.

'All right, fine. Follow me.'

Worthy led the way back through the door he'd appeared from, down a narrow corridor and into a large office, warm and welcoming. A beautiful, carved wooden desk stood at the back of the room, and with a groan, Worthy heaved himself into the chair that waited behind it. 'Ah . . . my back's playing up. Now,' he clasped his hands on the desktop. 'What's this all about? Do sit down. You are?' Catherine handed over their warrant cards as she and Anna sat down in the wooden chairs in front of Worthy's desk. He studied them.

'We're here because an employee of Worthy and Son has been reported missing,' she told him.

Worthy linked his fingers across his belly.

'Really, Sergeant? As far as I'm aware, all my staff are present and correct, except for my second-in-command, who's down in London.'

'It's Lauren Cook,' Anna said.

'Then I can't help you. Lauren has booked some days off.'

Catherine crossed her legs at the ankle.

'You're the owner of this business, aren't you, Mr Worthy?'

Worthy lifted his chin. 'I am indeed. Took over from my father fifteen years ago. He built this place up from nothing.' He stretched out a hand and picked up the receiver of the phone that sat on his desk. 'Can I offer either of you tea or coffee?'

Anna glanced at Catherine and replied, 'Coffee please.'

She gave a brisk nod. 'The same. Thank you.'

Worthy made the request, then sat back.

'What role does Lauren Cook have in the business?' Catherine asked.

'Role?' Worthy frowned. 'She's in packing and despatch. As you know, we're a printing firm, though we've had to branch out – diversify. You know how it is these days.' He gave a wistful smile. 'The printing side of things used to be our biggest source of income, but that's not so now.'

'So Lauren doesn't have a management position?' Anna asked, opening her notepad. Worthy frowned.

'No. She's a good worker and she's very willing, but I'd say she's not career-minded. I'm sure she would agree.'

'It's rare to find a managing director who takes such an interest in his junior members of staff, wouldn't you say?' said Catherine, keeping her tone light. Anna nodded.

'It's commendable, ma'am.'

Worthy hesitated.

'And what do you mean by that?' he asked finally.

'It's just that more often than not the owner of a company doesn't even know their employees' names, much less when their holidays are,' Catherine explained with a disarming smile. Worthy seemed satisfied with the reply.

'Well, we've always been hands-on here at Worthy's. I make it my business to get to know each employee, but then I've known Lauren since she was tiny. Her dad used to work here you see, he was my finance man for years. I've found it makes for a much more satisfied workforce if we take an interest in our staff, so we're like one big happy family.' He beamed at them, and Catherine raised an eyebrow as the receptionist bustled in with a tray. Worthy insisted on pouring their drinks himself, then settled back in his chair with a cup of thick coffee, liberally dosed with cream.

'Now, what's all this about Lauren being missing?' He smoothed a finger over his bushy grey eyebrows. 'It seems odd to me.'

'Why odd?' Catherine asked.
Worthy lifted his cup to his lips again, taking his time before replying.

'It's usually children who disappear, isn't it? I can understand the police getting involved then, but Lauren's a grown woman.'

'We'll need to speak to your staff, Mr Worthy - you'll understand if we don't give you any details until we've talked to everyone?'

'Well, I suppose so. I do own the place, you know.' He pouted, then took another mouthful of coffee.

'When is Lauren due back at work?' Catherine watched Worthy's brow crease as he thought about it.

'Tomorrow, I believe. Are you saying that we shouldn't expect Lauren to arrive? She's due to work some overtime on Saturday.'

'You're not overly concerned that no one has heard from her then?' Anna put in. Worthy's already florid cheeks flushed deeper.

'If she's genuinely missing, then yes, of course I'm concerned,' he blustered. 'I know Lauren – she's sensible, trustworthy. I find it hard to believe that she would just go off somewhere. I'm confident that she'll turn up for work tomorrow as planned.' He pulled a cotton handkerchief out of his trouser pocket and wiped his face. Catherine watched with interest - Worthy was rattled. Was it because he knew where Lauren was, or because he was realising it was possible that he didn't know his employees as well as he had thought?

'Did Lauren ever mention her home life to you?' she asked. 'Her husband, if she was happy with him? Any problems they might be having?'

Worthy shook his head. 'We're not on those sort of terms, Sergeant. I take an interest in my staff, yes, but not to that extent. You'd be better off talking to her colleagues.'

'Yes, sir. Is there somewhere we can speak to your staff individually? And could you provide a list of all your employees, please?' Catherine glanced at Anna, who closed her notebook, hoping Worthy took the hint.

'You may as well stay in here, I'll make myself scarce.' He got to his feet, lumbered into the centre of the room, then turned back. 'I don't understand.' His voice was plaintive.

Anna stood and shepherded him to the door. 'We'll talk to you again later, sir. Is there a Sarah on your staff?'

Catherine crossed the room to join them.

'Sarah? Yes, Sarah Watson. Good pals with Lauren.'

'Could you send her in first, please, Mr Worthy? And I know we can count on your discretion, you couldn't have built up a business like this without knowing who you could trust.' Catherine flashed him a winning smile as she opened the door.

'That's true enough, Sergeant,' Worthy preened. 'Don't worry, I won't breathe a word. I'll send Sarah along now, and I'll get that list you asked about. Anything to help.'

He backed out of the room and disappeared down the corridor. Closing the door, Catherine leant against it with a sigh.

'I thought he was never going to leave.' She sat in Worthy's chair and span around a few times. Anna joined her sergeant behind the desk, dragging a chair with her and settling into it.

A few minutes later, there was a tap on the door and Sarah Watson appeared. She wore jeans, a hooded sweatshirt, trainers and an apprehensive expression. Her hair was pulled back into a careless ponytail, her make-up discreet. She edged into the room, wary eyes fixed on the two officers. Catherine stood, held out her hand and introduced them.

'DS?' Sarah said uncomprehendingly. She gave Catherine's hand a limp shake, still standing. Gesturing that she should sit down, Catherine explained, 'DS just means detective sergeant.'

'Detective . . . So you're the police?' Sarah sank into the chair, her discomfort even clearer. 'Mr Worthy said someone needed to speak to me, I thought it was about work.'

'Are you a friend of Lauren Cook?'

'Lauren? Yes, we work in the same department. She's not in today though. I've sent her a text, but she hasn't replied.'

'Are you engaged, Sarah?' Catherine had already seen the ring on Sarah Watson's finger, but she wanted to tread gently. Watson seemed confused.

'Yeah, but . . . what's this all about?'

'Have you had your hen night recently?'

'Hen night? We've not even set a date yet. Are you going to tell me what's going on?'

Catherine took a deep breath.

'I'm sorry to have to tell you this, but it seems Lauren is missing. She told her husband she was away on a hen night this weekend and that the bride-to-be was called Sarah. You were the obvious place to start.'

Watson stared.

'She's missing? I don't understand.'

'Did she say anything to you about where she might have gone?' Anna asked.

'No. It doesn't make sense.'

'Did Lauren have a drug habit, as far you're aware?'

'Drugs?' Sarah looked at her shoes. 'No. Not Lauren.'

Hmmm, thought Catherine.

'Have you any idea why Lauren would have told her husband she was away with you over the weekend?' Anna questioned. She'd sensed that Sarah knew more than she wanted to say, as Catherine had.

'No, none. Unless she was going somewhere she didn't want him to know about.'

'Did she tell you she was going to lie to him, ask you to cover for her? Did she have a boyfriend? '

'No.'

'You're sure?'

'Of course I am. I'm not stupid, you know.'

'I realise that, Sarah, and I'm sure you know withholding information from police officers isn't a good idea. Still, if you're sure you can't help us . . .'

Catherine sat back in her chair and flipped a few pages in her notebook, scribbled and then held the pad out to Anna. She pretended to study the smiley face Catherine had drawn with a nod of agreement. Watson shifted in her chair.

'Look, you come in here, tell me my mate's missing . . .'

They waited. Sarah's face showed her internal struggle, her loyalty to her friend pitted against what she knew she should do. In the end, honesty won.

'Lauren did say . . .' She chewed on her bottom lip. 'I don't want to cause any trouble . . .'

'If you tell us what you know, it could help us find your friend. She could be in danger,' Catherine prompted.

'I do know she said she was going to earn some money to treat Mark to a weekend away as a surprise for his birthday. They'd not had a holiday for ages and she asked me not tell him. They'd been having a few problems, nothing major, just worries about Mark not being able to find a job. Lauren was worried that he was depressed, drinking too much sometimes. She was annoyed because it's not as if they had the money to spare, and Mark was snappy with her about it, defensive. Lauren never mentioned going away though, I just thought she meant helping out in a pub to earn some extra cash. She's done that before, you see.'

'She didn't tell you where she was going, mention any names?'

'Nothing, just that.'

'And what about drugs?'

Watson squirmed.

'What about them?'

'Come on, Sarah. We need your help. Please.'

'She . . . Oh, all right, I know she did a few drugs in the past, when she was younger. A lot of people do, you know, experimenting or whatever. Not recently though, or not that I know of.'

'What did she take?'

'Nothing serious . . . a few pills? Bit of dope? I don't know for sure, I didn't know her then.'

They spoke to her for a few minutes more, but it was clear she knew nothing else. The rest of the afternoon was spent in a similar vein; Lauren Cook's colleagues all described her as pleasant, hard-working, a "laugh" – only Sarah Watson had mentioned drugs, and no one knew of any marital problems or other issues. Catherine and Anna grew more and more frustrated, wondering if they were wasting their time.

'This is the last employee. Let's hope he or she wanders in and tries to sell us some heroin.'

Anna smiled as there was a hesitant tap on the door. 'Come in,' Catherine called. A young man entered and glanced around, his apprehension obvious. 'Have a seat, Mr . . . ?'

As he sat down, Anna glanced up from her notepad, then stiffened.

'Rob?' she said, frowning.

He started, staring at her.

'Anna? What are you doing here?'

'You two know each other?' Catherine didn't need to ask.

'We were at school together.' Anna's voice was soft. 'This is Rob Hunter.'

26

Catherine let Anna drive for a few minutes before she said, 'He's got a record, you know.'

Back in Worthy's office, they'd decided that it would better if Catherine interviewed Rob on her own to avoid any conflict of interest.

Anna hesitated. 'Sorry?'

'Rob Hunter. He's been out of prison less than a week.'

Changing gear, Anna reddened a little.

'It doesn't surprise me. How do you know?'

'He told me. It's only his third day at Worthy and Son, so he didn't have much else to say. He says he's never spoken to Lauren.'

'Don't you believe him?'

Catherine shrugged, gazing out of the window. 'I've no reason not to. He's determined to go straight apparently. John Worthy agreed to give him a job as part of his probation.'

'That's generous.'

'How well did you know him?'

'Rob?' Anna was blushing now. 'Very well.'

'Really?'

Anna nodded. 'He was my first proper boyfriend.'

'Okay.'

'We went out for a couple of years, only split up because . . . well, I knew I wanted to join the force and Rob wasn't a big fan of the police, even then.'

'A couple of years? Sounds serious.'

'You know what it's like at that age, Sarge, you think no one's been in love before. Then Rob started being mates with older blokes, flashing loads of money around. It didn't take a genius to work out what he was up to was dodgy.'

'So you split up?'

'I told him I wasn't going to be with a criminal and it turned out he preferred his new mates to me. I applied to join the force, stayed away from places I knew he might be. He wanted another chance, but I knew it wouldn't work, not with the things I thought he was getting up to going on.'

'He was done for robbery, served eighteen months in prison,' Catherine told her.

Anna sighed. 'Idiot.'

'He got drunk with a gang of mates. They went into a pizza place and threatened to burn it down if the blokes working there didn't hand over the takings. There was a CCTV camera in the shop and it picked them up as clear as day. Hunter didn't actually threaten anyone, he just stood there, but . . .'

'It's enough.'

'Yeah. They got away with less than a hundred quid between five of them. The shop closed down after that because the brothers that ran it were too scared to stay in town.'

Anna made a noise of disgust as she stopped at a red light. 'I thought you were going to say it was some sort of car crime.'

'Cars?'

'Rob was always into them and his dad's a mechanic, a decent one as far as I know.' The lights changed and Anna glanced in her rear-view mirror as she accelerated.

'It's not to say he hasn't been involved in car crime too,' Catherine pointed out.

'It sounds as if he was quite open about having been in prison?'

'Yeah, not boastful though, just matter of fact. He said he's pleased you're doing well for yourself.'

The blush stained Anna's cheeks again. 'None of his business.' They were almost back at the station.

'What about drugs?'

'Not when I knew him. I'd be surprised, but then it's been eight years since we left school. I went to college to do A levels and Rob started a car mechanic course. He didn't finish it though, dropped out when we split up.'

They swung into the station's car park and Anna reversed into a space.

'He'd have to be totally stupid to get involved with anything as soon as he got out of prison,' Catherine said as they climbed out. It was beginning to rain, the misty damp air clinging to them like cobwebs.

'Unless that was always the plan.' Anna locked the car. 'I just hope Rob's not that daft.'

Despite the chill outside, the air in the briefing room was warm and dense. Catherine felt her eyelids drooping as they waited for DCI Kendrick to appear. She glanced around with a frown. Dave Lancaster was missing. She half-turned in her chair.

'Has anyone heard from Dave?'

Chris Rogers frowned. 'I haven't.' He beckoned to Sullivan, sitting a few seats further down the row, and spoke to him. 'No, Si hasn't either.'

'Shit.' Catherine pulled her phone from her pocket and scrolled to Lancaster's number. He was enthusiastic and keen, but he wasn't overly experienced. She listened to his voicemail message and left a terse one of her own, asking where the hell he was.

'Try his radio,' Anna suggested, but then Keith Kendrick strode in.

'Hi-de-hi campers,' he said, clumping to the front of the room. 'DS Bishop, do you want to start?' Catherine stood next to Kendrick, who looked down at her. 'Problem?'

'No, guv.' Kendrick hadn't noticed Lancaster's absence. He would though, Catherine knew. He rocked back on his heels, hands in his trouser pockets, eyes scanning the faces of his officers. Catherine told the team what Sarah Watson had said. Kendrick raised himself onto his tiptoes and back down again.

'Interesting. So it looks like Lauren Cook could be drug mule number two?'

'It's a possibility.'

'There'll be more than two no doubt, possibly a whole herd. It'll be like the beach at Skegness if this carries on.' Kendrick smirked. 'So we know Lauren dabbled in drugs when she was younger?'

'No more than lots of people, if what Sarah told us was true. We need to know when she was offered the opportunity to earn a few quid and who by.' Catherine wrinkled her nose. 'When we know the identity of our body from the pond, we'll be able to see if she and Lauren have any friends in common.'

'But we don't know her identity yet.' Kendrick looked at his audience. 'Or do we? Any news?' He cupped a hand around his ear and waited.

'I've chased the DNA results up again,' Chris Rogers offered. Kendrick puffed out his cheeks.

'Chased them up nicely or kicked their arses?' he demanded. Rogers blushed.

'Fairly nicely. They said it should be tomorrow morning.'

'God Almighty.' Kendrick scowled. 'All right. Catherine – what about the rest of the workforce at Worthy and Son?'

She flipped through the pages of her notebook.

'Lauren's popular, no one had a bad word for her. No reports of any problems between her and her husband. Again, we need the ID of our body to see if there are any links. It's worth another visit when we know who she is.'

'Right.' Kendrick frowned. 'Simon, what about Mark Cook and the Chantrys?'

'Cook bit my head off when I asked if Lauren had ever been involved with drugs, and her mum wasn't far behind.' Simon grimaced. 'If her disappearance is linked to our mule, I don't think her husband knows about it.'

'That would make sense if she was trying to earn some money to take him away for his birthday,' Catherine put in, and Simon nodded.

'That's what I thought. Her mum wasn't having any of it, more or less told me to sling my hook. Her dad didn't say much. Even when I asked him a question specifically, his wife jumped in and answered. All I could get out of him was that his daughter had never taken drugs to his knowledge.'

Kendrick shook his head. 'This is bloody ridiculous. Is there anything to report?'

Silence.

The door at the back of the room opened and Dave Lancaster strolled in. Kendrick drew himself up.

'Good of you to join us, DC Lancaster. To what do we owe the pleasure?'

Dave stopped, blinking in confusion. 'Sorry, Guv. I lost track of time.'

Kendrick pursed his lips. 'You "lost track of time". I see. And how would it be if we all did that, Constable? What if I lost track of time while I was curled up under the cosy flannelette sheets with pretty pink flowers that I hate but my wife insists on having on the bed? If DC Rogers forgot the time on his run that we know he does every single morning, and just kept going all day long until he just dropped dead of exhaustion and sheer despair? If . . .'

Dave stepped forward, recognising that Kendrick would keep ranting until he exploded.

'I have some good news, boss.'

Kendrick stared at him.

'Good news? Are you joking?'

'Not at all.' Lancaster dared to step closer, and Kendrick suddenly flung an arm around his shoulders, grabbed his hand and shook it a few times.

'Dave Lancaster: Detective of the Year.'

'Well, it's . . .' Lancaster blushed.

Kendrick pointed a finger at him.

'Don't you dare try to wriggle out of it now.'

'I wasn't. It's just . . .'

Catherine raised her eyes to the ceiling.

'Come on, spit it out.' Kendrick opened his arms wide. 'We're on tenterhooks here.'

'It's just that I think I know who our unidentified body might be,' Lancaster stammered. Kendrick stared at him, then did a few energetic tap dancing steps, his huge shiny brogues thudding across the carpet tiles. Lancaster looked on, bemused, as his colleagues broke into laughter.

'Come on then, don't keep us in suspense. Who is she?'

'The name's Keeley Pearce. She lives with Shaun Simmington, who we know is a drug user. Her mum was looking for Keeley because she hasn't heard from her for a few days, but Keeley hasn't been home either. Her mum's waiting to talk to us downstairs.'

27

Lauren wrapped her arms around her body as she paced across the threadbare carpet. There was a tiny heater in the corner that was doing its best to spit out some warmth, but it seemed to make no difference. She shivered. There was a camp bed set against the wall with a grubby sleeping bag and a stained pillow bundled onto it. It had taken two nights, but in the end she'd given up. With the unzipped sleeping bag wrapped around her and her head resting on the damp, musty pillow, she'd cried herself to sleep.

She was losing track of the days, she was sure of it. The room was dim, the only window boarded up on the outside. Thin sunlight trickled through the gaps during the daytime, but night seemed to have fallen again. The door was locked, and no amount of kicking or pounding had any effect. She glared at it. There were a couple of two litre bottles of water in the far corner as well as enough packets of crisps, biscuits and cereal bars to last for days.

Would it really be that long? She aimed a kick at the camp bed, rattling it and causing the pillow to fall on the floor. Furious now, she stamped on it, then dropped to her knees, snatching it up from the floor, hugging it to her chest and weeping. Why didn't they let her go? She'd played her part, done all they'd asked her to. It had been a nightmarish sequence of events, but she'd done it. Why was she still here?

She knew, of course.

She'd seen.

Hearing the dull, wet thuds, she'd gone running, even though they'd told her to stay in the bathroom until she was empty. As if she were a container, a lorry or ship. Empty. She knew what empty felt like now. This gnawing ache, this crawling itch. She missed Mark. She even missed her mum.

She screamed, a high tear of despair, her throat feeling raw when it was over. There was no one there, she knew that. Just her, the cell-like room and the mess on the carpet.

28

The woman looked exhausted. When Catherine entered the room, she glanced up and folded her arms.

'I didn't want to come in, did that other copper tell you that? He made me.'

Her voice was low and deep with a scratchy dullness as if it was little used, brought out only on special occasions. She wore a grey hooded sweatshirt and new-looking jeans. Catherine sat opposite her. *This room again.* It was cold, the woman hugging herself as she hunched against the realisation that she was going to have to face the truth.

'My colleague said your daughter is missing?'

She sniffed and gave one quick nod.

'So they said.'

'Who told you?'

'Keeley's boyfriend and a friend of hers. They all live in a house together in the middle of the Meadowflower.'

Catherine nodded her understanding. The Meadowflower Estate was a run-down warren of council properties. Every police officer in the area knew it well.

'So you went to the house?'

'I had to. Keeley wasn't answering her phone and I've had her kids for over a week. Can't hear myself think. My sister's with them now and she's not best pleased either.' Ailsa Pearce ran her hands up and down her arms. One foot tapped on the floor. Catherine watched as her fingers discovered a scab on the back of her hand and started to pick at it. 'I thought their dad might take them, but he's bloody useless.'

'Didn't he wonder where Keeley was?'

The other woman made a sound of disgust.

'He doesn't care as long as he's got his . . . his beer.'

Catherine glanced at her.

'Beer?'

Pearce lifted her bony chin and met Catherine's eyes. 'That's what I said.'

'Okay.' Catherine pretended to make a note. 'How many children?'

'Two, boy and a girl. He's three, she's five months. Poor little sods.'

'When did you last see Keeley?'

Pulling a mobile phone out of her jeans pocket, Pearce frowned. 'She sent me a text asking if I'd have the kids for a couple of nights. I said all right. She pays me and it's better than them being left in that house.'

Catherine glanced up. 'She leaves them in the house?'

'With their dad,' Pearce clarified. 'She wouldn't leave them on their own.' She pressed a few keys on the phone, then announced, 'I got the text a week ago today, like I said, and I last saw her that night, when she dropped the kids off.'

'Did she say where he was going?'

'Away with a mate. I didn't ask.'

'That's all she said, away with a mate?'

'Like I said, I didn't ask. Between you and me, I was hoping it was a bloke. She could do with kicking Simmo into touch.'

'Shaun Simmington?'

'That's the one. Do you know him?'

'I know of him,' Catherine admitted. 'And he hasn't heard from Keeley either?'

'Said if she didn't come home soon, he'd change the locks,' Pearce sneered. 'You can see why I didn't want the kids there.'

'Do you have a photo of Keeley?'

'Loads on my phone.'

'Could you send me one and write down Keeley's phone number, please?'

Catherine scribbled her own mobile number on a piece of paper then pushed it and the pen over to Pearce, who nodded before scrolling through the pictures on her phone.

'That other copper said you've found a body? I saw it on the local news as well. Do you think it's Keeley?' Catherine met her eyes. The other woman blinked, her lips trembling. 'If Simmo's hurt her, I'll kill him myself.' Her voice was guttural and Catherine felt a shiver travel her spine. Her phone vibrated in her pocket and she took it out. The smiling face of Keeley Pearce greeted her. Blonde hair. Hazel eyes. The right build. Her stomach lurched.

'Good enough photo?' Ailsa Pearce asked, her voice rasping on the question. She knew.

'Excuse me a moment.' Catherine got to her feet. Jogging down the corridor, she called to Rich Smithies, just on his way out of the door: 'Rich, before you go, will you get someone to bring Shaun Simmington in, please?'

Rich groaned. 'Simmo? Do we have to?'

'I'm afraid so. There's a good chance our unidentified body is his girlfriend.'

'Bloke's a nightmare. I'll get the call put out,' Rich grumbled, shuffling back to his desk. Catherine ran up to the incident room and grabbed the first uniform she saw, told him what Ailsa Pearce had said and asked him to let the DCI know.

She pounded back down the stairs, pushed open the door of the room where she'd left Keeley's mother, then stopped, hands on her hips.

'Oh, you're kidding.'

Ailsa Pearce had disappeared.

Catherine yanked the seatbelt over her chest.

'She can't have gone far.'

PC Natalie Roberts started the engine and the squad car shot forward.

'Blues and twos?'

'No need.'

Roberts blew a raspberry. 'Spoilsport.'

'Child.' Catherine grinned.

'Got any sweets?'

'No.'

She laughed as Roberts stuck out her lower lip. They joined the main road through town, not many people on the pavements as the day passed into evening. The air was crisp, the sky clear and the moon loomed bright behind the grammar school. Roberts nodded at it.

'Full moon.'

'Not going to start howling at it, are you?'

'Good one, Sarge.' Nat rolled her eyes. 'Why are we looking for this woman again?'

'I hadn't finished talking to her.'

'Well, I've only seen blokes so far and a couple of female runners.'

'I don't see her as a runner.' Catherine thought back to Ailsa Pearce's scrawny, restless limbs. 'Anyway, she was wearing jeans.'

Roberts negotiated a sharp corner, then stamped on the brakes as a double decker bus pulled out of a side road.

'I don't know, she ran from you. Did you scare her off, Sarge?' Folding her arms, Catherine gave Roberts a stern glance.

'You can still go and bring Shaun Simmington in, you know.'

'Ugh, no way.' Roberts shuddered. 'He threw up on me last time.' Catherine turned as far as she could in her seat, craning her neck to scan the street behind them.

'No sign of her.'

'Maybe the huge day-glo police car wasn't a good idea?'

'Don't know what she was thinking.' With a sigh, Catherine turned back.

'I hate to break it to you, Sarge, but not everyone likes a cosy chat with a copper.'

'Thank you, Constable.'

Roberts lifted her hand in a smart salute. The bus dithered along in front of them and Catherine frowned. 'You don't think . . .'

'There's a bus stop a hundred metres from the station. If she was lucky . . .'

'Shit. All right, let's go up to the Meadowflower.'

'You're joking, aren't you? I think you've mistaken the car for a tank.'

'Stop complaining, we'll be fine. Ailsa Pearce lives on the outskirts anyway.'

'Third time this week,' Roberts grumbled, changing lanes as they approached a roundabout.

'What are you moaning about now?'

'Third time I'll have been up to the Meadowflower this week. A drunk and disorderly, an assault and now a . . . what? Absconding mother?'

'I'm pretty sure our unidentified body is her daughter, Nat. I think she is too.'

Roberts slowed the car as they approached a speedbump. 'Yeah, fair enough.'

Ailsa Pearce's house was a semi-detached with a neat front hedge. Nat pulled in close to the kerb.

'Looks respectable.'

'Unlike next door.'

Roberts leaned forward for a better look.

'Is it the massive inflatable snowman on the lawn that you object to, or the Santa hanging from the guttering that keeps flashing his arse?'

'Both. All of it.'

Pearce's neighbours were obviously fans of Christmas decorations, and it being the first week of December hadn't dampened their spirits. Catherine turned away as a huge 'Happy Xmas!' sign lit up in neon red and green above the front door.

'Half the bulbs have blown,' Roberts observed.

'Pity the rest haven't as well,' grumbled Catherine. 'Hang on, here she comes.'

Sure enough, Ailsa Pearce had just turned into the road. Catherine opened her car door and strode towards her. When Pearce saw the police car, she half-turned, clearly thinking about running again. Catherine hesitated but then Pearce shook her head as if annoyed with herself and turned back.

'Well, you've found me,' she said as Catherine approached.

'We hadn't finished.'

'I had. I just want to go home.' Pearce nodded towards her front gate.

'What about the children?'

'What about them?'

'I can get someone from Social Services to come down . . .'

'They're fine with me until . . . well, until there's news.'

Catherine nodded. 'We want to help you, Ailsa.'

Pearce's laugh was bitter, more of a snarl.

'Do you? Then leave me alone.'

'We're bringing Simmo in for questioning.'

'Good.'

'Do you know who his dealer is?'

Pearce made eye contact at last.

'You know better than that, Sergeant. Ask him. I've nothing more to say.'

'We still don't have a positive identification on the body we found.' Catherine's voice was gentle.

The other woman gave a small nod.

'So it could be Keeley.' It wasn't a question.

'It could. I'm sorry.'

Pearce pressed her lips together and tipped back her head. 'She never had a chance growing up around here.'

Catherine said nothing. It was a sentiment she'd heard several times before from different people; usually parents, but those she had arrested often had a similar point of view. Sometimes she agreed with them.

'Erm, Sarge?' Nat Roberts had edged her way towards them. Catherine turned. 'Shaun Simmington's done a runner.'

29

Back in the car, they headed deeper into the estate. There was a strange, charged atmosphere on the Meadowflower, as if the whole place was holding its breath, waiting for the next violent outburst. It was always the same, each resident eyeing each other and the world in general with an air of suspicion. Row upon row of tightly packed red brick terraces were dotted here and there with squat, oblong buildings that contained six or eight flats.

'My cousin lives along here.' Nat glanced at a tiny elderly man who was hurrying along the pavement, clutching a shopping bag.

'It's not all bad.'

A tennis ball bounced across the road in front of them and Nat braked hard as a small boy darted out to retrieve it. When he reached the safety of the pavement, he turned and shouted after them, gesticulating as they drove past. Nat glanced in her rear-view mirror.

'Not sure exactly what he was saying but the second word was "off."'

'Lovely.'

'I'm surprised we haven't seen Simmo yet.'

'Why?'

'According to Control, he's wearing a pink silk dressing gown.'

'What?'

'Yep. He went over the back fence and that's all he had on.'

'Nothing else?'

'Trainers?' Nat shrugged.

Catherine winced. 'I'll let you grab him then.'

'Thanks, Sarge.'

'Don't mention it.'

'Aren't we getting near his house anyway?'

'Yeah. Hang on, there he goes.'

There was a flash of fuchsia pink as a figure shot by, followed by two male constables in hot pursuit. Nat pulled the car up onto the kerb, threw open her door and joined the chase.

Several residents were hanging out of windows or standing on their doorsteps, pointing and laughing. Some joker had found the Benny Hill theme tune on the internet and was playing it full blast from their phone. Catherine hid a smile and slid into the driver's seat of the patrol car. She executed a quick three-point turn, then sped back in the direction they had come from.

Parking the car behind the wreckage of several burnt-out garages, she crept down a snicket that snaked between two blocks of terraces and waited, handcuffs at the ready. Within seconds, she could hear pounding feet and wheezing. Sure enough, Simmo appeared, his face almost the same colour as his dressing gown. He hurled himself into the alleyway, not noticing Catherine until it was far too late.

'Wait, I . . .' he spluttered just as Constable Nathan Collins rounded the corner and tackled him. The two men went down in a heap of stab vest, dressing gown, hairy legs and other flapping body parts that Catherine didn't even want to think about. As soon as she could identify a pair of pink-clad wrists, she snapped the cuffs on them.

'Evening, Simmo,' she said, standing back as Nathan hauled a panting Simmington to his feet. 'Nice outfit.'

'She can't stay there any longer.' The boss flicked ash from his cigarette into a silver ashtray that perched on the corner of the table. 'We need the room.'

The other two exchanged glances.

'We're carrying on with the operation?' the older man asked. The boss glanced up.

'Of course we are,' he snapped. 'What do you expect us to do, just pack it all in? There's a fortune to be made here now that Dougie Hughes has gone and I'm not missing out on it. I want to make enough money to get myself over to Spain and set up in a villa. Living in luxury for the rest of your life, it doesn't sound bad, does it?''

'But with the police involved . . . ?'
The boss stood up and marched over to them, hands on hips, glaring.

'We wanted the body found, you know that. Forget about her. Even if they find out who she is, which I suppose they're bound to, there's nothing to link her to us. She's the junkie girlfriend of a small time dealer, that's all. The police need evidence, that's what they work with, and they won't have any.' He turned back to the desk and stubbed out the cigarette as his mobile rang. '. . . You're joking. Christ, I'm surprised he could run that far . . . Right. Okay, thanks.' He put the phone back in his trouser pocket and turned to the two of them. The younger one glanced away. 'Talk of the devil, Simmo has just been taken in by the police.' His voice was calm, his eyes gleaming. 'You know what that means, don't you?'

There was a silence. He waited for a few more seconds, then drove his fist into the gut of the younger man, who collapsed with a cry. As he hit the floor, a kick glanced off his ribs.

'Fucking answer when I speak to you,' the boss snarled. The older man didn't look at his companion, keeping his eyes dead ahead. The boss stepped back and cracked his knuckles. 'She needs to go. Do it tonight, just in case.' He sneered at the man on the ground. 'And you: learn some manners.' He rocked back on his heels and lit another cigarette with a smile. 'Now get out.'

30

'This is police brutality, you know that, don't you?' Shaun Simmington held up his grazed palms for Catherine's inspection.

'No, Shaun, if we'd held you down and given you a kicking, *that* would be police brutality. What you have are accidental injuries sustained while resisting arrest when wearing a skimpy negligee.'

Shuffling in his seat, Simmington said, 'It's a robe, not a negligee. I was in bed, it was the first thing that came to hand. You think I'd normally wear one?'

Catherine pulled a face

'I don't even want to think about it, Shaun.'

'I wasn't resisting arrest either.'

'Enough. I want to talk to you about Keeley Pearce.'

Simmington gave a lopsided grin.

'Yeah, well, me and Keels have split up.'

'Does she know that?'

'You'll have to ask her. She will when she comes back to the house and finds her mate Jade in my bed.'

Leaning forward, Catherine caught a whiff of dope and body odour. Wincing, she sat back and took a breath of fresh air.

'Does Keeley have a dentist?'

Simmington gawped. 'A dentist? How should I know?'

'You live with her, don't you?'

'Her hygiene was never up to much, if you know what I mean.'
Simmington smiled and scratched his armpit.

'So you don't know?'

'She's got a toothbrush,' he offered.

'Well, that's a start. We'll be taking it then. There are officers at
your house now.'

He sat up straight, eyes wide, pupils huge.

'But I haven't done anything.'

Catherine studied her fingernails.

'That depends on your definition of "nothing", doesn't it?
Running away from police officers looks a bit dodgy, wouldn't you
say? What will we find in your house? Scales? Plastic bags? A big
roll of cash?'

Simmington squirmed. 'Look, what do you want to know?'

'Shaun, we have an unidentified body that we believe could
belong to your girlfriend. What do you think I want to know?'

'Wait a minute, there's a body?'

'Yep.'

'Keeley's body?'

'You tell me. She's missing, isn't she?'

He blinked a few times in confusion. 'Well . . . I mean, she hasn't come home.'

'And you didn't think it would be a good idea to report that to someone? Say, I don't know . . . us?'

'But you're the police.' Catherine gave a few slow handclaps. Simmington blushed, his eyes roaming the ceiling. He licked his lips. 'I didn't think anything of it, I thought she'd just got fed up of me and gone.' Simmington forced a laugh. 'I'm not the best boyfriend in the world, I know that.'

'You thought Keeley had left you? What about the children?'

'What about them?'

'Well, they're still at her mum's.'

'And?' Simmington sniffed, raising a grubby hand to rummage around one nostril.

Catherine closed her eyes for a second, the urge to thump him almost overwhelming.

'Let's start again, shall we? Did Keeley tell you where she was going?'

He looked away and one hand came up to scratch his ear. Catherine waited, knowing that whatever came out of Simmington's mouth next would be a lie.

'No, she didn't.'

Catherine inclined her head. 'Hmm. Really?'

'I've just said so.'

'And what if I said I don't believe you?'

He ran his tongue over his lips.

'Up to you. I can't make you.'

'What if I said I thought you knew exactly where Keeley was going, or at least what she was going to do?'

Simmington folded his arms in a pathetic attempt at defiance, treating Catherine to another whiff of his noxious armpits.

'Bollocks.'

'No thanks, I've had a good look at yours once today already.' She fixed her eyes on his face, holding his gaze. 'It's about drugs, isn't it, Shaun?' He stared at her, eyes wider than ever. 'Who was she carrying them for?'

He shook his head, terrified. 'I don't know what you're talking about.'

'Do you have a little stash in your house somewhere? Personal use, is it? Or are you dealing now as well? Anything up to life in prison for that you know.'

'I'm not dealing, I . . .'

'So who is? Keeley was carrying coke, lots of it. Who for? Who was paying her, Shaun? Was it you?'

'Look, I . . .'

'No, *you* look. You could be facing a prison sentence here, a long one.' She held up a hand and began to count on her fingers.

'Obstructing a police officer. Wasting police time. Drug possession. Drug dealing.'

'But I haven't done anything,' Simmington wailed.

She tipped her head to one side.

'Indecent exposure.'

'No way.'

'Wearing a horrible pink dressing gown in a public place. You could get five years for that alone.'

He covered his face with his hands.

'It was someone who worked at that factory with her. Worthy's,' he whispered.

Catherine's eyes narrowed, not sure if she had heard him correctly.

'What did you say?' she demanded.

He stared at her, tears forming in his eyes, his hands trembling.

'She worked there for a while, you must know where I mean. She said that someone there knew a way of making loads of money. When she told me what they wanted her to do I said no, no way, too risky. But . . .'At last he looked shamefaced. 'Well, we were desperate for money. Things are so expensive these days.' He glanced at Catherine to see if she was sympathetic, but her face hadn't changed, so he stumbled on. 'She said it was worth a try, that she could make more in a weekend than we would get in a year. The kids always need stuff and with Christmas on the way, well . . .'

Catherine felt her lip curling. 'So you let her do it?'

'I didn't let her, it was her decision.' He had the grace to look shamefaced.

'Who organised it? Who's behind it all?'

'I don't know.'

'Come on, Shaun,' she scoffed.

'I don't! I swear on my mum's life I don't. She wouldn't say, she didn't want me to know in case . . .' He spread his hands wide. 'Well, in case of this.'

'And you expect me to believe that?'

'It's true. She left on the Friday, said she'd be back on Monday morning, and off she went. She was really happy, said all our problems would be over.' He sniffed again and rubbed his hands over his eyes. Catherine watched the performance, unimpressed.

'Who told her about it? At Worthy and Son, I mean?'

'I don't know.'

'Man, woman? Vegetable, mineral?'

'What? I don't know, she wouldn't say. She was protecting me, like I told you.'

Catherine looked at him, not trusting herself to speak for a second.

'You honestly don't have a clue?' Her voice was taut, the fury held in check, but only just. Simmington squirmed.

'I don't. I swear, I've no idea.'

She looked hard at him again. He seemed to be telling the truth, slumped in the chair now, defeated.

'When was Keeley employed at Worthy's?'

'A year ago? Eighteen months? It was only for a few weeks, some sort of sickness cover.'

'Did she ever mention a woman called Lauren Cook?'

'Lauren? No, not that I remember.'

'You're sure? What about Mark Cook?'

'No. Never heard of either of them.'

Catherine stood up, sick of the sight of him. Simmington frowned. 'Is that it?'

'For now. I've a home to go to.'

'So is Keeley dead?' He blinked a few times. 'I know I'm a shit to her but I love her, you know?'

'Of course you do.' Catherine turned on her heel and marched out.

Dan Raynor set the magazine on the chair and got to his feet slowly, careful not to make a sound. He bent over his grandmother, kissing her cheek softly, laying his hand over hers for a second. As he left her bedroom, one of the care staff was passing and she smiled at him.

'Is your nan asleep?' she asked. He nodded.

'Dropped off while I was reading to her. She seems better today.'
Even as he said the words and saw the woman's reaction, the slight
tightening of her smile, he knew it wasn't true.

'She has good days and bad.'

Dan nodded. 'I suppose so.'

He walked quickly down the corridor and out into the car park. His
nan didn't have good days, not any more. Much as he hated
leaving her here, he had no choice. She needed nursing now, care
that he couldn't provide at home. He had tried in the early days of
her illness, much like he had with his mother, but in the end it had
been too much. She had insisted on selling her bungalow and
moving into the care home, though he had protested, not wanting
strangers looking after her in the last months of her life. The
standard of care was excellent though, at least as far as he had
seen. A smile crept across his face as he shoved his hands in his
pockets, waiting to cross the busy man road. No doubt Nan would
have let him know if the food or the nurses weren't up to scratch.
The money from the sale of her little bungalow was quickly being
eaten up by the nursing home's fees, but he would never have told
her. Soon he would have to pay for her care himself but again, that
would remain a secret. He hurried across the road, hoping the rain
would hold off until he reached home. He would do all he could to
keep her comfortable, including any overtime he was offered. Not

there was much of that anymore, but there were other ways to make money.

DCI Kendrick sat behind his desk, sipping from a mug of coffee. 'Your friends left early again,' he said to Knight.

'Shea and Allan?'

'They invited me into their little bolthole earlier,' he smirked. 'I told them if they wanted to speak to me, they could do it in here. They're still going on about those bloody photos. I told them I knew nothing about it and that they were wasting my time. They didn't stay long. Now,' he looked at Catherine, 'Simmington has given us another reason to go back to Worthy and Son?'

She nodded. 'I thought I'd go myself after the morning briefing and take Anna and Chris with me.'

'Fair enough. Right, what did Catherine miss while she was out playing kiss catch with Simmo?'

Knight smiled. 'We've got Lauren Cook's phone records, so Simon started going through them, and we've requested Keeley Pearce's records too. We've also started looking into where Keeley has travelled over the last few years, but like Lauren Cook, it doesn't seem as if she's left the country recently. We've had confirmation that there's been no activity on either of their bank accounts. We need to start thinking about where the drugs might have come from and where Keeley had been to get them. Did she travel in the back of a lorry, or under a different name? We think Lauren switched her phone off when she parked her car in the multi-storey because there's no signal after that. Forensics have removed the car with Mark Cook's permission, but as we know Lauren was fine when she left it, they're just storing it for now. We have Keeley Pearce's hairbrush and they're fast-tracking the DNA sample to see if it matches that of our body.'

'I think we're all agreed it will.' Kendrick's voice was sombre. There was a short silence, and then he said: 'We need to find Lauren Cook.'

'Or her body,' Catherine added.

'Glass half empty, Sergeant?' Kendrick asked. Catherine shrugged.

'It's a safe bet that Lauren's gone off to earn a few grand in the same way Keeley Pearce did.'

'Did they know each other?' Kendrick asked.

'Simmington says no. Mind you, I doubt he'd recognise his own family most of the time. He was coherent enough in the interview, but then he's not been fully sober for years.'

'Mark Cook doesn't recognise Keeley's name either, Anna phoned and asked him. Neither do Lauren's parents,' Knight added. 'Lauren's friends have never heard of Keeley and she and

Lauren haven't been in touch on social media or by using their mobiles as far as we can see. It's a safe bet that they didn't know each other, or at least not well.'

'Are the Chantrys still staying with Mark?' Catherine asked.

'Apparently so.'

She shuddered. 'Poor bloke.'

'We're also looking into any other arrests of drug mules that have been made over the last couple of years, especially fairly locally,' Knight said. 'I've got Anna checking if anyone of interest has been released from prison recently, seeing if they've come straight back and started up their business again. No luck so far.'

Kendrick drummed his thick fingers on the desk. 'We're getting nowhere. We've no witnesses, no leads except the person who told Keeley about the drug mule opportunity being at Worthy and Son. They might have left by now anyway. Didn't Simmo know anything else about them?'

'He said not, and I believe him.'

Kendrick pursed his lips. 'Let's hope we can find out ourselves tomorrow then. If not, we're stuffed. Helen Bridges has put a short article about the body having been found on the newspaper's website. It said there'd be more in tomorrow's paper.'

'Is it worth telling her we might have an ID?' Catherine asked.

Kendrick thought about it for a moment. 'Let's leave it for now. We'll tell her when we've got confirmation, let her think she's getting a scoop.' Kendrick set his cup on his desk and leant back in his chair, closing his eyes. Catherine remembered Helen's parting words about Claire and thought about sharing what she'd said with Knight and Kendrick. Knight glanced at her, but before she could speak, Kendrick opened his eyes and said, 'Right, come on, let's go. See you bright and early.'

31

The TV was blaring again, some cookery show with several contestants making ever more complicated recipes while a couple of chefs criticised their efforts. Mark thumped his mug of weak, sickly tea down on the coffee table just hard enough to make Celia glance at him, then turn back to the programme. Mark gritted his teeth. Geoff had offered to nip out and fetch fish and chips and he wished he'd gone with him. Even though the chippy was only a ten minute walk, it would be time away from Celia. Maybe he and Geoff could have had a pint too, killed another quarter of an hour or so.

He ran a hand over his mouth and chin, his stubble rasping against his palm. Celia didn't approve of stubble, which could be why Geoff had a beard, Mark thought; a tiny act of rebellion. Not really defying his wife and her unapologetic, unchanging opinions, but then not falling perfectly into line either. He glanced at Celia again, her profile softened by the glow of the television set, and wondered. Was she thinking about Lauren? Was the constant stream of soap operas, quiz shows and cookery programmes an attempt to distract herself from facing up to the fact that her daughter had disappeared? Mark crossed his legs, feeling restless. It had to be. It couldn't be because she enjoyed watching them, surely.

He picked up his phone from the arm of his chair and opened the photos. Lauren smiled back at him, wearing shorts and a t-shirt, a glass of wine in one hand and a half-eaten burger in the other. A barbeque, held only a few months ago, but it felt like longer, much longer. He scrolled again. Lauren in bed on a Sunday morning, the duvet pulled right up to her chin as always, smiling up at him as he brought her a cup of tea. His breath caught in his throat and he felt tears welling. He studied the photograph again; the easy, loving smile, the spread of her hair across the pillow. Her eyes, and the way she was looking at him as he raised the phone, wanting to capture the image of her, hold the moment for as long as possible. It had only been a few weeks ago, before the accusations and the argument. Angry again now, he stuffed the phone into his pocket. They had plans for the rest of their lives together. When he'd found a job, they wanted to have a baby, start the family they'd always talked about. Lauren couldn't wait. What would happen now?

The police had asked about drugs. What did that mean? They'd also found a body, a woman who must look like Lauren. Mark shuddered, wrapping his arms around himself. The central heating was on, had been all day thanks to Celia. She didn't have to worry about paying the bill, of course. It was still cold. Lauren didn't take drugs anyway. Mark thought about a few of his mates, hoping the police wouldn't knock on their doors. Lauren liked a glass of wine or a lager or two, but drugs had never been her thing.

Mark got to his feet and picked up the tea that he'd ignored, intending to chuck it down the sink and stick the kettle on again. He didn't feel like eating, but when Geoff had suggested fish and chips he hadn't liked to say no. It gave Geoff a chance to escape the house too. Mark felt sorry for his father-in-law. He was obviously worried about Lauren, but at least at home he would have been able to keep himself busy: pottering around, reading the military history books he loved, wandering down to the shop to buy a paper. Here, there was the TV and Geoff's daily walks and that was about it. Mark and Lauren did read of course, but Geoff liked factual books and they didn't have any.

As Mark reached the kitchen, he heard the front door open. Geoff called, 'Only me.' Mark started to take plates out of the cupboards. He and Lauren ate straight from the cardboard boxes that the chippy had recently started using, but he couldn't see Celia doing that somehow. Not, he thought, opening the drawer where they kept the cutlery, that they had had fish and chips for a while, not since he'd lost his job. Takeaways were a luxury they'd had to forgo as well as nights out, new clothes and their gym memberships. Mark had been for a few runs, but without people to chat to and the promise of a swim and maybe a sauna afterwards, it wasn't the same.

Geoff came in and plonked a plastic bag on the table, decorated with a grinning blue fish and a pile of garish yellow chips. Mark held onto the worktop for a moment as bile rose in his throat, and the room span. Geoff glanced at him, concerned.

'All right?'

Mark nodded, not knowing whether he was or not. He lifted his eyes to meet his father-in-law's gaze.

'Where is she, Geoff? She must know we're all worried sick.' Geoff began to unwrap the food, sharing the chips onto three plates.

'I don't know. It worries me that she hasn't been in touch with anyone, not you, her mum, her friends . . . It's just not Lauren.' His face was drawn, his hands trembling as he cut a battered fish in half. 'I just got one between Celia and me, she didn't want a lot.' Geoff paused for a second, studying the white flakes that were spilling from the batter. 'Oh Christ, I forget to get her cod. Don't mention it, for God's sake.'

Mark managed a smile. 'Wouldn't dream of it.' Geoff glanced at him, then hesitated. 'What?' Mark asked.

'It's just . . . I don't want you to take this the wrong way, but . . .' Geoff paused again, embarrassed.

'Do I think Lauren's left me?' Mark shoved a chip into his mouth. The other man raised his hands.

'I'm sorry, I . . .'

'It's fine, Geoff. It what everyone thinks no doubt, including the police. It's the only thing that makes sense, that and the fact that I'm a gormless bastard who hasn't realised yet that his wife's gone off with someone else.' His voice was flat, calm. He felt nothing, nothing at all.

Geoff shook vinegar onto his food, his eyes on Mark's, assessing his mood. 'Do you think she has?'

Mark sighed and began cutting up his fish. 'It doesn't make sense. Like I told the police, we're happy. She's happy, as far as I knew. If she wasn't, wouldn't she have said so?'

Geoff gave a tiny laugh. 'Knowing Lauren, yes.'

'Exactly. She doesn't hold back.'

There was a pause as both men chewed. The door clattered open.

'Did no one think to call me?' Celia complained, pulling out a chair and settling into it. Geoff was immediately contrite.

'I'm sorry, love, we were just talking about Lauren.'

Celia speared a piece of fish and brought it up to her mouth. 'I hope she's happy, wherever she is. Causing all this upset.'

Mark felt his jaw tighten but he kept eating, eyes on his plate. He wasn't going to bite, no matter what Celia came out with. She popped the fish into her mouth, chewed for a second and then thinned her lips. 'Geoff, this is haddock.'

Mark closed his mind to Celia's voice, raised in complaint as usual and Geoff's low, conciliatory tones. How much longer could he stand this?

32

Lauren opened her eyes. There was a noise in the hallway. Footsteps. And now a faint glow of yellow light creeping under the door. A torch?

This was her chance.

She sat up and swung her legs around to the side of the camp bed. After slipping her feet into her trainers, she crept over to the bottles of water, picked one up and weighed it in her hands. Two litres. It was only a plastic bottle but it was pretty heavy. She'd hardly drunk any of it.

There were voices outside the door now, male voices. They were both here. Her heart sank a little but she gripped the bottle and stood at the door, holding her breath. It was worth a try. She'd have the advantage of surprise at least.

A rattle as the door handle turned. Lauren raised herself onto the balls of her feet. When the door opened fully and the first man stepped inside, she swung the bottle with all her strength into the back of his head. He let out a cry and fell to the floor, clattering onto the filthy carpet as the torch flung across the room. Lauren staggered, then steadied herself just as the second man burst in.

She swung the bottle again but he was ready for her. He lurched out of the way and the bottle flew past his face. The momentum sent Lauren sprawling and as she fell he snatched hold of her, holding both arms behind her back and binding them together at the wrist. Cold metal dug into her flesh and Lauren roared in frustration. He gave her a shove.

'Shut the fuck up, Lauren. Crazy bitch, what were you thinking?' She glared at him. 'I was thinking it might be nice to get out of this shithole.'

He gave a nasty smile. 'Oh, you're going. Come on, time's up.' The other man, finally back on his feet, rubbed his stomach, then lifted his hand to explore the back of his head.

'Fucking hell,' he groaned.

His companion grinned. 'Not having much luck, are you, mate?' Lauren made a sudden dash for the open door but he grabbed hold of her again. 'Do you want us to just kill you here? You need to come with us.'

'Why should I?' Lauren spat.

He shrugged. 'We're going for a nice drive.'

'I doubt it.'

Reaching into the inside pocket of his jacket, he pulled out a knife and snapped open a wicked-looking blade. Lauren eyed it, fear closing her throat as he held it up, glinting in the torchlight. She'd never have believed it of him.

'You already know what this can do,' he said, still smiling. 'Now move.'

When she turned into her street, she was greeted by the bright headlights and loud engine noise of a gritter sweeping past on the other side of the street, sending salt skittering over the tarmac in front of her. A hot bath and straight into bed with a book. She couldn't wait.

For a change there was a parking space outside her flat, and Anna Varcoe shuffled her car into it, then locked up and turned towards the tall, Georgian building where she lived. Her flat was on the top floor and Mr Kemp downstairs was a perfect neighbour – quiet, friendly and happy to take in any deliveries. That, Anna reflected as she hurried up the path, blowing on her hands, was an important consideration when you ordered most of what you bought online and worked long hours most of the time. Having a police officer live above also made Mr Kemp, an elderly widower whose main aim in life now was to marry Anna off to his grandson, feel safe.

After collecting some boring-looking post from the hall table, Anna ran up the stairs, unlocked her front door and filled the kettle. The tall ceilings in the flat almost made up for the small rooms. Almost. It was much better now she had painted all the rooms white; the previous occupant had had a preference for dark, rich colours like plum and burgundy, but they had made the whole place feel stuffy and constricting, the way you'd imagine a funeral parlour to be decorated. Anna didn't know, never having been in one. Even the mortuary was more cheery than her flat had been. Only lack of funds and patience with living with her parents for another minute had made her sign the lease on the place.

With her tea made, she slipped off her shoes and went through into the bathroom, poured some of her favourite bubble bath into the tub and turned on the hot tap. With a book, her tea and a half-hour soak, she'd soon wind down and, more to the point, warm up. Then she could get into bed and relax. It wasn't that late, not compared to some nights, but she was tired and it had been a frustrating day. Thomas had sent her a couple of texts but hadn't pushed to see her, and she was glad, though a little disappointed too if she admitted it. She smiled as she remembered his grin when they'd been eating their curry and she'd teased him, telling him he was surrounded by police officers and that he'd better watch his step. And last night, the way he'd made her laugh with stories from his teaching jobs, his dancing eyes that were darker than his sister's. That might be weird, thinking of Catherine Bishop every time Thomas leant towards her. His hand, warm in hers as they walked back to her flat and his lips, gentle and teasing when he kissed her goodnight. She smiled to herself, aware that she was thinking like a soppy teenager. She didn't care. It had been a long time since she'd felt anything even approaching this, and she was determined to enjoy it for as long as it lasted.

Anna turned off the tap, set her drink on the side of the bath and took off her jacket. As her fingers found the top button of her shirt, the doorbell downstairs rang. She swore, checking her watch. She waited, but the bell rang again and she slipped her jacket back on with a sigh. She'd have to go down. Mr Kemp would be in bed already, keeping warm, and it wasn't fair to disturb him.

She slipped on the security chain, a precaution she had insisted on the landlord installing when she moved in, for both her and Mr Kemp's peace of mind. She worried about him as if he were a member of her own family. When she opened the door, a blast of cold air forced its way through the gap, making her shiver. On the step, his features masked by the gloom, stood Rob Hunter.

33

Thomas set a plate of lasagne and salad in front of his sister, then sat opposite her and took a long swallow from a bottle of beer. Catherine eyed the plate.

'Now you're really scaring me.'

'What do you mean?'

'Spaghetti bolognese, lasagne? You'll be making a soufflé next.' She picked up her knife and fork and tucked in.

'A what?' Thomas frowned.

'All right, maybe that's a step too far.' She chewed and swallowed. 'This is lovely, thank you.'

'You don't need to sound so surprised.' Thomas smiled. He reached into his trouser pocket and set a couple of twenty pound notes on the table. 'Here. I know it's not much, but when I get paid I'll give you some more.'

She waved it away. 'Don't worry about it, use it to take Anna out. Not seeing her tonight?'

He drank again, then shook his head. 'Didn't want to seem too keen. Anyway, she was working late.'

With a rueful smile, Catherine said, 'Better get used to it, Thomas, it happens quite often.'

'I understand that. She seems dedicated.'

Catherine piled lettuce and lasagne onto her fork.

'She is. Well, we have to be.'

'Anna says you're a good boss.'

'I'm not really her boss.' Catherine took a sip of water. 'Anyway, she's hardly going to tell you she hates me.'

'You know when you got hurt?' He raised a hand to his cheek. 'Your nose and face, I mean. Does that sort of thing often happen?'

'There's always a risk, I suppose, but I wouldn't say often. We're usually going in to find out what's happened when it's all calmed down, not when it's still kicking off. Uniform have that pleasure.'

'I couldn't do it. The things you must see . . .' He shuddered. Catherine smiled, then blinked hard as the image of the battered face of the woman they'd found at Moon Pond shot through her mind, followed by Keeley Pearce's smiling face. She opened her mouth, wanting to tell Thomas about it, to talk it through, share it. She couldn't.

'Are you worried about Anna getting hurt?' she asked instead, cutting off another square of lasagne. Thomas fidgeted in his seat.

'Not just Anna, but . . . yeah.' Catherine shot him a knowing glance and he grinned.

'You really like her, don't you?' She shook her head, amazed. 'I never thought I'd see the day. Thomas Bishop falls in love. Women across the globe go into mourning.'

He laughed. 'Don't be daft, I hardly know her yet. I just don't want to mess it up.'

'Cook her a meal, she'll be putty in your hands.' She swallowed the last mouthful.

'Only if she likes spaghetti or lasagne, that's my full repertoire.' He shrugged.

'Serve the lasagne, then get her a jam doughnut for pudding. She'll be bowled over.' Catherine stood and took her plate over to the sink as her mobile began to ring in her pocket. She sighed, pulling it free.

'Catherine.' His voice was quiet, distracted.

'Are you okay?'

There was a silence, then: 'Do you fancy a drink?'

Knight handed her the bottle of beer she'd asked for and slid into the booth beside her. The pub was out of town, quiet and old-fashioned with a log fire burning in a huge hearth and an elderly black Labrador snoozing in front of the bar. Opening a bag of salt and vinegar crisps, Knight offered them to her. She shook her head.

'Are you okay?' she asked again.

He chewed for a second, then said, 'I think I'm going to be suspended.'

Catherine stared at him. 'You're serious, aren't you?'

'Shea seems determined to get rid of me. I'm sorry, Catherine, I shouldn't have dragged you out here. You've got your own career to think about.'

'Don't worry about me.'

'I wasn't sure who else to talk to.' He looked wretched. Catherine remembered the kindness he'd shown her since his arrival in Lincolnshire and reached out a hand, laying it on his forearm for a second. He glanced up. 'I know Shea and Allan have talked to you. I'm not going to ask what they said, but they've got it into their heads that I covered up the photos Malc Hughes was sent, left them out of my investigation.'

'I know, but why would you do that?'

'Because I took them?'

Catherine snorted. 'That's ridiculous.'

Knight shook his head. 'They don't think so. They think I killed Paul Hughes to get back at his dad, sent him the photos to gloat, then used the investigation to cover my tracks and divert the suspicion away from myself.'

'I've never heard such crap. Kendrick told me Malc Hughes didn't even receive the photos until after he was questioned, not to mention the fact that you were with a team of police officers all day when Paul was killed. Anyway, if they really thought that you were involved, you'd have been suspended by now.'

'I doubt it'll be long.'

Catherine shook her head, feeling helpless. 'I don't know what to say.'

'You've seen the thing on my back. If Shea had, I'd be spending the night on remand.'

'Look,' she said. He was staring into the bottom of his glass of orange juice. 'Jonathan, *I* don't believe it, DCI Kendrick doesn't believe it, and no one who's ever worked with you would believe it either.'

He gave a bitter laugh. 'Oh, wouldn't they.'

'What does that mean?'

'I can think of a few ex-colleagues in London who would be only too pleased to have the chance to see the back of me once and for all. No pun intended.' His hand drifted towards his shoulder blade again.

'There are arseholes everywhere,' Catherine said.

'These are influential arseholes. A superintendent, a chief inspector . . .'

'What happened?'

He frowned. 'I shouldn't have phoned you, I'm sorry. How are you?' When she didn't answer, he glanced around. 'It's a nice pub. Cosy and traditional.'

'Jonathan . . .'

'All right. There was an investigation into the death of a teenage boy. I didn't like the way it was handled and I said so. They had it down as a gang killing, I thought his dad had done it. I still do. Anyway, I made some enemies.'

'I don't see what that has to do with the death of Paul Hughes?'

'Maybe I'm just paranoid.'

'Shea and Allan did ask me what I'd do if a DI's job became vacant,' Catherine told him. Knight smiled a little.

'That was subtle of them,' he said, sipping his drink.

'I told them I didn't know.'

'Really?'

'It's the truth. I like being a sergeant.'

'You don't aspire to be the next Superintendent Stringer then?' Catherine almost choked on her beer.

'What do you think?'

He grinned.

'Can't see it somehow.'

She raised her beer bottle and he clinked his glass against it. They sat, enjoying their drinks, the silence comfortable rather than awkward now. After a while, Knight cleared his throat.

'What?' Catherine asked.

'It's just that . . . Jo Webber gave me her personal mobile number,' he mumbled. She stared at him. Inspector Wallpaper volunteering more personal information? It had to be some sort of a record.

'And have you phoned her?'

He fidgeted.

'Not yet. I didn't want to rush it.'

'Rush it? You're sitting here with me when you could be spending the evening with the most beautiful woman in the county?' She drained her beer. 'I'm going to nip to the loo. Phone her now, it's only eight thirty. Pick her up and take her for a meal. I'll even let you drop me off at home first.'

Knight smiled as she hurried off towards the back of the pub. Catherine seemed to be much more herself tonight, not that he could say he knew her well. The fragile, haunted look that had masked her face was disappearing. He'd been worried about her. At Claire's funeral she'd been remote, desolate, her usual easy smile and humour having deserted her. He liked her, admired the way she had picked herself up in the few weeks that had passed since. She was determined to move on with her life, he could see that, and he respected her for it. Walking back into a station that had buzzed with gossip and rumour since Claire's death couldn't have been easy. He knew that the team were determined to help her through it in any way they could; they had told him as much. Anna, Dave, Simon, Chris, they'd all come up to him individually, shuffling their feet in embarrassment, asking how she was and when she was coming back. They all knew Claire hadn't been worth the heartbreak, but that was easy for them to say.

He waited for the call to connect.

They'd told Lauren to lie on the back seat of the car under a blanket and she wasn't going to argue, not with the memory of the other woman's body and that evil, gleaming knife blade so fresh in her mind. A sob rose in her throat and she swallowed it, pressing her lips together and blinking hard. It was her own fault that she was lying here, her filthy hair matted and stinking, her clothes even worse. The stench of her own body under the warm, scratchy blanket was unbearable. The two men in the front hadn't spoken since the journey had begun, and the atmosphere in the darkened, speeding car was tense.

She and Mark had been so stupid – the holidays, the clothes, the nights out. Their credit card bills were higher every month, but they'd been manageable until Mark had lost his job. Then there had been his bouts of drinking, the final argument . . . She sighed, not wanting to remember that, the threats and the mess on the kitchen floor. Vomit and whiskey, empty beer cans that she'd hauled out of the rubbish bin and thrown at her husband. She'd lost her temper, but then so had he, drunk and despairing. He'd stood there staring at her, his clothes filthy, vomit down the front of his shirt, mud clinging to his jeans. His elbow was badly grazed and bleeding, but Mark hadn't even noticed, he was well past the point of feeling pain. Perhaps that was the point. When she had found out that he had spent a good chunk of the money she had been saving on drink, she'd flown at him, clutching his arms, shouting in his face. Then she had grabbed her suitcase, already packed for the weekend away that couldn't now happen, and stormed out. One phone call was all that was needed, the chance that she sneered at before now seeming like a blessing. She could have gone to her parents for help, but she'd imagined the look of scorn on her mother's face, the outrage and disbelief, and she couldn't do it. Far better to take this route, a safe and quick way of paying off all their debts with even a little to spare.

Of course, it hadn't worked out like that. She'd known she was in trouble when she had rushed into the room and seen the two men's panicked faces, the shovel and the body on the floor. She retched, bile flooding her throat as she remembered the woman's ruined face. How could they have done it? She'd screamed at them, bent over the woman to see if she could help her. No chance. She'd tried to run then, to flee down the stairs, but they'd soon caught up with her. She didn't know who their boss was, but they were obviously terrified of him, talking in hushed voices about what he would do when he found out Lauren had seen the dead woman.

The car was slowing, and Lauren braced herself for whatever was going to happen next. She was numb; a detached, almost clinical feeling of helplessness. This was a film starring someone else, one she had no role in at all.

Lauren held her breath as the car's engine cut and she heard the doors open. She was completely at their mercy, her hands still cuffed behind her, the back doors of the vehicle locked. She heard the door nearest her feet open and the older man said, 'Right, get out.' The blanket was yanked away and she sat up slowly.

'Where are we?' she croaked.

'It doesn't matter. Get out.'

She scrabbled her way towards the door, trying to take in as much detail about her surroundings as she could without being obvious. Deciding she was taking too long, he lunged forward and grabbed a handful of her hair. Lauren let out a shriek and swung her feet at his shins. Swearing, he jumped back, then brought his hand around in a vicious slap across her face. She fell back, stunned for a second, her cheek burning, and blood starting to leak from her nose. He stood there, grinning down at her as she groaned.

'Are you going to play nicely now? You should know better than to try to piss me around.' She glared up at him. 'Come on, out.'

She lay for a few seconds longer, turning her face towards the car seat and allowing some saliva to dribble from her lips. She was no expert, but she'd seen enough crime programmes on TV to know that leaving as much trace of yourself as you could was a good idea. Hopefully there would be some blood from her nose too. He

grabbed her legs this time and hauled her out, set her on her feet
and kept a tight hold of her upper arms.

'Christ, you stink.'

The blood had reached her mouth.

'What do you expect?' Lauren snarled. 'It's not like I've been
staying at the Hilton.'

He marched her forward. In front of them was a building that
looked like a barn, red brick with several doors set at intervals
along the side. Lauren frowned. Where were they? She'd seen
another building behind them, two storeys with large windows on
the top floor. It looked like a house; there was even a conservatory
attached, then a low fence with a gate. The car had paused for a
minute or two just before she was ordered out of it; perhaps that
was when they had travelled through the gate?

He jerked her arm again and she kept walking. She risked a
glance at him, but his eyes were fixed ahead. She tried to let more
spit fall from her lips, knowing it was probably futile out here in
the elements. The blood was dripping too, she could feel it. She
flicked her head towards the man at her side, hoping some might
find its way onto the sleeve of his jacket.

Her eyes had adjusted to the darkness, and as they approached the
building she realised where they were. Her heart sank. The
younger man hurried forward and unlocked the door before
shoving her inside. Her breath misted the cold air in front of her

face. Plastic sheeting covered the floor and she shivered, wondering how many others had been dragged to this place before her. The door thudded closed and the room was illuminated as the single light bulb dangling overhead was flicked on.

He turned her to face him. She lifted her chin and met his eyes without flinching. She was beyond fear now, adrenaline coursing through her. Blood dripped from her chin, falling to the plastic-covered concrete with a tiny sound, like a clock marking the passing of a second. Smiling in a way that was almost fatherly, he lifted his hand and traced the line of her cheek with a fingertip. She hated him, with his leering mouth and his wandering hands. The way he always stood too close.

'Are you ready?' he whispered.

She forced out a laugh. If the ride in the car had felt unreal, this was the stuff of an awful gangster film. He took the knife from his pocket and held it out to the other man who came forward, his face pale in the flickering yellow light. Lauren's body tensed, her mind a mess of terror, regret and remorse. This was unthinkable, it couldn't be happening.

And yet, of course, it was.

The young man wiped his palms on his jeans and took the knife, his hand trembling. Lauren wanted to close her eyes but whichever part of her brain that controlled that action had shut down long ago.

The man behind her tightened his grip, holding her up like a human shield.

Another step closer. His Adam's apple jerked in his throat as he panted, ragged breaths slipping from his mouth. Lauren couldn't move, her feet feeling as if they were stuck in setting cement, every muscle and sinew taut as she tried to lean back against the brute strength of the man who held her captive. It was hopeless. He let out a laboured breath and hissed, 'Get on with it.'

He was one step away, his eyes narrowed, his forehead damp. Lauren felt her bladder release, urine added to the mixed stench of terror, sweat and filth that was swimming from her pores in waves. He swallowed again and raised the knife, clutching it in both hands like a sacrificial offering. Lauren's senses screamed, but no sound escaped her. Her mouth opened as her final seconds slipped away.

'Do it.' His voice was barely a whisper.

The breath shuddered from her as the blade touched her throat.

34

He stood there, an uncertain smile on his face. Anna glared at him.

'What are you doing here, Rob?' she demanded. 'How did you know where I live?' She kept the door on the chain.

He blinked a few times as if confused by her anger. 'I phoned your mum and asked her. She seemed pleased to hear from me.'

Anna sighed. Her mum had loved Rob, though she wouldn't be quite as keen on ushering him back into her daughter's life when she heard where he had spent the past eighteen months.

'Told her you'd just got out of prison, did you?' she snapped. His gaze fell to the ground.

'It . . . didn't come up,' he mumbled. Anna laughed.

'Strange that. She must have asked what you'd been up to?' Knowing her mum, she'd no doubt invited him around for tea.

'I just said I'd been away and changed the subject.' He shrugged.

'The new subject being my address?'

'I just want to talk to you, catch up, see how you've been.'

'I'm fine, thank you. You've been in prison, I'm a police officer. That's all we need to know about each other, I'd have thought.'

He gestured towards the door. 'Can't you take the chain off? I'm not going to force my way in.' She shook her head, her eyes fierce.

'The chain stays on. I've nothing to say to you, Rob. You made your choice and look where it got you.'

His laugh was bitter. 'Yeah, good for you, Anna. You told me so.'

Her eyes widened. 'That's not what I meant and you know it. Our relationship was over the day you started hanging around with those dodgy blokes. The day you started breaking the law.'

'I thought Mother Teresa was dead.' He smirked. She watched him, sadness creeping into her look of indignation. He blushed, scuffled at the ground with the toe of his trainer.

'Goodbye, Rob.'

She started to close the door, but just before she disappeared he said, 'Anna? I'm sorry.' She hesitated, holding the door still for a second. 'You know this missing woman?'

'What about her?'

'Is she dead? It seemed serious, the questions your boss was asking.'

'I can't talk about it, Rob, you must know that.'

His face twisted. 'Yeah, someone with as much experience of being questioned by coppers as me ought to.'

'I'm not going to feel sorry for you,' she told him. He met her eyes, then turned away. She just heard him as he began to walk up the path.

'I'm not asking you to.'

The Indian restaurant was quite busy again, the buzz of conversation and friendly waiting staff giving the place a cosy, welcoming atmosphere. Jo Webber glanced around.

'I've not been to this place for years,' she said.

'I was in here two nights ago,' Knight admitted, and she laughed.

'Hot date?'

'If that's what you call going out with five colleagues plus a wife and a woman they're trying to set your sergeant up with, then yes.' he smiled.

'Your sergeant? You mean Catherine?' When he nodded, Jo winced.

'Oh. How did she take it?'

'She didn't seem too pleased.'

'I'm not surprised. What happened with Claire Weyton had to hurt.'

'I was worried about her,' he admitted. 'She seems to be better than she was though.'

'I know what it's like to have people trying to matchmake,' Jo said. 'Mates of my friends, blokes they work with, even my assistant's brother.' She took a sip of beer. 'I think the job puts people off.'

'I can't think why.' Knight raised his eyebrows and she laughed.

'You get all the same old jokes: "Nice for you to meet a man with a pulse", "Watch out or she'll lock you in her freezer."'

'Funny.'

'The first time, perhaps.'

'I won't talk about your job at all then.'

She laughed.

'I bet you mention work within the next five minutes. Your colleagues, a point from my post-mortem report . . .'

'It was Catherine who said I should phone you actually,' he admitted.

'Ha. I'm glad she did.' She waited as he blushed, smiling at him.

'Catherine told me you have an ex in London.'

Knight swallowed nervously. 'Yes, Caitlin.'

Jo nodded. 'I think I told you that I'm divorced?'

'You did.' Knight fumbled for another topic of conversation.

'Caitlin's pregnant,' he blurted. Jo stared.

'Pardon?'

Knight groaned inwardly. Why the hell had he said that? There was no going back now though. 'My ex-girlfriend. She's pregnant.'

'I see.' Jo hesitated, then said, 'And how's that going to work?'

'Sorry, how do you mean?'

'Will you travel down to see the baby? Move back there?' She didn't seem too perturbed.

'Oh, it might not be mine,' he explained. Jo looked sceptical.

'Don't you know? Doesn't Caitlin?'

'She doesn't,' he admitted, feeling stupid. 'I could be the father, but so could the bloke she's living with now. She met him before we split up.'

A waiter arrived with their starters and Jo broke a piece off a poppadum.

'And you thought this was a good time to tell me about it?' she asked. Knight was studying the tablecloth, mortified. When he dared to glance up, she was struggling not to laugh, her eyes bright, her cheeks flushed. 'Your face . . .' She started to giggle and Knight joined in, relieved.

When she calmed down, she said, 'My husband was seeing someone else as well.'

Knight grabbed another chunk of poppadum. 'Really?'

She nodded. 'He worked in the hospital too, as a nurse in A&E, and he was sleeping with one of the consultants. She dumped him after a couple of months.'

'What an idiot. Him, not her,' he clarified.

'The worst part was,' she hesitated. 'While we're confessing . . .' He nodded, wondering what was coming. 'Just after he left, I had a miscarriage. I hadn't even known I was pregnant.' She kept chewing, her eyes blank. Knight had no idea what to say without sounding trite or inappropriate. Instead, he took her hand before he could doubt himself. Her face relaxed slightly, and she said, 'God, he was an arse.'

He pulled over to the side of the road, leaving the engine running as he turned in his seat.

'Lovely house.'

She shrugged. 'It's too big for me, but I couldn't face moving again.' She smiled. 'Thank you for a lovely evening.' He nodded, suddenly shy again, and she laughed at his expression. 'You're like a nervous teenager on his first date.' She raised a hand to his cheek, cupping his jaw and running her thumb over his lips. He closed his eyes, savouring it, then felt her breath on his face, knowing she was moving closer. Her mouth, her hands in his hair. Cold noses. The day disappearing, evaporating. The world outside ceasing to be for a short time.

She pulled away from him, then bent close again and kissed his cheek.

'I'm glad you phoned. Good night, Jonathan.'

35

The first phone call of the day confirmed what they'd known already – Keeley Pearce was their unidentified body. DCI Kendrick had taken the call, and as he relayed the message to the rest of the team, there was a moment of silence, a second of reverence. Officers would be despatched to inform Ailsa Pearce and to ask her to formally identify the body.

Then the noise started up again. Catherine sat at her desk, checking through her emails. As Knight headed for his office, she met his eyes and mouthed, 'Well?' He gave her a tiny smile and she resolved to interrogate him later on.

When Knight's door had closed behind him, Melissa Allan sprang out of the next office and treated Catherine to a dazzling smile before approaching her desk.

'Good morning. DI Shea would like a word.'
Catherine hesitated just long enough to make Allan's smile dim a few watts, then said: 'I've no time now, I'm afraid.'

'It can't wait.' Allan took a step forward.

'It'll have to.' Catherine beamed, switching off her monitor. She felt Allan's resentful eyes on her back as she crossed the room to Anna Varcoe's desk.

'Don't ring me again, do you understand?' Anna snapped at whoever had called her. Catherine perched on the corner of her desk as she slammed the receiver down.

'All right?'

'That was Rob Hunter, phoning me at work as if that's a perfectly reasonable thing to do.' She looked up at Catherine, furious. 'He even came to my flat last night, wanting to talk. I told him to get lost. I'm so bloody annoyed.'

'I'm sure he realised. Are you ready?'

Anna held up her notebook.

'As long as I can stay away from Rob.'

'I think we can arrange that,' Catherine replied. Chris Rogers fell into step with them as they passed his desk.

'Sarge . . .' he said. Catherine held up a finger.

'Is this going to be about Ellie?'

'No.' He looked wounded.

'Carry on then.'

'It's just that Faye . . .'

Catherine strode ahead as the two DCs broke into laughter and jogged to catch her up.

This time when they arrived at the premises of Worthy and Son, there was no welcoming smile from the receptionist. John Worthy hurried to meet them as soon as they arrived, smoothing down his waistcoat.

'Back already, Sergeant Bishop?' He smiled. 'And with two colleagues this time. How can we help you?'

'We'd like to speak to your staff again, Mr Worthy. I'm hoping your second-in-command is back in the office?'

'Alex? Well, yes he is, but . . .' Worthy shuffled his feet.

'Could you let him know we're here, please?'

'I think he's on a conference call at the moment,' he replied with an apologetic shrug. There were footsteps behind him and he turned.

'It's all right, John, we've just finished.' He was tall with his hair cropped short and wore a casual navy blue shirt and jeans. Standing beside him in his shabby tweed jacket and cord trousers, John Worthy looked like a poor relation.

'I'm Alex Lambert.' He came towards them, hand outstretched, a broad smile fixed in place.

'Mr Lambert, we'd appreciate it if you could answer a few questions.' Catherine kept her tone neutral. Lambert nodded.

'No problem at all. Shall we go through into my office?'

'Thank you. Mr Worthy, would you be able to show DC Rogers the rest of the building, please?'

Worthy nodded, bewildered. 'I'm not sure what any of this has to do with . . .'

The rest of his protest was lost as Lambert led Catherine and Anna away from the reception area.

The room was a contrast to the old-fashioned style of Worthy's office. Lambert sat in a chair that looked like it would have been more at home on a space shuttle than in an office. His desk was made from curved silvery metal with a black glass top. The carpet was also black, the walls painted a light grey. There was a lime green sofa along one wall, as well as two armchairs of the same colour facing Lambert's desk.

'Please sit down,' he said, the smile still evident. He unbuttoned his shirt cuffs and rolled up his sleeves, revealing an expensive-looking watch. No wedding ring, Catherine noted. She was silent, wanting Anna to take the lead.

'John said you were asking about Lauren Cook?' Lambert tilted his head to the side, smiling at Anna. 'I don't know her well, I'm afraid. I've only been with the business a couple of years.' Catherine made a note and Lambert's eyes followed her pen across the page. 'I hadn't realised that I was so interesting.' He laughed.

'Mr Lambert, do you remember a woman called Keeley Pearce coming to work here?' Anna asked.

It was subtle, but his eyes narrowed for a second.

'I don't, I'm afraid.' His voice was smooth, unflustered. 'Was she a temp? We do have them from time to time. I don't have much to do with the packing staff, I'm more interested in the web design and marketing side of the business.'

I'm sure you are, Catherine thought. Lambert didn't seem the type to get his hands dirty somehow.

'She worked here for a few weeks about eighteen months ago, we understand,' Anna continued.

'I'm sorry. As I said, I don't remember the name.'

Yet you knew she worked in the packing department.

'But she did work here?' Anna had noticed his mistake too.

'I don't know for sure.' Lambert ran a hand through his hair, looking up at Anna through his eyelashes. 'Margaret on reception deals with all the HR stuff, you'd be better off checking with her. Shall I call her in?' He stretched out a hand and picked up the receiver of his desk phone.

'That won't be necessary at the moment.' Anna paused for a second and made eye contact with Lambert. 'Tell us more about Lauren Cook.'

'There's nothing to tell. She's reliable as far as I know, turns up and does her job. I don't know anything else about her.'

'What about your other members of staff?' Catherine put in.

Lambert's eyes flicked from her to Anna and back again.

'Who should I answer first?' He gave a broad, easy smile.
Anna nodded towards her sergeant. 'She's the boss.'

'You haven't given either of us a straight answer yet in any case,
Mr Lambert,' Catherine pointed out.

He gazed at her for a few seconds.

'I think I have, Sergeant, but let me try again. Firstly, I know who
Lauren Cook is but have never spoken to her, other than "good
morning" or "good night". I think I once said "excuse me" when I
had to squeeze past where she was working. Secondly, I don't
know this woman . . . what was her name? Keeley?'

'Thank you for clarifying that, Mr Lambert.' Anna's smile was an
effort.

'Please call me Alex.'

'Could you tell me about disciplinary procedures here at Worthy
and Son, Alex?'

'How do you mean?'

'Well, if an employee turned up for work drunk or under the
influence of drugs, for example?'

Again, the reaction was subtle, but it was there. Lambert blinked a
few times before forcing a smile. 'I'd be very surprised if they
did.'

'Come on, Mr Lambert, you're not running a convent,' Catherine
snapped.

'Playing the bad cop, Sergeant Bishop?' he asked with a smirk. She gave a hollow laugh.

'You caught me out.'

Chris Rogers was chatting with John Worthy and Margaret from the reception desk. Catherine kept her distance, took out her phone and scrolled through her emails, not wanting to interrupt. *Shit.* She hadn't replied to Ellie's text yesterday. Opening the message, she read it again: **Good to talk last night**. She had no idea what to say to that. Just "You too" seemed almost rude, especially a day late. Glancing over at Chris, she closed the text again.

After another minute or so, he joined her.

'All right, Sarge?' he asked in an undertone. She nodded.

'How's it going with them?'

'Interesting. John Worthy plays the role of bluff country gent quite well, but I don't think he's a naïve as he makes out. And a fly couldn't fart around here without Margaret knowing about it - she's switched on. She doesn't like Alex Lambert.'

'She's not the only one.' Catherine screwed up her face.

'Arrogant prick?'

'Yep. I've left Anna talking to him because I was either going to slap him or throw up on his horrible chairs. Anna's letting him think she likes him.'

'I suppose you want me to go in there now?'

'He might respond to a man-to-man type approach. He wasn't going for mine.'

'Which was what, bull-in-a-china-shop?'

'As if. What about the staff out there?' She jerked her head towards the packing and printing part of the building.

'All very chirpy. I made myself noticed, did a lot of looming over people's shoulders like you said.' He grinned.

'I'm going to go through and do some myself.'

Rogers laughed.

'With respect, Sarge, you're too small to loom. You'd be better off giving them a tap on the kneecap.'

'Ha bloody ha. Go and give Alex Lambert a grilling with Anna.'

'Will do.'

He turned away and she took her phone out again: Enjoyed chatting too. Coffee?

The packing department was cold, a bitter draft blowing through a pair of double doors that stood open as a delivery driver heaved a pallet of brown cardboard boxes out to his waiting lorry. A conveyor belt about half a metre wide snaked through a hole in the wall and ended in a semi-circle. Stacks of cardboard and rolls of tape were scattered around the place. The cement floor was painted a dark green with a yellow line warning employees not to stray too close to the conveyor while it was moving.

A group of people huddled in one corner where an old kitchen unit and a sink stood. She'd caught them at breaktime. Perfect. There were two women and two younger men. As Catherine approached, Sarah Watson, the woman she and Anna had spoken to the previous day, looked up and smiled.

'Back again?' the taller man asked, the hostility clear in his voice.

'That's right. Can I have a quick word?'

'Why not?' he shot back. 'Not like we've got anything better to do. Not as if we've been working all morning in this bloody icebox and these are the only fifteen minutes we get to ourselves.' He took a mouthful from his cup and said, 'Well?'

'Come on, Billy, she's just doing her job. Aren't you bothered about Lauren?' Sarah asked.

Billy gave a scornful laugh.

'She'll have gone off with some bloke, I don't know what all the fuss is about.'

Sarah shook her head. 'Not Lauren, she wouldn't do that to Mark.'

'God knows why, he's a proper thicko,' the other woman spoke up.

'Would you like some hot chocolate?' Sarah offered. Catherine accepted and thanked her.

'Could you remind me of me your names, please?' she asked, raising her voice over the whine of the kettle.

'Can you tell us why we should?' Billy retorted. He had broad shoulders and wore a belligerent expression. Catherine sighed.

'Because it'll be so much easier if we do this here rather than at the police station.'

'Is that a threat?'

'No, not a threat. More like a fact.' Catherine had met people like Billy hundreds of times before. The best approach was to ignore the hostility. It was usually all hot air. He sniffed.

'Let's get it over with then.'

Billy Kilner, Dan Raynor and Josie Hayward. Catherine scribbled them all down, though they had a full staff list already. Sarah handed her a mug and she took it with a smile, the rich scent of the chocolate welcome in the chill air.

'How can you work in here? It's freezing.' Catherine cupped both hands around her drink.

'I'll go and close the doors,' Dan Raynor said, hurrying away.

'Two pairs of socks, fingerless gloves, and we move around a lot.' Josie Hayward smiled.

'You're busy?'

'Not as busy as we were; there were ten of us working in this department a few years ago. It's busy enough though, with Lauren away.'

'You're missing her then?'

'It's easier with five, especially when you're loading pallets. We're supposed to have two to a box, but we can manage them on our own if we need to.' Josie shrugged her shoulders. 'Don't tell Margaret that, she's Health-and-Safety mad.'

'Do any of you remember a woman called Keeley Pearce? She worked here for a few weeks a while ago?'

Billy frowned. 'The name's familiar . . .'

'I remember her. Bit of a dreamer,' Dan put in as he rejoined them.

'Spent more time in the loo than out here working,' Josie sniffed. 'Think the job centre told her they'd stop her money if she didn't turn up. She couldn't wait to get out of here.'

'That's right.' Sarah was nodding. 'She was lazy, but nice enough.'

'Did she make any friends here? Did you see her talking to anyone in particular?' Catherine asked. Headshakes all round.

'Why do you ask?' Billy wanted to know.

'I'm afraid Keeley's been found dead.' Catherine was blunt, wanting to see their reactions. There was a short silence.

'The poor lass,' Sarah said after a few seconds.

'Drugs, was it?' Josie asked.

'Why do you ask?' Catherine hoped she sounded casual.

'Just a feeling. She always seemed jumpy, she couldn't seem to concentrate, and she was always moaning about having no money. I don't know, it was just the impression I got.'

'She was on drugs.' Billy was firm. 'She was spaced-out most of the time, you can see it a mile off.'

'I bumped into her in town once and she was off her face then too,' Dan offered.

'Did she talk about drugs at all? What she was taking, where she got it from?' Catherine knew it was a long shot, but she had to ask. Billy laughed.

'She lives on the Meadowflower, there's a drug dealer in every other house up there. I should know, I live there too. Hate the place, but what can you do? Can't afford anywhere else in town.'

'What about money?' Catherine asked.

'Keeley? She never seemed to have any, but then who does?' Dan gave a short laugh.

'She was really skint though,' Sarah said. 'She told me her mum helped her out with food and clothes for her kids.'

'None of us are rolling in it, that's for sure.' Billy took a gulp of hot chocolate.

'Well, some have more than others,' Josie sniffed. 'Our resident blue-eyed boy for one.'

The others nodded. 'Money's never been a worry for Alex, with his cars and holidays and designer clothes. Talk about born with a silver spoon,' Sarah commented.

'What do you think of Alex Lambert?' Catherine wanted to be sure. There were a few low groans and noises of disgust.

'He's a twat,' spat Billy. 'Looks at us who work through here like he's found us on the bottom of his shoe.'

'Thinks he's a cut above us lot. Thinks we all fancy him too,' Sarah agreed. 'As if.'

Catherine drained more hot chocolate. 'What about John Worthy?'

'What about him?' Billy butted in again.

'Is he a good employer?'

Dan cleared his throat. 'I'd say he's fair,' he said. 'He cares about his staff, which is more than you can say for most bosses.'

The others nodded. Billy glanced around. 'He likes to give people a chance, I'll say that for him. A few of us have been in trouble, some have been in prison.'

'Including you?'

Billy smiled for the first time. 'Don't tell me you haven't already checked.'

Catherine said nothing, finished her drink, thanked them for their time, and went through to the printing room. The two men who were working in there eyed her with suspicion, throwing quick glances in her direction and then turning back to their work. She moved closer, careful not to get in their way as they moved around the machinery. Rob Hunter was also there, watching the men as they worked.

'Learning the ropes,' he said with a shy smile. 'I had a few hours in packing, now I'm through here.'

'Can the three of you spare me a few minutes?' Catherine asked. The nearest man pulled off his baseball cap and ran a hand over his balding head. 'I thought we'd been through it all yesterday.'

'We've got an order to get out by lunchtime,' his mate complained.

'I won't keep you long.' They left their task and came to stand around her in a semi-circle, clearly not happy about it. 'Thank you. Does the name Keeley Pearce mean anything to you?'

For a second or two, no one spoke. Catherine felt the already icy temperature fall another few degrees. When Phil Richards spoke, his voice was controlled.

'Why do you ask?'

'She's dead. We want to know why.' Catherine kept her eyes on his face but his expression didn't change.

'She wasn't welcome here,' the other man, Sid Benson, spoke up. 'Not welcome?'

'The first day she came to work, things started go missing,' Benson elaborated. 'As soon as she left, the thefts stopped. Seems a coincidence, wouldn't you say, Sergeant?'

'Thefts? What sort of thefts?'

'Cigarettes, money. Most of us have worked at Worthy's for years and we trust each other. When Keeley was here we had to start using the lockers again.' Benson shook his head as if disgusted.

'Sid's right. Keeley was a sneak thief and we didn't like it. She didn't stay long,' Richards confirmed.

The two men exchanged a grin. Rob Hunter was frowning.

'You're certain it was her?' he asked.

'Who else? Listen to me, none of us would steal, not from the people we work with.' Richards snapped. 'We're all struggling to get by as it is.'

Hunter held up his hands.

'I'm sorry, I didn't mean . . .'

Richards glared at him, but Benson smiled. 'Forget it. You're new here, but you'll learn. We look after each other. Understand that and you'll fit in fine. Keeley didn't. Can we get back to work now?' he asked. When Catherine nodded, the two older men went back over to the machine. Rob eyed her, his face wary.

'Glad you're here?' Catherine grinned. He gave her a rueful smile.

'Better than being inside. They like to sound tough but they're decent blokes. I didn't bring any food on my first day and they shared their sandwiches with me.'

'No one's put your head through the window yet then?'

'Not quite.'

'Anything else you want to tell me?'

'Nothing.' He was uncomfortable, unable to stand still. 'Will you tell Anna I'm sorry I phoned her? I've already apologised for turning up at her house . . .'

'I'm not a message service, Mr Hunter.'

He blushed.

'No, I . . . I'm sorry.'

She nudged him. 'I'm joking. I'll mention it.'

'Oh. Oh right. Thank you,' he stammered. Rolling her eyes, Catherine left him to it.

Back in the reception area, she plonked herself down on the sofa to wait for Anna and Chris. Margaret on reception turned her back on Catherine, who had to smile. She had a reply to her text: **Are you free at lunchtime?**

When the door had closed behind them, he counted to a hundred just to be sure they weren't coming back, then snatched up his mobile and scrolled through his messages. Finding the one from her, he deleted it and then wiped her contact details too. His heart was pounding as he turned his laptop back on and opened up his banking software. Just seeing the figures there calmed him, the black type bold and unmistakable. He reached out, ran his finger down the column, then tapped it twice on the numbers that showed the final balance, satisfied.

She was dead now. She couldn't say a word.

36

Catherine sat with Chris at his desk, both of them frowning at his monitor.

'So three of the staff at Worthy's have done time in prison. Rob Hunter, Phil Richards and Josie Hayward. Hunter we know about already. Hayward – shoplifting and handling stolen goods. Phil Richards was done for burglary. So much for him telling me he wouldn't steal. They've all done one stretch each and that was years ago, except for Hunter,' Catherine confirmed. Chris gave a low whistle.

'You could look at Worthy employing them in different ways.'

'Generous, stupid, suspicious.'

'It's quite a lot out of a workforce of what,' he ran his finger down the list as he totted them up, 'eighteen.'

'What about directors?'

'There's just Worthy himself and Alex Lambert.'

'What's Lambert's story?'

'His dad was at school with John Worthy and they were friends right up until Victor Lambert's death. Alex took over his dad's role at Worthy's two years ago when he became ill. He's got a degree in business studies, he's a qualified accountant and has plenty of industry experience. Worthy doesn't have any children of his own, and it looks like Alex will be managing director one day.'

'Can't be bad.' Catherine shoved her hair behind her ears.

'He doesn't have a criminal record?'

'No. He mentioned being involved in the management of a club when he was younger though?'

'Yeah, some place in Lincoln. You're thinking about the drug angle?' Chris asked.

'Coke and nightclubs go together like . . .'

'Beans and toast? Beer and kebabs? Bacon and brown sauce?'

'Was that your stomach rumbling?'

'Might have been.'

'Right, go and get some food, then see what you can dig up about Alex Lambert's nightclub.'

He stood up.

'Got a feeling in your water about him, Sarge?'

'That or indigestion.'

'Hunger pangs.'

'That'll be it.'

She took out her phone.

Ellie was sitting in the same seat that Helen Bridges had occupied the day before. The same man was behind the counter too. He gave Catherine a cheery wave. 'Back again?'

She smiled at him and slid into the chair opposite Ellie, who said, 'It's good to see you.'

'You too. Have you ordered?' Ellie shook her head.

As they sat back down with their drinks, Catherine asked, 'So is Ellie short for anything?'

She laughed in surprise.

'I've never been asked that before.'

'Not by anyone?'

'Not that I remember. My full name's Eleanor.'

'But you don't use it?'

'My parents have always called me Ellie.'

There was a short silence. Catherine glanced around, picked up a fork and turned it a few times in her hand.

'What do you do at the council?' she asked.

'I work in accounts.'

Catherine wrinkled her nose. 'That sounds . . . interesting.'

Ellie laughed and the awkwardness evaporated.

'Not as interesting as your job, that's for sure. How's it going?'

'At the moment it's frustrating.'

Their food arrived and they tucked into chip butties with enthusiasm. Catherine squirted tomato ketchup onto her plate, dipped a chip into it and said, 'I didn't tell Chris I was meeting you.'

Ellie met Catherine's gaze, her eyes dancing. 'I didn't tell Faye either.'

They smiled, feeling like conspirators. Catherine bit into her chip butty again, not sure why she was here but pleased all the same. Ellie wiped her mouth.

'You said work is frustrating?'

Catherine nodded, swallowing her mouthful.

'It happens more often than not during an investigation. You reach a point where you've followed every lead, spoken to every person. We're not quite there yet, but it can feel like you're treading water until a new piece of information comes in.'

'A bit like when a client dumps a year's worth of receipts on your desk and expects you to do a tax return for them. It happened a lot in my last job.'

'All the answers are in there, it's just putting them into some sort of order.' Catherine nodded. She hesitated for a second, then asked, 'Have you always lived in Northolme?'

'I grew up in a village on the other side of Lincoln. I moved over here when I met my girlfriend.' Ellie paused and gave a tiny smile. 'When she died, I'd just started a new job at the council. They were good to me, Faye especially, so I stayed.'

'What happened?' Catherine asked, her voice gentle. 'Don't tell me if you don't want to.'

'It's fine. She had cancer, stomach cancer. Quite rare at her age. Nine months from her being diagnosed to her death, almost to the day. We were together for three years, just about.'

'It must have been terrible.'

'It was. She never complained, didn't even speak about it. Told me that I should still do all the things we'd planned to do together: the holidays, the weekends away. She wanted me to be happy. I suppose a lot of people tell their partners that when they know they're dying.'

'She sounds lovely.'

'Yeah, she was. I was so angry, not with her but with life, with cancer. She never felt like that, or if she did she didn't say so. I couldn't believe it. We'd just found each other, we were planning the rest of our lives, and then . . . then she was gone. I felt numb for months. I just went to work, went home, lost touch with my friends, didn't talk to my family. Then, one day I went to her grave and it dawned on me that she would hate the way I was living. It wasn't even living, just ticking off a day and getting through the next one.' She smiled, looking up from beneath damp eyelashes. Catherine felt like a fraud. This poor woman was pouring her heart out and Catherine's own mourning seemed trite in comparison, almost an insult. She didn't know what to say. The truth?

'I'm sorry.' She felt helpless. Ellie took a deep breath.

'No, I am. You didn't need to hear all that.'

'It's just that . . . well, it makes me feel stupid.'

Ellie frowned, concerned.

'Stupid? What do you mean?'

Catherine took a breath and started to talk, starting from the minute she and Claire had met and ending with the day of her funeral. Ellie listened without interrupting until Catherine fell silent.

'I'd no idea. What a nightmare,' she said at last. 'How it must have felt, to be betrayed like that . . . A killer. It's unthinkable.'

Catherine managed a crooked smile. 'It's different, that's for sure.'

Ellie glanced at the clock on the wall opposite and groaned.

'I'm so sorry, Catherine, I'm going to have to go.'

Turning in her chair, Catherine saw they'd been sitting there for almost an hour.

'God, so am I.'

They hurried to their feet, pulling on coats and scarves. Ellie picked up her bag, hesitated, then moved to Catherine's side and kissed her cheek.

'Thanks for listening.'

Catherine smiled. 'You too.' Talking about Claire had calmed her. It was as if the whole thing had happened to someone else, someone she didn't have to worry about. It had been like telling a story rather than a tearful account of the tragic events of her own life.

Her phone was ringing. Catherine watched as Ellie gave another smile and left the café, waving as she passed the window.

'Sarge, it's me.'

'How's it going, Chris?'

'I'm at the club Alex Lambert used to own. It sounds like cheap cocktails weren't the only thing on the menu.'

37

They met at a bus stop just down the road from Worthy and Son, each of them taking a circuitous route. It stood on a quiet residential street and with woollen scarves disguising the bottom half of their faces, shoulders hunched around their ears and padded winter coats on, who would look at them twice? Just two blokes waiting for the bus into town. Much less conspicuous than a pub or café where there would be witnesses and no doubt CCTV. There were no cameras out here.

'What are we going to do?' His voice sounded strained, even to himself.

'You're panicking again.'

'What do you expect me to do? The police turn up at work twice in two days and you're wondering why I'm anxious? It's all right for you.'

'What does that mean?'

He turned away, glancing up and down the street, half expecting a police car to pull up and officers to drag them inside at any moment. 'You're like a robot. Doesn't anything bother you?'

His companion laughed; a dry, throaty chuckle that made his flesh crawl.

'Not much. There is one tiny thing though.'

'Surprise me.'

'What the boss is going to say when he finds out . . .'

He swallowed.

'Does he need to know?'

'You're joking, aren't you? I've got to speak to him about the police anyway.'

'What if they come back with a search warrant?'

'There's nothing to find, you know that.'

'If they look in the right place . . .'

'We'll move it tonight.'

'Are you going to tell him?'

Running a hand around his jawline, the other man sucked in a noisy breath through his teeth.

'I'll have to soon, unless . . .'

'Unless?'

'You know what. I'm not lying to him.'

His stomach cramped, his mouth filling with acrid bile that burned like shame.

'I'll do it tonight.' The voice didn't sound like his own, more like the choking gasps of a person being submerged under water, watching as the sky disappeared.

The other man clapped his hand down on his shoulder. 'You'd better.' All at once, the thick, strong fingers dug into his flesh, sharp and painful. 'I'll pick you up at six.' Then he was gone, strolling away as though they'd just been chatting about the weather.

Turning away, he took a shaky breath. This was a nightmare. He was being sucked deeper and deeper into a situation he couldn't control and couldn't escape from. He glanced at his watch. Ten minutes. He'd have to go back in.

38

Lauren hurled the empty water bottle against the far wall as hard as she could. She was furious, sick of being shut in here, the same four walls, the stink and the frustration.

They hadn't been able to kill her. She supposed she should be grateful. He'd touched the knife to her throat, staring into her eyes. She had gazed back, chin up, not giving them the satisfaction of knowing how terrified she was. If this was to be how she died, she just wanted it over with. After a silence, a second that seemed never-ending, his eyes had filled with tears and he'd dropped the knife to the floor with a clatter before turning away with his head in his hands. The bastard holding her had bellowed at him, but it made no difference. Eventually, he'd thrown her onto the floor and seized his companion by the throat, raging at him. They continued to argue, shouting and threatening each other but not taking any action.

In the end, they left her alone. She'd rushed over to the door as it slammed behind them, pounding her hands on it as she heard the soft scrape of the padlock being threaded through the metal latch.

She'd screamed in frustration, thumping her fists on the door until they throbbed.

The room was freezing cold, the floor bare concrete, the only insulation the plastic sheeting. She'd wrapped it around herself last night but it had made little difference. If they left her in here much longer she would die anyway, if not of the cold then of thirst. They had left one tiny bottle of water, lobbed in as an afterthought. They must have learnt their lesson about the big bottles. She'd done her best to sip it, but she had drunk it all in the end. There was no toilet either, not even a bucket. She'd had to squat in the corner, as far away from the small cocoon she had made herself in the plastic as possible. She swallowed a few times, her mouth already parched. She hadn't drunk enough, she knew that. If only she had made the most of the supplies in the room in that house. Too late now.

Blowing on her hands, she dragged herself to her feet. She knew she needed to try to warm up, and the best way to do that was to start moving. The room was about ten feet square but that was big enough to march around in. She swung her arms and lifted her knees; big, exaggerated movements that would raise her heart rate and get her blood pumping.

'I'm not going to die in here.' She said it out loud, to the walls, to the floor. She stamped her feet a few times, then began a series of star jumps.

As her feet hit the concrete for the twentieth time, she heard the roar of an engine, a low familiar drone. She pressed her eye to the doorframe, trying to peer through the tiny gap. No luck. She turned away, guessing what it was. They wouldn't hear if she shouted for help, not over the noise and not from that distance. She paced again, attempting to tame her tumble of thoughts into some sort of order. The men would have to come back. They couldn't leave her here forever. They had been instructed to kill her, but by whom? Whoever it was wouldn't be happy to discover that Lauren was alive and kicking. Baring her teeth in a savage grin, she clenched her fists. She was kicking all right. He wouldn't kill her, she knew that now. She had looked into his eyes and seen it. The other one might, psycho bastard that he was, but then why hadn't he done it already?

Perhaps they'd come back with a different weapon? A knife was messy and you had to be close to your victim. Too personal. What then? A rope? Then they could turn her around and would not have to watch her face, see the light fade and the life drip from her. They could be brutal, she had proof, and that knowledge was the reason she was still here. In a way though, she was pleased that she had seen it. If she ever had the chance, if she did walk out of here, she would go straight to the police, tell them the whole story and face the consequences. Keeley, lying dead and battered on the floor deserved no less. A prison sentence would be a small price to pay for justice for her. She hadn't remembered her name at first, but it had come to her in the end. Keeley hadn't worked at Worthy's for long. Long enough for them to get their claws into her though, obviously.

Were the police looking for her? Mark would have gone to them, in his innocent, unimaginative way. She loved him, but Lauren had to admit Mark was easy to deceive. Not that she was proud of having done so, but she could see no other way of digging them out of the pit of debt they'd thrown themselves into. Drugs ruined lives, yes, she could accept that, but then no one forced people to take them. She had committed a crime, done the unthinkable. A few years ago, even a few months, the thought of bringing cocaine into the country, of stepping outside the law in any way would have been ridiculous. Now though, she had done it and she had no real regrets.

'Except for being stuck in this fucking room,' she muttered, giving the door another thump.

How long would they leave her here? Would they just wait for her to die? The few drops of water they'd left with her would suggest not, but she couldn't be sure. Her lips felt tight and parched and her throat itched. How long could you last without water? A couple of days? It would be one way of getting rid of her without bloodying their hands.

Maybe it wouldn't be like that. They might return with a gun, or that shovel. A syringe filled with whatever drugs they were peddling this week. A bucket of water. A noose or a plastic bag. There were lots of ways to kill someone if you thought about it.

Lauren swallowed a couple of times, attempting to create some moisture in her mouth. No chance. She took a few deep, controlled breaths, forcing herself to calm down. Hysterics would not help and neither would panicking. She tried more star jumps then threw a few punches, the quick movements of her body wafting its stink around her face and making her retch. She kept moving, not allowing her brain to process the fact that she was here alone in a bitterly cold building with no water, no food and no means of escape.

If she began to scream again, she wasn't sure whether she would stop.

39

They pushed desks together in the incident room, dragged a whiteboard closer and took their seats. Jonathan Knight, his face pale, wandered into the room and sat down next to Catherine as she flipped to a clean page in her notebook.

'Still here then?' she asked with a smile. He nodded.

'Just about. Allan was looking for you again earlier.'

'And she didn't find me. What a shame.'

Knight laughed. 'Chris, do you want to start?' He seemed to be addressing the table top. Chris Rogers grinned.

'I went to the nightclub Alex Lambert was a part owner of in Lincoln and got talking to a couple of the staff there.'

'They're open during the day?' Catherine interrupted. He nodded.

'They have part of the bar open for breakfast, coffee, that sort of thing. Anyway, there were a couple of bar staff there and a cleaner. Two of them remembered Lambert, neither had a good word for him and get this – Lambert offered the bloke I spoke to drugs.'

'Good work, Chris – so was he dealing or sharing or what?' Catherine asked.

'Sounded like dealing to me, Sarge. He offered them a taster and said he could lay his hands on more if they wanted it. Told them they could tell their friends if they were discreet.'

'How long ago was this?' Knight wanted to know.

'Two years, give or take a few months.'

'About the time he started working for John Worthy,' Anna observed.

'It shows Lambert has form though,' Simon pointed out.

'Did this person you spoke to buy anything from Lambert?' Catherine asked.

'Apparently not, but then you wouldn't say, would you?'

'Suppose not. Okay, Dave, what about Lauren Cook? Anything useful? Finding her is still our priority, of course.'

Dave looked around the table like an eager child with a good school report to share.

'The story's in the local paper today, as promised. We've had a couple of calls but nothing concrete. A bloke phoned and said he'd seen Lauren getting into a car, but we're still getting a full statement.'

'Getting into a car where? When?' Catherine asked.

'Down a side street, just after we lost her on the CCTV footage. There are no cameras on that actual road, which they no doubt knew,' Dave replied. 'We haven't got the registration number, but he's given us a good description of the car and a sketchy one of the driver and passenger.'

'There were two of them?'

'So he says. Lauren got in the back of the car.'

'And we're checking everyone who owns a similar vehicle?' Knight asked.

'We are, boss. It's not a long list, shouldn't take much longer,' Dave confirmed. 'We're checking the stolen vehicles reports too as well as the CCTV footage as near as we can get it. We might be able to see where they headed, but they seem to have been careful and it all takes time.'

'Are the descriptions any use at all?' Catherine's hopes weren't high.

'They're not brilliant. They were wearing baseball caps for a start. Our witness was sure they were two blokes, but that's about all.'

Kendrick let out a sigh.

'Great. Step forward, Hercule Poirot. Catherine, I think it's time we spoke to Helen Bridges again. Get photos of Keeley Pearce and Lauren Cook in the paper as well as our witness's description of the car and these men.'

She nodded. 'Will do. Helen should be able to get the information on the website straight away.'

'And let's circulate the descriptions to Lauren Cook's family, Keeley Pearce's mum, horrible Simmo, and at Worthy and Son too.' Kendrick cleared his throat. 'That place smells fishy to me.'

Chris said, 'Particularly Alex Lambert.'

'Let's bring him in,' Kendrick decided. 'It's now a week since Mark Cook last saw his wife. Unless she's left him for good without telling him, that's a long time. We need to find Lauren.' There were nods around the table. 'We know Keeley Pearce was offered the chance to earn some money bringing drugs into the country by someone at Worthy's. Let's find out who that was. Anyone else in the frame apart from Lambert?'

'Pretty much everyone at Worthy's. They weren't giving anything away this morning, but we should go back over there.' Catherine sighed. 'All the staff have worked there for at least two years, so any of them could have spoken to Keeley Pearce, except Rob Hunter.'

Anna shifted in her chair as Kendrick pursed his lips.

'Ah yes, Mr Hunter.' He glanced at Sullivan. 'Do some digging, will you, Simon? Let's find out where he worked before he went to prison, if he knows Keeley Pearce or Lauren Cook. He's local and it's a small town.'

Catherine glanced at Anna, whose cheeks were red, her expression unreadable. Sullivan nodded. 'No problem.'

'The rest of you, keep chasing up the other leads, such as they are. I've got a lovely conference call with the Super to trot along to.' Kendrick gave Catherine a pointed look. 'Let's see what Alex Lambert has to say for himself.'

Knight stretched his back. 'I thought I'd go over to Worthy and Son myself.'

The squad car arrived just as a delivery van was being unloaded. The driver gave the marked vehicle an appraising glance as it drove past and parked.

'Have you had some trouble?' he asked.

Billy Kilner, a heavy box of paper in his arms, grunted.

'Not again. Christ, when are they going to leave us alone?' He staggered towards the building, his boots scuffing over the uneven surface of the car park.

Two uniformed officers climbed out of the car, one male, one female. They put on their hats as they strode around the corner, heading for the entrance. Dan Raynor shook his head.

'What do they want now?'

Billy was back. He picked up the delivery note and scanned it, running his gaze down the column of items.

'They'll be still bleating on about Lauren bloody Cook. I wish someone had made a fuss like this when my wife ran off.'

'Didn't think you were that bothered, Billy.' Josie Hayward nudged Dan.

Kilner glanced up. 'I wasn't, but she took the dog.'

They broke into laughter, then stifled it as the two police constables reappeared, walking back towards their car with Alex Lambert in tow. Kilner let out a low whistle.

'Bloody hell.'

Lambert saw them staring and raised his hand in a casual wave.

'Hold the fort, I won't be long,' he called with a grin. The female officer scowled, opened the car door, and Lambert climbed inside.

'Cocky sod,' Josie muttered. 'He could do with taking down a peg or two.'

'What do you think they want him for?' Dan asked.

'Maybe he's Lauren's new boyfriend.' Billy shrugged.

'Alex and Lauren? I can't see it,' Josie scoffed. 'He'd never look twice at the likes of us.'

'I didn't say he was going to marry her.'

The delivery driver cleared his throat.

'Look, I don't mean to be rude, but can we get a wriggle on? I've other deliveries to get to.'

They turned back to the van as the squad car pulled away.

He'd sent her a text, but hadn't received a reply. She was no doubt up to her elbows in some poor unfortunate, he reflected, starting his car engine.

As he drove through the town, his phone rang and he answered it, hoping it was Jo.

The deep, booming voice that echoed through the car was the last one he had expected.

Alex Lambert sat in the interview room with his legs crossed. When Catherine and Dave Lancaster came into the room, he smiled.

'You know, Sergeant Bishop, if you were this keen to see me again you could have just phoned,' he smirked. She ignored him, but Dave offered a smile as he sat down.

'Mr Lambert, thanks for coming in.'

'I wasn't aware I had a choice. I'm waiting for my solicitor.' Catherine turned on her heel and walked out again, closing the door with a thump behind her.

'I don't think she likes me,' Lambert said, straightening the cuffs of his shirt.

Dave lowered his voice. 'She can be a bit moody.'

Lambert nodded.

'Is she your boss?'

'Yeah, sort of.'

'Feel sorry for you then, mate.'

'You're in charge at Worthy and Son, aren't you?' Dave asked.

'More or less. John's the owner but he leaves the day-to-day running of the place to me. He'd rather be out on the golf course these days, he's semi-retired.' Lambert waited a beat and then added, 'I'm hoping he's soon to be fully retired.' He grinned, displaying straight white teeth.

'Bet you can't wait.' Dave wanted Lambert to keep talking.

'There'll be some changes, that's for sure. I've got plans for the place – more web design and marketing, SEO stuff. Get rid of the printing side for good.'

Dave nodded.

'Sounds sensible.'

'You've got to keep moving with the times. John's problem is that he's stuck in the past. He struggles to use email.'

'Do you play golf? I'm more of a football man myself.' Dave kept his tone casual. Lambert laughed.

'Not my cup of tea either. All those tank tops and tartan trousers? It's an old man's game.'

'What then? You go out? Clubbing, drinking?' Dave held his breath. Had he pushed the matey act too far? Lambert's eyes narrowed a little, but he answered readily enough.

'Not as much as I used to.'

'Lincoln's a decent night out.'

'Yeah, not bad. I prefer London or Manchester myself.'

'Bit out of my price range,' Dave told him. 'You owned a club in Lincoln didn't you? That's impressive.'

Lambert eyed him, trying to figure out if this was just a friendly chat or if there was more to it. In the end, his ego took over.

'Yeah, well, if you're willing to work hard, you can pretty much do anything. My dad helped me out with a loan to get the place on its feet and I had a few good years there. In the end I sold my share. Made a massive profit too,' he preened.

'Nice one,' Dave commented. He imagined Catherine Bishop watching on the monitors, pretending to gag at his sycophancy. Sometimes it had to be done. Lambert thought a lot of himself, that much was clear, and they might as well try to use it to their advantage. Lambert wasn't stupid though and would no doubt see through any attempts to flatter him.

'Yeah well.' Lambert smiled. 'There were always plenty of people up for having a good time, so the money kept rolling in.'

'Must have been handy for meeting people?' Dave held his breath as Lambert watched him.

'Women, you mean?' he asked.

'Yeah. I mean, we meet plenty of girls in this job, but they're usually running as far as they can in the opposite direction.' Dave forced a laugh, but Lambert was sneering.

'Not a problem I've ever had, mate. Look, I thought we were waiting for my solicitor?'

Dave folded his arms. He'd lost him.

'We are.'

'So this is an innocent chat?' Lambert's eyes were cold.

'Just passing the time of day, Mr Lambert. I'll leave you to it.'

Outside in the corridor, Catherine was waiting.

'That was smooth,' she grinned. 'See what I mean though? Talk about arrogant. He's lying too.'

'Yep, I reckon so. He's a smart-arse, like you said. It's not going to be an easy interview.'

'You'll be fine.'

He glanced at her.

'You want me to do it?'

She nudged him. 'Don't want someone as moody as me in there, do you?'

40

Patrick Shea looked plumper than ever, the familiar smirk
lingering around his face like a bad smell. Allan flicked back her
hair as she brushed past, then deliberately allowed the palm of her
hand to make contact with Catherine's backside for a second on
her way over to her own seat. Catherine ignored the performance,
furious. Being sexually harassed by another woman was a new and
unwelcome experience.

'Detective Sergeant Bishop, we need another word.' Shea's voice
was sickly sweet, his pale little eyes entreating.

'Fine.' Catherine's voice was even. 'But can we make it quick? I
have a bloke waiting to be interviewed downstairs.'

'Oh, you do make arrests then?' Shea guffawed. 'I thought most
of your suspects escaped through windows?' Catherine clenched
her jaw as Allan gave an appreciative titter, but said nothing. Shea
gave another little laugh, then picked up a few sheets of paper from
the desk in front of him. Catherine saw he had spilt mayonnaise
down his gaudy tie. The room was hot and oppressive and as
Catherine's eyes flicked towards Allan, the other woman bit her
lower lip. Catherine felt nauseous; Allan was about as seductive as

a pool of sick. The whole thing was pathetic, a scheme designed to make everyone so uncomfortable that they turned on Knight, reasoning that if he went, Shea and Allan would too. Why else would the two of them still be here? They seemed to have done precious little detecting.

'Now, we've spoken to DCI Kendrick as well as the various detective constables you have littering the place up. Not the brightest sparks in the world, are they?' Again, Catherine ignored the jibe. Shea smiled. 'No, they wouldn't say a word against you either, even though you made a pretty catastrophic error of judgement a few weeks ago, didn't you? In fact, they all seem to think you're great.' He tapped out a little tune on the desk top with his fingertips. 'Standards around here must be lower than what DS Allan and I are used to. Anyway, they did have some interesting things to say about DI Knight.'

'The DCs did?' Catherine smiled. 'Amaze me.'
Shea bared his teeth. 'Not the DCs as such, but people have told us he's odd, weird, and that he's not a team player.'

'He is odd.' Catherine nodded. 'Weird too. Aren't we all?'

'Speak for yourself,' Allan sniped. Catherine beamed at her.

'And as for not a team player, well, did any of his actual team say that?' Shea studied his notes again but didn't speak. 'Thought not. However much you pry and poke around, however much you want DI Knight to be bent or whatever you're trying to make out he is, you're not going to find anything, and you also won't find one officer in this station who will take your side.' She stood up. 'Can I go now?'

Shea waved a hand. 'Suit yourself. I'll tell you what though, Sergeant Bishop.'

She gripped the door handle, then turned back, angry with herself for taking the bait. 'What?'

'I don't think you know Jonathan Knight at all.'

Alex Lambert's solicitor was a smart suited woman in her late twenties. Back in the interview room, she introduced herself as Sophie Townsend.

'Can we get on with it, Sergeant Bishop?' Lambert asked. 'I have an important meeting this afternoon.'

Catherine ignored him again, flipping through the pages of her notebook, taking her time. Townsend eyed her.

'My client is right, Sergeant. Is there a point to us being here?'

'Mr Lambert, where's Lauren Cook?' Catherine barked. Lambert stared for a second, then recovered himself.

'How should I know? On holiday, isn't she?'

'You tell me.'

Lambert's laugh was scornful. 'She works in packing, she's not someone I chat to. How should I know where she is?'

'You've no idea?'

'No, Sergeant, I haven't. Blackpool? Benidorm? Somewhere cheap and tacky with lots of booze, I'd have thought.' Lambert sniffed.

Catherine met his eyes. 'It's good to see you have such a high opinion of your staff.'

Lambert spread his hands. 'I'm not judging, it just seems to be what they like to do.'

'You're not a drinker then?'

'I prefer a decent wine or a good whiskey.'

'Of course you do. What about drugs?'

'Drugs? I never touch them.'

'You never touch them now, or you've never touched them ever?'

'Never. What has this got to do with anything?' demanded Lambert.

'So you're saying that you have never taken any form of illegal drug?' Dave put in.

'That's exactly what I'm saying.'

'What about selling drugs?'

'Selling them? What are you talking about?'

'It's a simple enough concept, Mr Lambert. Someone gives you money in exchange for drugs. Like a shop?' Dave added helpfully. Lambert glared.

'This is ridiculous. I'm not a drug dealer.' He turned to Townsend. 'Can they do this?'

The solicitor tapped her notepad on the table. 'Is my client being charged with anything, Sergeant, or are these accusations entirely baseless?'

'We're not making accusations, Ms Townsend. We have a witness who is willing to swear that Mr Lambert offered to sell him drugs.' Catherine watched Lambert, but he didn't seem perturbed.

'A witness? Is his name Jason Garner, by any chance?'

'His name is irrelevant.'

'This whole conversation is irrelevant. Garner hates me because I . . . well, I slept with his girlfriend. He'll say anything to get me in the shit.'

'You deny offering to sell drugs to employees of the club you part-owned?' Catherine asked. Lambert's eyes burned. 'Yes, I do deny it. It didn't happen.'

'What about offering them a sample, with a view to purchasing later?' Dave persevered. Lambert switched his glare to him.

'What?'

'A small sample of your wares, just as a taster.' Dave raised his eyebrows. 'Like pieces of cheese in a supermarket.'

'I did not offer anyone drugs,' Lambert spat. There was a pause and then Catherine opened a brown folder that she held on her lap.

She took out a photograph and lay it on the table in front of
Lambert, who glanced down at it.

'Who's that?' he asked.

'Again, Mr Lambert, you tell me.'

'I don't know her.'

'You're sure?'

'I've just said so, haven't I?' The smooth manner had gone;
Lambert was on the defensive.

'How about this one?' Catherine slid another image over the table
top. Lambert looked at it then turned his head away, his horror
appearing to be genuine.

'Jesus Christ.'

Sophie Townsend also averted her eyes.

'Unacceptable, Sergeant.' Her voice was tight.

Catherine ignored her. 'Both photographs are of Keeley Pearce, Mr
Lambert,' she said. 'Do you remember her now?'

'No.' He wouldn't look at the photograph.

'She worked at Worthy and Son for a couple of weeks.'

'So what?' Lambert ran a hand across his lips.

'Did you offer her drugs too?'

'I don't even know who she is.'

'Did you offer her drugs?' Catherine wasn't going to let it go.

'No, I fucking didn't!'

'Did you do this to her face?'

'No! What do you think I am?' It was a plea, but Catherine ignored it.

'As you can see, Keeley Pearce is dead. She died of a drug overdose. What do you say to that, Mr Lambert?'

Townsend butted in. 'Sergeant Bishop, my client has already told you he doesn't know who this woman is.'

'I've never seen her before,' Lambert bleated.

'And once she was dead, someone destroyed her face with a shovel. Was that you, Alex? Did you do that?'

'Sergeant, I really must . . .' Townsend tried again.

'Have another look at the picture, Alex. Did you smash Keeley's face in? Were you angry with her? Tell us what happened.'

Lambert shoved the photos away with a sweep of his hand and they fluttered to the floor, Keeley's smiling face covered by the terrible image of her battered one. Lambert rubbed his hands over his eyes, then took a deep breath.

'I swear to you, I didn't do that. I remember her face now, yes, I admit it. I don't think I even spoke to her though. I promise you, I swear on my life. I couldn't do that to anyone.' He nodded towards where the pictures lay without actually looking at them. Catherine exchanged a glance with Dave, who said: 'So did you get someone else to do it?'

Lambert turned to him. 'Someone else?'

'Yeah. You don't seem the sort of bloke to get your hands dirty.' Dave gave a guileless smile. Lambert laced his hands on the scratched table top with a sigh. 'I haven't battered anyone and I haven't told anyone else to do it either. This is stupid.'

'You seem quite wealthy, Mr Lambert,' Catherine said. 'Nice car, designer clothes?'

'My client's financial circumstances are none of your business, Sergeant,' Townsend sniffed.

'That depends on where the money came from, doesn't it?'

'I earn a decent salary, plus bonuses,' Lambert sneered, rallying a little. 'Four or five times more than you do.'
Catherine laughed. 'Good for you.'

'So your only source of income is your wages from Worthy and Son?' Dave probed.

'My salary, Constable. I don't earn wages. I also own a couple of properties which bring in rental income. My accountant deals with all the details.'

'I thought you were an accountant?' Catherine shot back.

'I am.' Lambert raised his chin.

'Properly qualified?'

'Chartered,' he smirked. 'Good enough?'

'Yet someone else deals with your rental properties?'

'I've a full time job with Worthy and Son, I don't have time to deal with tenants as well.'

'So you just take the money?'

Lambert gave a scornful laugh.

'The market's not what it used to be, Sergeant, believe me.'

'I'll have to take your word for it. Do you have other business interests?'

'Not really. I own two shops in town and three small houses, all of which are rented out. I'm trying to sell the shops, as a matter of fact, but it's not proving easy.'

'Why not?'

'Because they're empty half the time and no one wants them. Look around you - Northolme isn't exactly a shopper's paradise.'

'Some businesses are thriving though,' Dave said.

'Such as? Fast-food places and cheap clothes shops. Not my idea of business.' Lambert shook his head.

'Drugs are always popular.' Catherine stared at him.

'Sergeant, Mr Lambert has told you he isn't involved with drugs and never has been. Can we move on?' Townsend was firm.

'Of course. In fact, let's take a break.' Catherine stood up and smiled at them. 'We'll speak to you again soon, Mr Lambert.'

41

'Would you like a biscuit, Inspector?' Margaret Saddler pulled a packet of chocolate chip cookies from her desk drawer and offered them to Knight.

'Thank you.' He bit into one, then took a mouthful of tea, struggling to fit his finger through the tiny handle of the bone china cup. Margaret replaced the packet, sat down and smoothed her skirt.

'Of course I keep them for Mr Worthy, but he'll never know if we have a couple.' She smiled. 'Now then. I hear that Alex Lambert's been taken in for questioning?'

'Well, he went voluntarily.'

Margaret made a sound that was somewhere between a snort of derision and a laugh.

'We all know what that means. He went before you dragged him.' Knight laughed. 'We don't tend to drag people around, Mrs Saddler.'

'Well, you know what I mean.'

'What do you think of Mr Lambert?'

'Alex?' She sighed. 'Cocky. Full of himself. Charming though, and he's always been polite and courteous to me. I speak as I find, you understand.'

'Yes, I see.' Knight raised his cup.

'I'm not sure he's quite the businessman he thinks he is though. Not up to his father's standard, at any rate.'

'The elder Mr Lambert was John Worthy's business partner?'

'Well, in a way. They were best friends, had been for years. They were both widowed at a young age too. Mr Worthy remarried, but Victor never did. Mr Worthy was distraught when Victor died. Heart disease, you know. So sad. We lost my brother to a heart attack a few months ago.'

'I'm sorry.'

She rallied.

'Well, you're not here to talk about me.'

'How did Alex Lambert take his father's death?'

'I don't judge, you understand, but . . . well, Alex was sitting behind his father's desk within three weeks. He spent a fortune redecorating it too. I'm still not sure what he does here.'

Knight smiled.

'What about the other members of staff? Do they like Alex?'

She lifted her shoulders. 'I'm not sure. He's charming, as I say, but he does tend to get people's backs up. He's . . . well, crass, I suppose.'

'Crass?'

'Always going on about his new car when other people are struggling to pay their bus fare, strutting in wearing new clothes every week when most of us have one or two decent outfits for work. Thoughtless.'

'I see. He's not popular?'

She eyed him.

'Now, Inspector, I'm not sure what you want me to say. People mutter about him, of course they do. He's rich, successful and good-looking. Jealousy makes people spiteful. Then again, there have been rumours . . .'

'Rumours? About what?'

'Someone said he'd had an affair with a young girl who worked here. She's gone now.'

'Can you remember her name?' Knight asked.

'Jemima. I can't recall the surname, but I can check. She was just a kid, all of sixteen. Barely legal, you know.' Her face screwed up in disgust. 'Alex is thirty-eight.' She got up, went across to a filing cabinet and opened a drawer. 'Here we are. Jemima Morley. I've got her address too?'

'Please,' Knight replied, scribbling the name down. She handed him a form with all of Jemima Morley's personal details on it.

'Mr Worthy was furious when he found out. He looks on Alex as a son but he won't stand for that sort of thing.'

'How is John Worthy as a boss?' Knight asked. He had a feeling he knew what the response would be.

'Well, I've worked here for almost thirty years now and I've never had a cross word from him.' Margaret smiled, finishing her tea and setting the cup and saucer on her desk.

'That can't be bad. I have cross words from my boss every day,' grinned Knight.

'He has been a little quiet these past few months,' Margaret mused. 'I think he's worried about retiring and what will become of the place if Alex takes over the reins.'

'What do you think will happen?'

'I dread to think. Maybe he'll turn it into a wine bar,' she laughed. 'I have heard . . .' She glanced around. 'Now, this won't go any further, will it?

Knight replaced his cup on the saucer. 'I can't promise to keep secrets, Mrs Saddler. If it's pertinent to the investigation, I'll need to disclose it.'

She nodded. 'Of course, I understand. It's just that the business is struggling. The website design, the printing - none of it is bringing enough money in. I think Mr Worthy is concerned.'

Knight absorbed this.

'And Alex Lambert is your accountant?'

'He has an assistant too, but yes.'

'Could I speak to his assistant then, please?'

In a small room just down the corridor from Alex Lambert's office, Luke Christie sat at a crowded desk, hemmed in by filing cabinets and bookcases. As Knight approached the open door, he looked up and smiled.

'Can I help you?'

Knight shuffled forward.

'You're Alex Lambert's assistant?'

'I am, yes.' Christie made no attempt to hide his curiosity as Knight held out his warrant card. 'You're a police officer?' He pushed back his chair, concern creasing his face. 'Has there been an accident? My parents . . ?'

'No, no,' Knight reassured him. 'I'm here to ask you about Mr Lambert.'

The young man sank back into his chair, relieved.

'Alex? Is there a problem?'

'Would you be surprised if there was?'

Christie blushed.

'I'm not sure what you mean. I'm sorry, there's not a spare chair. You're welcome to have mine?'

'It's fine, thank you. This shouldn't take long.' Knight moved into the centre of the room and gestured over his shoulder with his thumb. 'Plenty of paperwork.'

'Alex is always going on about having a paperless office, but we're some way off that yet.'

'What do you do here?'

'I deal with accounts receivable and payable, invoices, financial reporting, entering data onto the computer system – all the tasks that don't involve actual money,' he smiled.

'You don't control the bank account?'

'No, and I don't open the bank statement. They still come in the post – paperless, you know.' He rolled his eyes and Knight laughed.

'What's Mr Lambert like to work for?'

Christie hesitated.

'He's fine.' Knight eyed him sceptically, and he reddened again. 'A little impatient sometimes,' he allowed. Knight waited. Christie glanced at the door, lowered his voice and said, 'All right, he's a nightmare. I'm looking for another job.'

Knight walked over, closed the door and turned back to Christie.

'A nightmare in what way?'

The young man sighed. 'He never does anything he says he's going to. Payments are a good example. A supplier will chase an invoice, I'll speak to him, promise payment as he's said and then he doesn't do it. We owe money all over the place.'

'He won't pay, or he can't pay?'

'I . . . I'd have to say both.'

'How involved is Mr Worthy in the financial side of the business?'

'I think I've seen him twice since I've worked here, which is over a year now.'

'Not exactly hands-on in this department then?'

'You could say that. He prefers the printing works, I think.'

'Do you know when the last audit was done?'

'No, sorry. I think we're exempt because of our turnover.'

'I see. So Mr Lambert has a free rein when it comes to company finances?'

'More or less, I suppose. He produces reports for the board meetings, but . . .'

'Thank you for your time.' Knight turned away.

'Sorry, but . . . is Alex in trouble?'

'Nothing to worry about.'

'Okay.' Christie didn't sound convinced.

Knight gave a brief smile and crossed the room. Back in the reception area, he called to Margaret Saddler, now tapping away at her computer again. 'I'm leaving now. Thanks again.' She smiled and waved a hand in farewell. Knight pushed open the door and then stopped. Frowning, he turned and strode back over to Margaret's office.

'Can I help you, Inspector?'

'I just wanted to have another look at this photo.'

Following his gaze, she shrugged. 'Oh, that's a few years old now.'
Knight took his mobile phone out of his pocket. 'You don't mind if
I take a picture of it?'

'Why should I mind? It's up there for everyone to see,' she
replied, her eyes not leaving her computer screen.

'Sarge, look at this,' Anna Varcoe said as she hurried towards
Catherine's desk with a few sheets of paper in her hand. Catherine
put down the report she was reading.

'What is it?'

'Keeley Pearce's phone records. The last call she made was three
days before we found her body. Guess who to?'

'Surprise me.'

'Alex Lambert.'

'You're kidding.'

Catherine took the sheet Anna was holding out to her.

'Highlighted in blue. It's the only call she made to him that I can
see though. They spoke for almost two minutes.'

'Bloody hell. Good work, Anna. Are any of the other numbers
Keeley called any use to us?'

Anna shook her head.

'Not that I can see. She didn't seem to phone people too often, she just sent texts like most people do. She did ring her mum and Simmo a few times, but that's about all.'

'Where was she when the last call was made?' Catherine squinted at the data.

'That's the interesting thing. She was in the same area as Lauren Cook when her phone was switched off.'

'So they might have been picked up in the same street?'

'It's possible.'

'We need the CCTV footage then.'

'I've put the request in.'

'We've had Lambert in custody for three hours already.'

'Do you think it's him?'

'He's got some explaining to do, that's for sure. The lifestyle fits, but then as he says, he's on decent money from his job at Worthy's plus bonuses and his rental income, as well as any money he inherited. Have we heard from DI Knight?'

'No, Sarge.' Anna hesitated. 'I hope Rob's not involved.'

'Don't worry about Rob. I don't think he has anything to do with this, but if he has he doesn't deserve your concern.'

'Thanks, Sarge.' Anna met her eyes. 'It's not that I feel anything for him, it's just . . .'

'I know. He's an old friend.'

Anna nodded, grateful for her sergeant's understanding and Catherine took out her phone.

Back in the car, Knight had another look at the photograph he'd just taken, emailed it to Catherine and DCI Kendrick and then tried her mobile.

'Are you still at Worthy and Son?' she demanded, not bothering with a greeting.

'Just about to head back. Have you seen my email?'

'Not yet. Let me have a look.' There was a silence and then she said, 'Oh.'

42

Lauren lay on her side, her knees drawn up to her chest. She pulled the plastic sheeting around her, as tight as it would go. It might as well have been tissue paper for all the warmth it was providing. The concrete floor was like ice, leeching the warmth and strength from her limbs. She shivered, her head empty of thoughts other than those linked to her pain and discomfort. Clamping her teeth together, she managed a sketch of a smile. Lying in the foetal position. What a cliché. She stretched out her legs, then pushed herself onto her hands and knees. She managed to get to her feet and lurched over to where the plastic bottle lay on the floor by the door. After unscrewing the cap laboriously, she tipped back her head and held the bottle over her open mouth, willing just another drop to emerge.

Nothing.

A low moan crept from her as the bottle fell to the floor, bounced, rolled and then lay still. She slunk back to her plastic nest. The puddle in the corner had long since disappeared and she hadn't needed to go again. Not a good sign.

Curling up again on the floor, she closed her eyes. Where was Mark? Why wasn't he looking for her? Where were the police?

A sob choked her throat but her hand was cold and dry as she wiped her eyes. No tears. What did that mean?

She couldn't remember the last time she had cried, before all this had begun. When Nan had died? When Katie Thomson pushed her over in the park? No. No. That was years ago. Pigtails and plaits. Patent leather shoes and mud pies. Katie Thomson was coming around to play. Her mum was having a baby soon and Katie hoped for a brother, because she already had a sister. Lauren had a brother. His name was Mark.

Lauren lifted her chin, blinking hard. No. Mark was her husband. She didn't have a brother, she was an only child. What was happening? Her vision blurred, the plastic sheeting rising from the floor to meet her.

Her heart seemed to thud against her chest, the beat rattling the pain in her head around like a pinball.

'Where are you Mark?' she screamed, startling herself. 'Where are you, you selfish bastard? Don't leave me here. I'll die, you know. I'll die.' She raised her hands and tucked them under her armpits, whimpering. 'Mum. Mark. Mummy. I can't see you. I can't see you now.'

43

Alex Lambert looked relaxed as Catherine and Dave resumed the interview.

'Mr Lambert, you told us earlier that you couldn't remember Keeley Pearce, that you didn't even know who she was. Correct?'

'Back to this again?' he sighed. 'Yes, Sergeant, that's what I said. I've no idea who Keeley Pearce is.'

Catherine nodded. 'And yet when she rang you on your mobile a few days ago, you spoke to her for almost two minutes.'

'Quite a long conversation to have with someone you don't know.' Dave smiled. Lambert sat up straight, his face stricken.

'What are you talking about? I told you, I've never heard of her.' Catherine pushed the sheet of paper Anna had given her over the table towards him. 'I'm showing Mr Lambert a print-out of Keeley Pearce's mobile phone records.' She indicated the relevant line with a fingernail. 'That is your phone number, isn't it, Alex?'

He stared, his face growing red. 'This is bollocks, I've never . . .' he blustered. His solicitor glanced down at the sheet, then scribbled in her notepad. Lambert ran a hand over his face. 'All right,' he said at last. 'Looks like I'll have to tell you, doesn't it?'

'Mr Lambert, I . . .' Sophie Townsend interrupted. Lambert held up a hand.

'The sooner I explain, the sooner we get out of here.'

Dave smirked.

'We're waiting, Mr Lambert.' Catherine was stern.

'Okay, I lied. I admit it. I lied.' Lambert looked at the two officers in turn, expecting some kind of reaction. There was none. 'Keeley phoned me, desperate for money. I didn't know who she was at first, didn't even know she had my number. Anyway, she begged and pleaded for a while, saying her kids were hungry, she'd no money for the electricity, she hadn't eaten for two days, blah blah blah. A real sob story. I kept telling her I wasn't going to lend her anything. I had to hang up on her in the end.'

'You expect us to believe that this woman phones you out of the blue, asking for money, then happens to turn up dead a few days later?' Dave shook his head.

'It's the truth,' Lambert said, maintaining eye contact. Catherine stretched her arms over her head and yawned.

'We'll see you again later, Mr Lambert.'

'Wait a minute, you can't keep me here.' Lambert sounded outraged. Catherine gathered her papers again with a smile.

'We can, I'm afraid.'

A print-out of the photo Knight had taken lay before DCI Kendrick on his desk. He studied it for a few seconds, turning it this way and that with his fingertip.

'Interesting,' he said. 'So what's your theory?'

'That this is how they brought the drug mules into the country.' Knight was staring at a spot on the wall just above Kendrick's head.

'But why bother to have them swallow the coke then?' Kendrick demanded. 'Why involve the mules at all? Couldn't they just have packed it into a bag and flown it over? It would have saved them money too.'

'It makes no sense,' Catherine agreed. 'Unless it was just a safety precaution, some extra insurance if anyone caught them.'

Kendrick picked up the photograph and frowned at it.

'What do you know about these things?'

Knight shrugged. 'Not much if I'm honest. Looks like a death trap to me.'

'It might have been for Keeley Pearce,' Catherine reminded them. 'And Lauren. I keep expecting her body to be found.'

'We've still no evidence that she's involved,' Kendrick pointed out.

'She must be though.'

'Then where is she? She's had plenty of time now to get the drugs out of her system and trot home with her cash, hasn't she?'

Catherine screwed up her face. 'Yes, if it was that straightforward. We know it wasn't for Keeley. They're taking a massive risk.'

'So who are we looking at?' Kendrick preferred action to speculation. He set the photo back on the desk top. 'Alex Lambert?'

Catherine nodded. 'He's arrogant enough to believe he can get away with anything. We know he's been involved with drugs before, however much he denies it. Our witness has signed a statement saying that Lambert offered to sell him drugs. Also, we know he's charming and persuasive and that he knew both Keeley Pearce and Lauren Cook.'

'Have we tracked down this young girl he's supposed to have had an affair with?' Kendrick wanted to know.

'Anna and Chris have gone to see her,' Knight told him.

'Excellent.' Kendrick pinched his lip. 'We need to get some more information on these kite things too.'

Catherine began to stand up. 'I'll do it now.' She hesitated. 'There is another possibility.'

'Which is?' Kendrick shoved back his chair and got to his feet. Catherine was quiet, thinking it through. Kendrick tutted in exasperation and pushed out of his office door, only to barge back in holding three plastic cups of water which he doled out. 'Well, Sergeant?'

'I'm not sure if it makes sense . . .'

Kendrick gulped his water. 'Let's hear it.'

'Okay. The eyelash has been bothering me.'

'Lauren Cook's eyelash?'

'Yeah. We know it means that Lauren was near Keeley's body after she died, unless they met before Keeley's death and Lauren's eyelash was transferred onto Keeley's clothing somehow.'

'It seems more likely that she was near the body after the incision was made, based on what Jo told us,' Knight added. Catherine glanced at him with a half-smile. She still hadn't had a chance to grill him about his date with the pathologist.

'Yes, agreed,' she said instead. 'So, did Lauren do the cutting? Was she present when it took place, or did she somehow find the body afterwards? We know that Keeley didn't die at the side of Moon Pond.'

'We still need to find out where she did die,' Kendrick pointed out. 'What have we got?'

Knight fidgeted. 'We made a few enquiries but we didn't get very far. There was nothing to go on, either from the post-mortem or from the crime scene reports.'

'Wait a minute,' Catherine interrupted. 'Alex Lambert owns several properties, he told me so himself.'

'Would he have done that if he knew a woman had died in one of them? I suppose it looks less suspicious than if we found out and he'd said nothing,' Kendrick answered himself. 'Let's get some addresses and we'll take it from there. '

'Would Lambert use a property he owned though?' Knight queried. 'He seems too clever for that. I know we need to check, but . . .'

'What else do you suggest we do?' Kendrick made Knight meet his eyes. 'All lines of enquiry are leading to Alex Lambert at the moment.' Knight nodded, acknowledging the point. Kendrick held up a finger. 'What are you thinking?' he asked. Knight smiled a little. 'Come on, none of your mystery man rubbish. Tell us.'

'There's another man in the photograph, that's all.' Kendrick's gaze flicked over the image once again.

'John Worthy? You think we need to have another look at him?'

'He knows Keeley and Lauren. He has property and we know he likes to give offenders a chance to earn an honest living. I'm just wondering if that's all there is to it.' Knight switched his gaze to the wall again as Kendrick sighed.

'Catherine, what do you think? You've spoken to him.' She frowned.

'It's difficult to say. As Jonathan says, he has access to all that Lambert has.'

'Including a plane,' Kendrick nodded.

'It's a microlight, Guv.' Kendrick flapped a hand.

'Right, let Lambert go, but have someone follow him. I want to see what he does next. Bring Worthy in. Find out about all of his property too. Let's poke him a few times and see how he reacts.'

Catherine checked her mobile as she sat down at her desk. There was a voicemail from the journalist, Helen Bridges, wanting a progress report. Catherine smiled. *Dream on, Helen*, she thought, switching on her clapped-out old monitor. If only they had made any progress. She found a mobile number for the local flying school and tapped the digits into her desk phone. It rang a few times before going to voicemail. She put on her best clipped tones and asked for a call back as soon as possible. Simon Sullivan glanced over from his own desk.

'Scary, Sarge. You should have been a teacher.'

'No chance,' she smiled. 'Can you do me a favour, Si?'

'Tea or coffee?' he winked.

'Now you mention it . . . No, I need you to look at Alex Lambert's property, see where it is and if it bears any relation to the locations we already know about, like Moon Pond. Also, find out if it's standing empty or if it's occupied by tenants or shopkeepers. We're looking for the place where Keeley Pearce died.'

He nodded understanding. 'And where she was cut open?'

'That too.' She shuddered.

'No problem.' He turned back to his keyboard. Catherine tapped her feet on the floor a few times, looking at the phone and willing it to ring. She decided to give it five minutes, then try another flying school. It was early evening, but someone would be answering their phone. She stood up.

'Si?' He span his chair around again. 'Tea or coffee?'

He didn't even go home to pack in the end. There was a bus stop outside the factory and he stepped onto the first one that approached, heading for the railway station and a one-way ticket out of Northolme. If he could get to Retford, he was on the mainline to London, and from there he would be safe.

He might be safe, there was no certainty. He knew too much and he was entirely dispensable. Not a good combination if you wanted to stay alive.

The first step was getting out of town. He sat on the back seat, slumped in the corner, keeping his head down and his baseball cap pulled low. There were a few other people on the bus but no one he recognised. He flexed his hands and cracked his knuckles. Pulling his phone out of his jeans pocket, he checked the display. Ten to six. Almost time. Would he guess that he'd done a runner? No doubt. Not much got past him.

He huddled further down into his coat, his mind racing. What would he do even if he reached London? Get a job, he supposed. Anything would do. Washing pots, cleaning, kitchen work. A straight job, he knew that much. No way was he getting into anything dodgy again. The rewards weren't worth the risk.

The bus trundled through the town centre. He kept his face turned away from the window in case anyone saw him, but kept flicking wary glances at the pavement outside. Groups of young women with pushchairs, laughing and smoking. Men striding along swigging lager or energy drinks from tall cans. A few elderly people dotted here and there, dragging shopping trolleys or carrying a couple of plastic bags. Thick winter coats and boots, trainers and thin, fashionable jackets. He thought about Lauren, locked inside that freezing room, biting down on his lip as guilt coursed through him. She hadn't deserved that. She certainly didn't deserve to be killed. The whole mess sickened him. That girl, Keeley. She'd been so pleased, so eager to have the chance to earn some money. She had plans, she'd said.

She had kids.

He swallowed and checked the phone again. Six o'clock. Nausea rose in his throat and nudged him. He'd be waiting. How long until he gave up and came looking? They were still a few streets away from the railway station. His eyes fixed on the cab in which the driver sat. *Come on mate, put your foot down.* It was hopeless of course. The traffic, even in a one-horse town like Northolme was choked at this time of day.

At least he wasn't due at work until Monday. He'd miss the place, and the people.

Some of the people.

The bus slowed again as it approached a mini roundabout. He took some deep breaths. Another few hundred metres and they would reach the station. The bus trundled forward and he shuffled in the seat, preparing to move down the aisle. He had no bag, no clothes, just his phone and his wallet. He'd lose his flat; no doubt the council would soon realise he wasn't living there and move some other poor bastard in. He didn't envy them. The black spots of mould on the walls that grew back whatever paint or cleaning solution you slapped over them, the constant noise and turnover of neighbours.

He stood as the bus finally lurched to a stop across the busy main road from the station. He thanked the driver and stepped out onto the street, pulling his hat even further over his face. Cars hurried by as the bus indicated hopefully for a while, then gave up and pulled out into the streaming traffic regardless. He glanced from right to left and made a run for it, hesitating in the middle of the road for a few seconds before nipping through the slowing traffic.

The car park had half a dozen spaces and each one was occupied. He hurried across the tarmac, towards the platform. As he drew level with a dark blue estate car, the window was wound down. He hesitated for a second. It couldn't be.

Then he heard the voice: controlled, almost amused.

'And where do you think you're going?'

44

'Which interview room is he in?' Kendrick asked.

'Two,' answered Catherine.

'Nasty.' He cringed. 'Is it warm in there?'

'A bit. It still smells like sweaty Simmo too.'

'Delightful.'

'He doesn't want a solicitor with him.'

'Let me guess.' Kendrick slipped his thumbs through the front belt loops of his trousers and bent his knees. '"I don't need some Fancy Dan with a string of letters after his name babysitting me when I've done nowt wrong."'

Catherine shook her head. 'Uncanny.'

'Where's DI Knight?'

'I've no idea.' Catherine realised she hadn't seen him for ages. 'Who do you want to talk to John Worthy?'

Kendrick bounced up and down on his toes a few times. 'I thought I'd do it myself.'

Catherine looked at him. 'Really?'

He looked wounded. 'Why not?'

'Well, because you're a DCI.'

'A mere puppet master, I know. Come on, you can sit in, give me a nudge if I ask the wrong questions.' He set off across the incident room, gleeful as a five-year-old on Christmas morning. Catherine trotted behind him. 'Did you speak to someone about the little planes?' he asked.

'Yeah, eventually.'

'Is it possible?'

'He said so, yes.'

Kendrick clapped his huge hands together, making a couple of uniforms who were chatting on the stairs jump. 'Excellent. What about property?'

Catherine was hurrying now, trying to keep up with him.

'Similar to Lambert – a couple of houses. No shops though. One house is out in the countryside.'

'Aha. And is it occupied?'

'We're not sure. A squad car is going to do a recce.'

'Just a casual drive past, in no way infringing the privacy of anyone who might be lurking inside the house?'

'In no way whatsoever.'

They were outside the interview rooms now and Kendrick wheeled around to face her.

'Okay. I'm going to be blunt with him because I think he'll respond best to that, looking at the reports and what's been said about him. Do you agree?'

'Yeah, old boys at the golf club is the way to go.'

He looked at her. 'Steady on, Sergeant. Less of the old, thank you.'

She grinned as he stepped up to the door.

John Worthy had his back to them when they entered the stuffy, claggy little room, absorbed in draping his jacket over the back of his chair. As he turned, his face registered alarm for a second at the sight of the DCI, who didn't leave much space in the doorway. Catherine poked her head around Kendrick and chirped, 'Hello again.'

Worthy dredged up a smile.

'Sergeant Bishop. To what do I owe the pleasure?'

Kendrick stomped over to Worthy and arranged himself in the chair opposite him, which creaked and groaned a little but held firm. Catherine sat in the one remaining seat, over to the side of the room, out of Worthy's eyeline. Kendrick was filling most of that anyway. He bared his teeth in an expression distantly related to a smile. 'I'm Detective Chief Inspector Kendrick. I thought it was time we had a chat, Mr Worthy.'

Worthy nodded. 'As I said – a pleasure.'

'Good man. Now, you understand why you're here?'

'Some follow-up questions, they said. I wanted to stay in my office, but the officers you sent were quite insistent that I came down here.' He allowed a little outrage to colour his tone. 'I'm a busy man, Chief Inspector. I trust this won't be a waste of my time.'

'I hope not, nor a waste of ours. Sergeant Bishop has her crochet class tonight.' Kendrick sat back and folded his arms while Worthy tilted his head, trying to figure out whether the DCI was serious. Catherine cleared her throat.

'Starts at eight o'clock, sir.'

'Best crack on then. Mr Worthy, tell us about your relationship with Lauren Cook.'

Worthy stared.

'I've been through this before. She works for me.'

'In what capacity?'

'In my packing department. She knows.' Worthy nodded at Catherine, who bent her head over her notepad.

'And is that all Lauren did for you?'

Worthy narrowed his eyes. 'What do you mean?'

'Not blunt enough? Okay, did you offer her any out-of-hours opportunities?'

Leaning forward, Worthy set meaty elbows on the table in front of him.

'Are you trying to be funny?'

'Not any more. Where's Lauren?'

'How should I know?' Worthy snapped. 'She's not being paid for the extra day she's had off, I can tell you that.'

Kendrick gave another nasty smile. 'You think she's coming back.'

'Why wouldn't she?'

'Do you read the local newspaper, Mr Worthy? Watch the news?'

'When I have the time.'

'So you know the body of a young woman has been found?'

'Yes, Keeley Pearce. Alex told me you were asking about her. She didn't last long at Worthy and Son, I'm afraid. Some people just don't seem to want to work. I haven't seen her since she walked out.'

Catherine raised her eyes to the ceiling as Kendrick frowned. 'Walked out of where?'

'My office. I'd just told her we were letting her go.'

'I thought she was providing some sickness cover?'

'She was supposed to be, but she wasn't even capable of that.' Worthy shook his head in disgust. 'We didn't want her sort.'

'Keeley Pearce died of a drug overdose.' Kendrick's eyes were fixed on Worthy's face. The other man's expression didn't change, though his cheeks flushed a little. He pulled a white handkerchief out of his trouser pocket and wiped his face.

'That's sad, Chief Inspector, but I'm not sure what it has to do with me. I don't employ people who use drugs.'

Catherine snorted and Kendrick let out a chuckle. 'Keeley didn't have a drug habit, Mr Worthy. She died when one of the many packets of cocaine she was carrying in her stomach burst.'

Worthy stared at him, his jaw working. 'What does that mean?'

'It means she'd been employed as a drug mule, paid to carry cocaine secretly into the country.'

Out came the handkerchief again, and Worthy took his time formulating a reply.

'Again, this has nothing to do with me.'

'Can you fly, Mr Worthy?' Catherine asked. He glanced at her.

'Not without an aircraft, Sergeant Bishop.' He gave a nervous titter, then swallowed a few times. 'Yes, yes I have a licence. It's all up to date, I assure you.'

'I'm sure it is. Do you pilot planes?'

'Mostly microlights these days. They're cheaper to run.' He attempted a smile.

'Interesting. And the cost is a factor, is it?'

'Well, yes. We all have to watch what we spend these days.' Worthy blinked a few times and ran a hand over his balding head.

'Especially when your business is struggling?' Kendrick enquired, his tone friendly. Worthy glared at him.

'Now, just a second . . .'

'Are you denying that your company is in trouble?' Kendrick pressed.

'It's not doing as well as in previous years I admit, but it's not struggling.'

'You can see why we've brought you in?'

He glanced from Kendrick to Catherine. 'I've no idea.'

'Let me spell it out. You have access to people who are struggling for money. Your own business could do with a cash injection. You fly planes, small planes that could sneak in and out of the country undetected. A woman who was employed by you dies, and another woman, also employed by you, is missing. We have a witness who states that Keeley Pearce was offered the chance to earn some money as a drug mule by someone at your company. Are you beginning to see our reasoning?'

Worthy's eyes were wide, his face pale. 'It's nonsense.'

'Who are you working with?' Catherine asked now. 'Alex? We know he can fly too. There would need to be two of you to have carried Keeley down the path to where you left her. Two men were also seen with Lauren Cook just before she disappeared.'

Worthy gulped. 'I don't know what you're talking about. Anyway, there are lots of people who can pilot planes around here.' He hesitated, then a look of cunning crossed his face. 'Perhaps I could help you after all . . .'

There was tap on the door and Simon Sullivan stuck his head into the room. 'Can I have a word please, Ma'am?'

45

Maybe when they had to stop at traffic lights he could jump out? No, that wouldn't work. Too risky.

'How did you know where I was?' he asked, finding as he spoke that he didn't much care. Chances were he wouldn't live to see the morning anyway, so what did it matter? The other man laughed.

'There's an app on your mobile that I can use to track you. Haven't you seen it?'

He shrugged. 'I hardly use my phone.'

'No, not blessed with friends, are you?'

'I used to be.'

'Whatever you say. Should have turned your mobile off anyway.' He drummed his fingers on the steering wheel, smiling to himself.

'Where are we going?'

'Do you really want to know?'

They were driving along the side of the River Trent, the blackness of the treacherous waters flowing below them. He turned his head and stared out at the darkened sky. It was bright and clear, thousands of stars visible. It would freeze tonight.

'To see the boss?'

'Well, he is keen to hear your explanation for your top secret trip to the railway station. You've got a date first though.'

He closed his eyes.

'A date?'

'Don't tell me you've forgotten about Lauren?' Fat chance. He couldn't stop thinking about her, alone and no doubt freezing. 'Look on the bright side,' his companion continued. 'She'll be half-dead already.'

'Great,' he mumbled, opening his eyes and fixing them on the road ahead.

'Makes your life a lot easier. I've even brought you some rope.'

'Rope?'

'Look, I understand stabbing someone's a big ask. Strangulation though, you don't even need to look at her, you just keep on pulling.'

He almost laughed. 'Much easier then.'

They were approaching the police station now. He felt the bile in his mouth again, the sense of his life disappearing before him. Stupid. Stupid and pathetic. Why was he sitting here, allowing himself to be driven like this, as passive as a child? Why had he even got into the car? He swallowed as an idea crawled into his mind. It was ridiculous, suicide, but it had to better than being a murderer. It all depended on chance now though.

He slid his left hand from his lap to the side of his leg, careful not to make any sudden movements, then held his breath. The other man hadn't noticed. He was whistling again, irritating and tuneless.

Another second passed before he made a similar movement with his right hand, allowing it to hover near his trouser pocket. It was out of his control now. He stared at the traffic, hoping, willing it.

And then it happened.

The car in front of them braked, then halted. A few people were waiting to cross the road at a pelican crossing fifty meters or so away. Swearing, his companion brought their car to an abrupt standstill. He gulped and moved, knowing he had seconds to act. His left hand snaked out and grabbed the door handle just as his right released his seatbelt. When the door flung open, the other man grabbed his wrist, yelling, 'What the fuck are you playing at?' He yanked away, tumbling onto the pavement hard on his hands and knees. His palms burned as he scrambled to his feet. The driver stared at him for a second, then shook his head. 'You're a dead man,' he snarled, wrenching off his own seatbelt.

Move! he told himself, and started to run. The police station was a couple of hundred metres away. If he made it, even if he reached the pavement outside, he'd be safe.

His bruised knees screamed out as he pounded along, his cheap plimsolls allowing every stone to punch painfully into the soles of his feet. He could hear the grunts of the other man pursuing him.

He kept running, dodging an elderly man walking a Jack Russell, skirting round a group of laughing teenagers. One girl shouted, 'My mate fancies you!' as he ran by. Their giggles rang in his ears as his breathing became laboured. He was slowing, a stitch burning his body, his saliva thick and choking.

He held a hand to his side, panting. Why was he so unfit? He was jogging now, limping along, willing his aching knees to move a little faster. He couldn't hear the other man – had he given up?

There was a squeal of tyres behind him, and a theatrical scream rose from the gang of teenagers as the car he had just escaped from accelerated up the road, its engine roaring. The rest of the group cheered, waving their hands in the air like football supporters whose team have just scored a goal. He covered his face with his hands. At least the other man didn't have a gun – or did he? He waited for the crack, the pain.

Nothing happened. The car flew past as he stood there panting, its lights disappearing around the corner. He swallowed again, tasting blood on his tongue. The police station stood in front of him, a few lights flickering. He wanted to turn and run again but he knew what he had to do. Glancing up at the stars again for a second, he turned and began to limp down the path.

He tried to push open the door, but it held fast, and he stared stupidly at it before noticing the sign. The police station was closed.

He let out a roar of frustration. What now? He could call 999, but that didn't seem right. Turning back to the station door, he spotted the out-of-hours number. Without giving himself time to think, he tapped it into his phone and waited until a pleasant-sounding male voice answered. He panted that he was outside Northolme police station and that he had important information regarding a missing woman.

46

Mark Cook sat seething as Celia flicked the TV onto yet another soap opera. Why were they still here? It was obvious that Lauren wasn't coming back, so why didn't they pack their things and piss off?

Geoff stood up and smiled at Mark. 'Think I'll put the kettle on.' Mark watched him leave the room and then followed him into the kitchen.

'How are you bearing up?' Geoff asked as he took the milk out of the fridge. Mark shrugged.

'Okay. I just wish Lauren would let us know what's happening.' Geoff stroked a hand over his beard and said, 'You think she's left you.' It wasn't a question.

'There's no other explanation, is there? The police would have found her by now otherwise. It's been over a week, she obviously wants to stay away.'

Geoff winced as Celia's voice rang out in the other room, telling someone on the screen they were 'a bloody fool if you take him back.'

'Why don't we go down to the police station now?' Mark suggested. Geoff looked at him, surprised. 'Just one last time. If they send us away again, that's it, I'll assume Lauren's left me and start trying to move on.'

'Won't they be closed by now?'

'I don't know. Surely there'll be someone around?'

Geoff thought about it, then nodded. 'It's got to be worth a try. All right. I'll tell Celia we're nipping out for a pint.'

Celia's eyes didn't leave the screen, she just waved a hand in her husband's direction. Geoff smiled to himself and closed the door.

'Come on then,' he called to Mark.

'Are you okay to drive?' Mark asked, shrugging on his coat. 'God knows when we'll get our car back.'

'Of course. If they can't help us, Celia and I will leave tonight, I promise.'

Mark smiled in spite of it all. 'Putting your foot down?'

Geoff managed a laugh as they left the house and stepped out into the cold air. 'I'm not sure I'd go that far.'

In the corridor, Catherine waited.

'What is it, Si?'

'I thought you'd want to know – John Worthy owns a house in the middle of town, smack bang in the area where we lost both Keeley and Lauren's phone signals.'

She beamed at him. 'Brilliant, thanks. I think the DCI's got him on the ropes already.'

Sullivan grimaced. 'I wouldn't want him interviewing me.'

'Worthy's none too keen either. A search warrant for this house you've found and we might just have him.' Catherine smiled.

They heard hurried feet approaching and PC Nathan Collins turned the corner.

'DS Bishop, I've been looking for you.'

'What's up, Nathan?'

'We've had a call from Headquarters. They say that there's a bloke here wanting to talk to someone – he told them he knows where Lauren Cook is.'

'He's here?' Catherine frowned.

'Standing outside the main door.'

She stared at him for a second, then began to run.

'Tell the DCI, Si,' she called over her shoulder. 'Come with me, Nathan.'

They raced down the dark, echoing corridor, the lights above them suddenly glowing as their movement was sensed.

'What else did they tell you?' Catherine gasped.

'Nothing. I thought you'd want to talk to him straight away.'

They ran out into the car park, their breath dancing around their faces in the chill night air. When they rounded the corner of the looming building, they saw him standing there, his shoulders hunched against the cold in his thin jacket. Catherine slowed to a brisk walk as he turned to face them, tears coursing down his cheeks.

'Sergeant Bishop,' he croaked. 'I'm sorry.'

She stared at him, not understanding, trying to work out what they'd missed.

'Do you know where Lauren is? Is she okay?' she demanded.

He straightened his back, wiped his hands over his face and finally met her eyes. 'We'll have to be quick.'

'Nathan, we need a squad car.'

47

Geoff adhered to the speed limits, keeping a strict two car lengths between himself and the vehicle in front. In the passenger seat, Mark was biting his nails in frustration. He'd forgotten about Geoff's driving style - it would have been quicker to walk. Geoff's car was less than a year old, top of the range, and deserved a driver who knew how to handle it. Mark's palms itched as he thought about offering to take the wheel.

'We take a left here, don't we?' Geoff asked.

'Yeah, then the next right.' Mark tapped his fingers on his knees. 'I'm not sure if they'll be open by now though.'

Geoff didn't take the hint, slowing down even more as a jogger approached a pedestrian crossing, then changed his mind and ran on. Mark sighed.

After another minute or so dragged by, Geoff's mobile phone began to ring in his pocket. Mark hid a smile as his father-in-law's eyes searched for a safe place to stop.

'I'd better answer, it'll be Celia. Maybe Lauren's been in touch.' He indicated and pulled in at the side of the road while Mark bit back a smart reply. He doubted it somehow.

'Blues and twos?' PC Natalie Roberts asked again as she gunned the engine.

'Definitely,' Catherine replied, leaning forward and hitting the button to start the siren and flashing lights. The car leapt forward, onto the main road. Catherine turned in her seat, glaring over her shoulder at Dan Raynor who slumped in the back, his grazed hands now cuffed in front of him.

'So tell me how you fit in,' she demanded. 'I can't think you're in charge.'

Raynor squirmed. 'No, I'm not.'

'Well?' Catherine barked. Natalie executed a sharp left turn and Catherine grabbed the seat for support. Dan wasn't so lucky and was flung to the side, hitting the car door next to him with a thud.

'Sorry about that,' Nat muttered. When Dan managed to right himself, Catherine leaned closer.

'Look, Dan, if you want to help yourself, you need to start talking. You've made the right decision in coming to us, but now we need all the information you can give us.'

'I just want to make sure Lauren's okay,' he sniffed. 'None of this was meant to happen, no one was supposed to get hurt.'

'Yeah, well someone did.' Catherine's tone was brutal and Dan shrank back against the seat. 'Because you were greedy, because your wages weren't enough for you, Keeley Pearce is dead and Lauren Cook probably isn't far off, if she isn't there already. Tell me who's in charge, Dan.'

He was crying again, tears and snot mingling on his face as he raised both shackled hands to try to wipe the mess away. Catherine sighed, exasperated. Glancing over the top of Raynor's head she could see another squad car in hot pursuit, with Nathan Collins behind the wheel and Kendrick's bulk filling the passenger seat. In the back were most of the rest of the team: Anna, Dave and Simon. Knight was still absent and no one seemed to know where he'd gone. Chris Rogers and more uniformed officers were also on their way, as well as an ambulance. Catherine gritted her teeth.

'Tell us what we're dealing with here, Dan,' she urged. 'Are your friends going to be waiting for us? Will they be armed? John Worthy's out of action, locked in a cell back at the station, so you don't need to worry about him.'

Dan looked puzzled. 'Mr Worthy?'

Catherine clung on again as the car lurched to the right. They were out of town now, heading into the quiet country roads that surrounded Northolme. Hedgerows flew by, illuminated every second or so by the wheeling blue lights.

'Two miles, Sarge,' Natalie said, her jaw clenched in concentration.

'Why have you locked Mr Worthy up?' Dan whinged, his voice that of a confused child. Catherine glared at him.

'Because he's behind all this, isn't he?'

Confused, Dan shook his head.

Mark watched as Geoff pulled his mobile out of his cardigan pocket. It was a battered old thing; Lauren had often teased him about it, asking when he was going to get a smartphone, and Geoff had just smiled. Checking the display, Geoff frowned a little and lifted it to his ear. Mark could hear an agitated male voice, though he couldn't make out what was being said. He glanced at Geoff, whose expression had changed, his skin seeming paler than it had before. Mark held his breath – not more bad news? He knew Geoff had an elderly aunt that he worried about.

'I'm on my way. You'll get there first - you know what to do.' Geoff shoved the phone back in his pocket and stamped on the accelerator. Mark's head was thrown back and he gripped the door handle, fear pitting his stomach.

'Okay, Geoff?'

Geoff gave a quiet laugh.

'Not exactly, Mark, no.'

'Where are we going? Is it your aunt?'

As the car screeched around a mini roundabout and his father-in-law bent over the wheel, Mark took out his own phone.

'I'll ring Celia and tell her . . .'

'Turn it off,' Geoff snarled, wrenching the steering wheel to the right.

'But . . .'

'Do as I fucking say.'

Mark, terrified now, did as he was told. Geoff was almost unrecognisable as the mild-mannered, gentle man he knew. His teeth were bared like an angry dog as he urged the car forward. Mark folded his shaking hands in his lap, not wanting to do anything to further antagonise Geoff. Whatever was going on, he wanted no part in it.

As they sped along, Geoff leant even closer to the windscreen. He smiled a little, the sort of leer a predator might give its prey.

'Almost there,' he muttered.

Mark sat up straighter, squinting out into the darkness.

'Almost where, Geoff? I can't see anything.'

His father-in-law glanced at him, his eyes cold.

'You've been wondering where Lauren is for days, haven't you? Well, it's your lucky day. You're going to be reunited.'

48

Catherine gawped, speechless for a second.

'Say that again?'

'It's nothing to do with Mr Worthy, or Alex Lambert either. Geoff Chantry is our boss.'

'Is that good news or bad news?' Natalie asked, changing gear. She turned into a single-track lane littered with huge potholes, most of them filled with water. 'Hold on to your hats.'

'Geoff Chantry? Are you sure?'

Dan widened swollen eyes.

'Don't you think I should know?'

'But that's ridiculous. You're telling me he's known where Lauren's been all this time?' Catherine demanded. 'He's her father, for God's sake.'

'He's Lauren's step dad, not her father,' Dan told her. 'He married Lauren's mum when Lauren was ten.'

Catherine shook her head in disbelief. 'Oh well, that's all right then. Perfectly fine to offer your step daughter a job as a drug mule as long as you're not a blood relation.'

Natalie muttered to herself as they bounced over a particularly savage pothole.

'And he does have a connection to Worthy's – he was the Financial Director until he retired two years ago,' Dan went on, wincing as another jolt threw him up in the air.

'And Worthy told us that himself.' Catherine raised a hand to her face and rubbed her forehead for a second as Natalie swung the car in through an open gate and bumped down a short stretch of concrete.

'This is the place.'

'Thanks, Nat. Right, we need to find Geoff Chantry. He's been staying with his son-in-law, Mark Cook. Have him brought in please.'

'Okay, Sarge.' Nat fumbled for her radio.

The other squad car arrived alongside them and doors started opening, the blue lights still whirling over the brick building that loomed in front of them. Kendrick was out of the car and by Catherine's window, tapping on it.

'Where is she? It's getting colder by the minute.'

Catherine turned to Dan. 'Right, you. Out. Show us where Lauren is.'

He couldn't take his eyes off Kendrick hovering in the window, his face lit up like a Halloween lantern every few seconds. Dan held up his hands piteously.

'Can't you take the cuffs off now?'

'No chance,' she snapped. 'Come on, before DCI Kendrick decides to help you.'

Dan's eyes widened again and he began to slide towards the door. Catherine yanked it open and he clambered out, blinking in the glare of the blue lights. Kendrick grabbed him by the elbow.

'Show us where she is.'

The wail of another siren cut the air and more blue lights were visible in the distance.

'Sounds like our ambulance,' Natalie observed. Kendrick gave Dan a shove.

'Come on.' He marched off, dragging the younger man along with him.

'Guv, Geoff Chantry's the man in charge,' Catherine called after them. Kendrick's step faltered for a second.

'Chantry? As in Lauren's father?' His face was a mixture of disgust and disbelief.

'Step father, but yeah, that's the one,' Catherine confirmed.

'Jesus. Strange how family ties don't matter when drugs and money are involved,' he muttered.

Nathan, Anna, Dave and Simon clustered around Catherine.

'Geoff Chantry? And we never . . .' Dave exhaled.

'I know. Nat's putting a call out for him. Come on, let's find Lauren.'

They caught up with Kendrick and Raynor.

'He says she's locked in that barn thing over there.' Kendrick nodded towards a dilapidated building that stood in one corner of the field.

'Lauren's in that place? I wouldn't keep a dog in there,' Simon sounded disgusted. Raynor said nothing and kept his head down.

'She'll be freezing too,' Anna added, glaring at Raynor.

'Can we get them to bring the squad cars closer?' Kendrick asked. 'We might be glad of the light.'

Anna nodded and spoke into her Airwave handset.

'On their way.'

They kept walking, both squad cars driving behind them. All at once though, another set of headlights sped onto the airfield, the engine screaming.

'Who's this?' Dave Lancaster turned and shielded his eyes.

'Any ideas, Dan? Another of Geoff Chantry's assistants perhaps?' Catherine gave him a prod. 'Well?'

Raynor was terrified. 'It'll be Sid.'

Blank faces.

'Sid?' Kendrick said, shoving his huge face close to Raynor's. The younger man shrank back.

'Sid Benson. He works at Worthy's as well.'

Catherine groaned. 'Of course he does. So you and Sid are the muscle and Geoff Chantry's the brains?'

'You could put it like that,' Raynor sniffed.

The two squad cars had moved quickly to pen the vehicle in. Between them, Collins and Roberts had wrestled Benson out of the car and were now in the process of handcuffing him. Raynor let out a sigh.

'I thought he was going to kill me,' he said. No one bothered to reply and they kept walking.

One squad car was on the move again, Natalie's vehicle waiting by the entrance to the airfield, Benson now locked into the back seat. Nathan kept driving, reaching the squat building at the same time as Raynor, Kendrick and the others.

It was built from red brick; a functional, military-style storeroom that looked derelict.

'It's the other side,' Raynor nodded.

They crept around and sure enough there was another door set into the brickwork with a bright new padlock hanging from the handle. Kendrick kept a tight hold of Raynor as Nathan brought his car right up to the building, then marched him around to the back of it and shut him in.

Catherine was at the padlocked door. 'Lauren?' she called. No reply. 'Lauren, can you hear me?' Nothing. 'It's the police – we're going to break down the door. Stand clear, Lauren, okay? Lauren?' She turned to the others, her face set. 'There's a terrible smell in there.'

'Come away for a minute, Sarge.' Anna took her elbow as Nathan Collins came forward, gripping the handle of a heavy-duty hammer.

'Where's that come from?' Kendrick demanded.

Collins grinned. 'Thought it might come in handy.'

'Just get on with it,' Kendrick snarled, standing well back. 'Where's that bloody ambulance?'

Collins hit the padlock once and it flew off into the grass. 'Pathetic,' he muttered as Simon handed him a torch. He ducked through the door. 'Lauren?'

Catherine stepped forward. 'Is she there, Nathan?'

'She is. She's alive, but she looks bad.'

'I'm coming in,' Catherine said, slipping on some nitrile gloves. Her shoes touched plastic sheeting, crackling underfoot as she gazed around the freezing room. The smell was overwhelming: urine, faeces and fetid, closed-in air. She swallowed a few times. Collins crouched in the middle of the room, where the plastic had been gathered.

'She's tried to use it to keep warm I think.' Collins swallowed.

'For the good it's done her. Gloves, Nathan.' Catherine shoved a pair under his nose.

'Thanks.' He pulled them on as Catherine leant over Lauren. Her eyes were closed, her blonde hair dark with grease and filth. A stench rose from her, unwashed, rotten and terrible. Catherine touched a fingertip to Lauren's cheek. 'You're safe,' she whispered.

Both officers looked up when they heard an engine outside.

'The ambulance.' Collins was on his feet.

'About time.' Catherine hurried after him, knowing the paramedics would need room to work. As she neared the door she noticed a light switch and flicked it, not expecting it to work. A yellow glow fell across the room, flickering and stuttering. She turned back to glance at Lauren. She hadn't moved.

Outside, she didn't see the ambulance she had been expecting, but a civilian car. As she frowned at it, wondering why Natalie had let it through, the passenger door was flung open and Mark Cook leapt out. Geoff Chantry was in the driving seat.

'Where's Lauren?' Mark yelled. Kendrick hurried towards him.

'Mr Cook, you need to calm down.' The police van had finally arrived and was lumbering over the grass towards them. Catherine saw Geoff Chantry's eyes flick up to his rear-view mirror as it approached, as though trying to decide what to do next. She wondered why he had approached the building when it was obvious that the police had already arrived on the scene, then realised that on the single-track road with the police van close behind him, Chantry would have had no choice but to keep moving forward.

'Where is she?' Mark shouted, trying to run past Kendrick, who grabbed his arm.

'Mr Cook, please. Your wife is safe, but we're waiting for the ambulance. You need to stay out here.'

Cook tried to wrestle himself away.

'I want to see her, let me go.' He continued to struggle, but Kendrick held him tight. Anna was approaching the driver's door of Chantry's vehicle.

'Mr Chantry, please get out of the car,' she commanded.

Chantry ignored her, still staring at the police van. Nathan Collins met Catherine's eyes and glanced at his squad car. Catherine gave a tiny nod and Nathan began to move. Chantry's hands gripped the steering wheel and a strange, beatific expression crossed his face.

'Guv . . .' Catherine warned. As Kendrick looked at her, Mark Cook saw his chance, broke free of the DCI and sprinted towards the building. At the same moment, Geoff Chantry made up his mind and floored the accelerator.

With a sickening thud, Chantry's car collided with Mark and flung him to the side. He rolled over and lay still, face down in the grass. Chantry kept going, pulled the car into a sharp turn and sped off in the direction he had come from.

Uniformed officers spilled out of the van, rushing over to Mark Cook who lay motionless. Chris Rogers ran up to Catherine, his eyes wide.

'What the hell's going on?' he shouted. Catherine could only shake her head as the ambulance finally arrived at the gate. She took out her phone and requested another.

49

They stood in a huddle in the incident room, hot drinks cradled in their hands as the shock kicked in.

'That sound when the car hit him . . .' Dave shuddered.

'Don't,' pleaded Anna.

'Have we heard anything from the hospital?' Chris wanted to know.

'Not yet. The paramedics said Lauren was dehydrated, but that she should be fine once they got some fluid and food into her. They didn't say much about Mark though.' Catherine was staring at the grubby carpet tiles. No one spoke for a few seconds, the image of the car's impact and Mark's tumbling body still fresh. Chris cleared his throat. 'Geoff Chantry didn't put up much of a fight, did he? Didn't even have to call the helicopter in.'

There were a few weak smiles. 'Crashing into a hedge after half a mile wasn't the best start,' Dave smirked.

'Now he'll be at the hospital for hours avoiding being interviewed,' Chris complained.

'I'd rather wait for him to be given the all clear by a doctor now than have him say later that he had concussion and no idea what he was talking about when he spoke to us,' Catherine pointed out.

'Yeah, I suppose.'

'So we're just going to hang around until Chantry is brought back here?' Simon was keen to get home to his wife and baby.

'No, you lot go,' Catherine said. 'I've agreed it with the DCI, he's on the phone with Superintendent Stringer now, singing all of your praises. We won't start interviewing Chantry until tomorrow morning anyway. I'm going to have a quick chat with Dan Raynor now to get some basic facts, but other than that there won't be much else happening tonight. We'll want everyone here in the morning, say eight o'clock.' She smiled round at them.

They all finished their drinks and trooped over to rinse their mugs out, then started filing out of the door. Dave hesitated for a moment.

'Sarge, if you do hear anything from the hospital about Lauren and Mark, will you text us?'

She nodded.

'No problem, Dave.'

He nodded and closed the door behind him. She could hear them talking and laughing as they went down the corridor. She pulled out a chair, weariness overtaking her.

As she finished her last mouthful of tea, her mobile phone began to ring. Checking the display, she frowned.

'Jonathan?'

Knight's voice sounded odd, tight, as if his throat were constricted.

'Catherine, do you remember how to get to my house?'

'Of course, but . . .'

'I know it's a lot to ask, but could you come here, please? It shouldn't take long.'

'Come to your house? Why? What's going on?' She heard a deep voice rumbling in the background and then what sounded like a slap. 'Jonathan? Are you all right? Tell me what's happening.'

'Please Catherine, just come here. I'm fine, I promise. There's been a . . . a development.'

'But we've arrested Geoff Chantry, he's the one behind Keeley Pearce's death and the drug smuggling. What other developments can there be?'

Knight paused. 'Chantry? Christ, I never . . .' The deep voice again, impatient and commanding. Catherine felt unease creep through her. What was going on? She trusted Knight, but he was doing himself no favours at the moment, it had to be said. She sighed. What choice did she have?

'All right. Give me two minutes to let them know downstairs that I won't be interviewing just yet and I'll be there.'

'Thank you.'

She ended the call, angry with herself. Why had she said that? She wanted to talk to Dan Raynor, find out what had been going on at Worthy and Son. Now she'd allowed Knight to drag her into one of his mysteries. This wasn't the time.

She sent a quick text to DCI Kendrick, explaining she had to nip out and that she'd be back soon. He would be on the phone with the Super for a while and she might be back at the station before he even realised that she'd gone.

She hoped so, knowing Kendrick wouldn't be amused by another of Knight's "mystery man" routines. She pulled on her coat, shouldered her bag and ran down the stairs. Whatever Knight was up to, it had better be worth her while.

Knight lived in a small village, accessible only by negotiating a maze of country lanes. Catherine threaded her way through them as quickly as she dared, knowing that these roads were never gritted. She wouldn't be able to be quite so smug about Geoff Chantry smashing up his car if she ended up doing so herself a few hours later.

Finally she spotted Knight's grey stone cottage. His car was parked on the driveway, and another vehicle had been shoved in behind it, a huge, menacing-looking black four-by-four. Catherine frowned. What was going on here? She pulled up onto the kerb and sat for a second. Taking out her phone to snap a picture of the unfamiliar car, she felt her heart rate quicken. She only had Knight's word for it that he was here, at his house. What if Shea and Allan were right? What if Knight had killed Paul Hughes? She had believed, during their last case, that she was beginning to know him a little better, but could she truly say she did?

Get a grip, Catherine, she told herself, forcing down the doubts. Kendrick had faith in Knight, and she knew she did too. She climbed out of her car and locked the door, still watching the black vehicle as if it were a vicious dog snarling on a chain of unknown length. It looked empty. There could be someone lying in wait on the back seat, of course, waiting to grab her as she walked by.

She gave the car as wide a berth as possible, even though she knew she was being ridiculous. There were lights on in Knight's house – he was there. She hurried towards the front door and gave it a hearty thump.

It swung open and a middle-aged man in a smart suit stood grinning at her, one leather gloved hand resting on the door frame.

In the other hand, he held a gun.

50

Catherine gulped, her heart apparently trying to escape from her body via her throat. For a second, she thought she was going to throw up all over his pointy black shoes.

'Sergeant Bishop? I'm Malc Hughes. Thank you for coming.' He waved the gun airily, beckoning her inside. It was the last thing she wanted to do, but she wasn't going to say so, not to him, and not to the gun. He stepped back as she stumbled forward, closed the door and turned to her.

'Your boss is in the living room with some associates of mine.' Swallowing hard, Catherine took a couple of steps, then faltered. Hughes stopped too and gave a chuckle. 'I'm not going to hurt you, if that's what's worrying you.'

Catherine half-turned and looked him in the eye.

'And I'm supposed to believe that?'

He smiled and waved the gun again. She set her jaw and marched into the living room, his footsteps heavy on the wooden flooring as he walked close behind her. Knight stood in the middle of the room with his hands in his trouser pockets. He didn't look worried, and Catherine felt panic clutch her stomach again. Why had she come here alone? Knight was odd, people kept her telling her so. What if his oddness was a cover for more sinister behaviour? Had he been working for Malc Hughes all along? It wasn't unheard of, of course. The memory of that rough, jagged tattoo lurking on his back again flitted into her brain. A warning, a threat as Knight himself had said, or a brand of ownership? She clenched her jaw and held her head high. She wasn't going to let them see how frightened she was.

Then Knight turned his head and met her eyes, and at once, she knew she could trust him. She had no idea why; he didn't speak, didn't even mouth words of reassurance, but she was certain all the same. She risked a shaky smile, and Knight nodded. Hughes stepped forward.

'You're no doubt wondering why you've been asked to come here, Sergeant Bishop?' he asked, his tone pleasant.

'It's crossed my mind,' she admitted, pleased to hear that her voice didn't betray her fear. Hughes laughed before raising his voice to a shout. 'Come in here.'

Catherine heard footsteps in the hallway and two men shuffled into the room, one fairly short, the other tall and thin. They were handcuffed together, their faces bruised and bleeding. Catherine stared at them, then at Knight. Hughes glared at his prisoners, his eyes venomous, his lips drawn back over his teeth in a snarl.

'These are then men that murdered my son.'

There was a silence. The men didn't deny it, just stood looking down at their shoes. Hughes walked over to Knight and held out the gun.

'This belongs to him.' He nodded at the taller man. 'Might come in handy for evidence?'

Knight came to life at last.

'Catherine, do you have any gloves?'

Catherine stared at him, then rummaged in her bag, feeling as though she were sleepwalking. These men had killed Paul Hughes? And Malc was just handing them over as if they were some lost property he'd found?

'Here.' She handed Knight a pair of gloves and an evidence bag.

'Thanks.' Knight slipped on the gloves, took the gun from Hughes and dropped it into the bag.

'Then there's this.' Hughes nodded at the smaller man, who swallowed. With his free hand, he removed a digital camera from the inside pocket of his jacket and held it out.

'Those photos that that wanker Shea has? They were taken on this camera. No doubt their prints are all over it and maybe even some of Paul's blood,' Hughes said. His voice was quiet, emotionless. Catherine wondered what he was feeling under the surface, what he saw when he closed his eyes at night. She pulled out another evidence bag and allowed the man to meekly deposit the camera inside.

Hughes jerked his head towards his prisoners. 'Their names are Miodrag Adzic and Petar Latas,' he said. 'They killed my son. They've confessed, and I'm sure you'll be able to prove it was them with DNA or whatever magical tests you use these days.' Knight and Catherine kept quiet. Hughes lifted his arm and glanced at a huge, expensive-looking watch. 'Now I have to go, it's past my bedtime.' He moved close to Catherine, and though her instinct was to run, she held her ground. He held out a hand and she shook it. 'Good to meet you, Sergeant Bishop. We won't be seeing each other again though, more's the pity.' She caught a whiff of expensive aftershave as he turned away, and her breath caught in her throat. 'And Jonathan.' Hughes didn't shake Knight's hand, just leant close and whispered in his ear. Knight shied away like a startled horse and Hughes laughed. He marched up to the two men and suddenly, his arm whipping out as fast as a striking snake, grabbed the smaller one by the throat. 'I hope I never see you two again. You remember what I've said.' Both men nodded, their faces clenched tight like fists. Hughes smiled in satisfaction and let go. 'I'll see myself out.'

He sauntered away.

Catherine waited until she heard the front door close and the engine of the black four-by-four roar as Hughes sped away. She let out a breath she hadn't been aware of holding and rounded on Knight.

'Well?' It was almost a scream. Knight came closer and took her arm.

'Let's go into the other room.'

Catherine glanced at the two men.

'What about them?'

'They're not going anywhere.'

In the kitchen, Catherine ran her hands through her hair.

'Do you want to tell me what's going on, why you've got a gangster as a house guest?'

'He's not a house guest. I doubt I'll ever see him again.'

'So what happened? How are you going to explain this? That you just came home and found two murderers and two bags of evidence in your living room? Maybe Father Christmas left them for you, I don't know.' Knight was trying to speak but she kept ranting, all of the frustrations of the past few days spilling out. 'This is the end of your career, you know that, don't you? Shea and Allan are dying to get you sacked and here you are having a fucking dinner party with Malc Hughes. Why did you phone me? If you want to end your own career, then that's up to you but I don't see why I should be dragged down with you.' She ran out of steam and Knight stepped forward.

'Catherine, I know how it looks . . .'

'Really,' she spat.

'Listen, let me explain. Shea had me in the Super's office again earlier, going on and on about those stupid photos again. While I was in there, my mobile rang. Shea got a bit shirty and told me I might as well answer it. It was Hughes.'

'While you were still talking to Shea?'

'Yeah, great timing. He'd phoned me earlier as well, but I cut him off. God knows how he got my number. Anyway, he said since Shea and Allan interviewed him he'd been making some enquiries of his own. When I asked where he was, he told me he was sitting on my sofa.'

'What?'

'He was too. I walked in and there he was, as large as life, with the gun on his lap and those two blokes sitting on my kitchen floor.'

'Bloody hell. So how did he find them?'

'I've no idea. I don't want to know. I'm sorry to drag you into it, but I wanted someone else to witness what happened. Hughes wanted that too.'

'That's fine, but how are we going to explain it to DCI Kendrick and the Super?'

'I've thought about that. They'll have to take the camera and the gun out of the evidence bags first though.'

51

Dan Raynor had been crying again, the dried snot and tears covering the lower half of his face like a half-shed skin. He glanced up as Catherine and Knight entered the interview room. Catherine readied the recording equipment, and they ran through the preliminaries.

'Now, Dan. You've decided to proceed without having a solicitor present?' Catherine asked.

He sniffed.

'I don't want anyone.' He looked up at them, his eyes red and puffy. 'Is Lauren okay?'

'We've heard from the hospital. They're going to keep her in for a few days, but she'll be fine.'

'What about Mark?'

Catherine cleared her throat. 'His legs were badly damaged and he suffered internal injuries.' Dan's lips quivered but he fought for control as he watched Catherine's face. She met his gaze. 'I'm afraid Mark Cook died before the ambulance reached the hospital.'

'I can't believe Geoff would do that to him.' Dan whispered. Then he hesitated, a tiny, mirthless smile creeping across his face. 'No, wait. Of course I can.'

'We need to ask you some questions about Geoff Chantry,' Knight said.

'Of course,' Dan gulped.

'Explain to us how Keeley Pearce died.' Catherine's voice was flat. Raynor bit his lip.

'She was carrying packets of coke in her stomach. She was supposed to get the ferry back, but she phoned Sid and said she was feeling ill, so Geoff agreed to go and fetch her.'

'Go and fetch her? How?' They already knew the answer, but Catherine wanted the full story.

'He can fly planes. He and Mr Worthy started learning at the same time. It was like a competition. Whoever qualified first could choose the plane they ended up with. They bought it between them. They used to run a raffle at work every month and they'd take the winner up in it. I never won, I'm not that lucky, but it kept people interested, you know? Anyway, all that stopped when Geoff retired and Alex took over. Alex flies as well, but he'd never take any of us up.'

Catherine glanced at Knight. Auditors would be arriving at Worthy and Son's premises on Monday morning. John Worthy had taken their warnings about Alex's lifestyle and Worthy and Son's diminishing cash flow seriously. Meanwhile, Jemima Morley had confirmed that she had been underage when Lambert had first taken an interest in her, during her work experience at the factory, and that he had paid her to keep their relationship a secret. They might never know if Keeley Pearce had really phoned to beg Lambert for money; Knight had suggested that she could have been blackmailing Lambert if she knew he had been stealing from the company, but at this point it was guesswork.

'Tell us about your relationship with Geoff Chantry,' Catherine asked Dan.

Raynor licked his lips. 'I've always worked in packing – it's not a bad job, keeps you fit and they're a good bunch of people. Anyway, I got a call from Geoff one day, out of the blue, just after he retired. He asked me if I'd do him a favour. I said yes, of course. He'd always been good to me, good to us all. He said he had a package to send, a present he'd bought for his wife's birthday he was returning because it wasn't suitable. He didn't want her to see it, so he said if he dropped it off, would I make sure it went out with the rest of the post.'

'And you said yes?' Knight probed.

'Well, yeah. Why not? I had no reason to suspect anything. It was just a small box, well-packaged. He told me it was an ornament and to be careful with it, then gave me twenty quid. That was it, or so I thought. I did the same thing a couple more times over the next few months, thought nothing of it. Then one day, Sid came up to me at breaktime and said he wanted a word. I was terrified. I thought he'd realised what I was doing and was going to tell Mr Worthy. He said he wanted a chat and that he'd pick me up at my flat later that night.'

'And did he?' Catherine asked. Raynor met her eyes and nodded. 'For the recording, please,' Catherine reminded him.

'Sorry. Yes, he did, and we went to a pub. I'd never been there before, it was quiet. Sid bought me a drink and asked if I wanted to earn a few quid. I said yes. My nan's ill and I . . . You have to understand, I didn't know that there was anything dodgy in it, Sid had always seemed such a straight bloke. We drove straight to the ferry port in Hull and collected a young lad.'

'His name?' Knight wanted to know.

'I never knew it, I'm sorry. We took him to this house, scruffy little terrace in town. Sid told him he'd pick him up in the morning and that he knew what to do, then locked him in the bedroom.' He paused and ran his tongue over his lips again. 'I should have come to you then, I should have known . . .'

'How many times did you do that, Dan?' Catherine asked him.

'A couple of times a month for over a year. I'd say around thirty in total.'

'And was it always the same person?' Knight doubted it but wanted to be sure.

'Oh no, loads of different people. Young, though a few were older. I never knew their names. The operation ran like clockwork. I thought Sid was in charge, I never realised the packages that Geoff was asking me to send had anything to do with it.'

'You were still sending them?'

'Yes, at least once a week. I know I must sound like an idiot, but Geoff told me it was stuff he'd sold or he was returning . . . I never doubted it. Then, we had to get Keeley back quickly.'

Catherine sat forward. 'Why?'

'She was ready to come back on the ferry like the others, but some kid was done for drug smuggling the day before and Sid panicked, because we knew how risky what they were doing was and how much all the stuff was worth. Sid phoned Geoff while I was in the car, and it was then I realised who was in charge. Anyway, Geoff ranted and raved for a bit, but he said he'd go and bring her back. I don't know the details, I didn't go in the plane. They bribed people, I know that much. Geoff had his own microlight by then and it could get across the Channel, but not much further without fuel. He must have landed somewhere. We took Keeley to the house and left her to . . . Well, you know. Wait for the stuff to come out. Anyway, I went up to check on her and she was dead.' His eyes widened as he remembered. 'It was awful, terrible. She'd seemed fine, we had no idea that there was anything

wrong. I couldn't believe it. Then they made me . . . Sid made me
. . .'

'What?' Catherine was blunt.

Raynor glared at her. 'Cut her open like a fish, then smash her face
in. Happy now?'

'Ecstatic,' she said, her tone dry. 'What then?'

'Geoff said we had to leave her by the pool so the other dealers in
the area would know we meant business. He wanted her found, but
not identified, to give us some breathing space. I thought it was
stupid, asking for trouble. He talked about some bloke that used to
run the area, said he wanted to make a go of it around here now
this Dougie Hughes had gone.' Neither Catherine nor Knight
moved, and Raynor took a gasp of air. 'Lauren came in and saw
Keeley's body while she was waiting for the drugs to work
through. She shouted at us and tried to get out of the house, but we
couldn't let her. Later, we took her to the airfield. We'd already
seen that old building and Sid said she'd be all right there until we
figured out what to do. Anyway, when you found Keeley, Geoff
said we had to get rid of Lauren.'

Catherine stared at him. 'Geoff told you to kill her? His own
daughter?'

'Step daughter. Yes, he did. He knew who she was by then. When
they were just bringing the drugs in, he never wanted to know their
names. Protecting himself, I suppose. He had to know Keeley's

name and Sid had already asked Lauren if she wanted to do it, because he knew she was short of money. She said no to start with, but she'd had an argument with Mark because he'd spent some of their savings and she was desperate. She didn't know about Geoff and he didn't know about Lauren – he paid some French bloke to fly her back after all the trouble with Keeley. He was always paying people to do things and then giving them a load more money to keep quiet.'

'Including you?' Catherine couldn't resist. Raynor gave a watery smile.

'No point in denying it now, is there?

'There are more people involved in this than we thought.' Knight shook his head.

'So what made you come to us?'

'I was going to do a runner, get out of town, but Sid caught me at the railway station. As we drove through town, I decided that if we went past the police station and I had a chance, I'd jump out. I know I'm in all sorts of trouble and that I'm going to prison, but I thought . . . Well, that way Lauren would still be alive and it would be over. I know it sounds stupid.' He hung his head.

'Was Geoff just in it for the money?' Knight asked.

'He got a kick out of using Mr Worthy's factory for distributing the stuff as well, I think. They had some sort of argument about the payment Geoff got when he retired and I think Geoff saw it as getting his own back, doing it all under Mr Worthy's nose without him suspecting a thing. He wanted enough money to retire in Spain, talked about getting a villa out there.'

'I wonder if he'd take Celia?' Catherine muttered.

'I doubt it.' Dan shook his head. 'Not the way he talks about her.'

Catherine exchanged a look with Knight.

'I think that's enough for now.'

'What's going to happen to me?' Dan's fear was evident in his voice.

'You'll stay here tonight,' Knight told him. 'Tomorrow you'll be interviewed again. After that, we don't know.'

'Prison?'

'Think about what you've done, Dan.' Knight stood up. 'What do you think?'

52

As they emerged from the interview room, a group of people were coming down the corridor towards them. The two men that Hughes had brought to Knight's house earlier were in front, now handcuffed separately. Bringing up the rear were a smiling DI Shea and a scowling DS Allan.

'DI Knight, what a pleasant surprise,' Shea simpered. 'Allow me to introduce Miodrag Adzic and Petar Latas.'

Catherine and Knight looked at the two men, who kept their eyes fixed on the dirty tiled floor, showing no signs of recognition. No doubt Hughes had briefed them well.

'And they are . . .?' Knight asked. Shea drew himself up.

'We've just arrested these two gentlemen for the murder of Paul Hughes,' Shea announced. 'We're going to have a little talk and then hand them over to your custody sergeant for the night, then in the morning we'll take them back to our own station.'

'Where was that again?' Catherine gave an exaggerated frown and Allan's eyes were on her immediately. She gave an innocent smile as Melissa Allan turned away.

'Well, congratulations,' Knight said.

'Solid police work, you see, DI Knight.' Shea smirked as he led his prisoners towards the cells. Allan gave one last spiteful glance over her shoulder before they disappeared.

'"Solid police work."' Knight scoffed under his breath. 'Latas phoning and confessing, you mean.'

'Let's presume he forgot to mention that.' Catherine's face was expressionless.

As they crossed the car park, the wind blowing icy drizzle in their faces, Knight said, 'Thank you for tonight. I'm sorry about what happened, but I swear, if anything comes back about this you'll be kept out of it.'

'I suppose they did murder Paul Hughes?' She didn't want to ask, afraid of the answer.

'It's certain. Hughes says they've even got the clothes they wore while they did it hidden away. There'll be CCTV footage of them buying the petrol, fingerprints on the camera. They admitted it to me before you arrived. I don't think they were lying.'

'If Hughes had threatened them though . . .'

'It was them, Catherine.'

'But why did they kill him?' Catherine shivered, pulling her hands up inside the sleeves of her coat.

'Paul Hughes and a sister of Latas were mentioned. I don't know the details, but I'm sure Shea will find out.'

'I don't like it.'

'Neither do I, but what can we do? They killed Hughes and now they've been arrested. Case closed.'

'But what did Malc Hughes do to find them? What if it all comes back to bite us in the arse?'

'It won't do. It can't. Hughes told me tonight that he's retiring.' Catherine snorted. 'Really? Got a pension, has he? Does a person like Malc Hughes ever retire?'

'When his son is tortured and murdered and he's no doubt made more money than you or I could ever dream of, why not? Anyway, you weren't there tonight, and you don't know anything.'

She gazed at him.

'So I'll have to trust you.'

'Hughes wanted a witness. I'm sorry.'

'And it had to be me.'

He shuffled his feet.

'I trust you too, Catherine.'

Sleet gathered in her eyebrows and she wiped a hand across her face. 'Maybe we're as daft as each other then. Come on, let's go. I'm freezing.'

She turned away and ran towards her own car. As Knight watched her go, a feeling he couldn't define tightened his throat. He got into his car and started the engine before it could choke him.

Regret.

53

Catherine lay back in the bath, closed her eyes and let the warmth of the water seep through her. Thomas was out, she hoped with Anna. They both deserved some happiness. She moved her toes in the water, remembering shared baths, long lazy Sundays, picnics, holidays. She wanted to have that again, the security of knowing that someone was there. She could never have had it with Claire, she knew that. She didn't want it with Louise, and Ellie was a friend. There would be no romance there.

It had been a long, difficult day, and she still wasn't sure how she felt about what had happened. Knight was right, of course: If the two men had killed Paul Hughes they deserved to be brought to justice. She was worried though, caught up in a situation in which she wanted no part. If it had been left to her, she would never have become involved. Had those men really killed him? And even if they had, why would Malc Hughes hand them over to the police? Hughes was a career criminal. Knight had said before that no crime was beyond him, so why hadn't Hughes meted out some justice of his own? Catherine didn't like it, feeling very uncomfortable about her own role, however unaware she had been. Knight had said

Hughes was retiring, but the idea seemed ridiculous. Then again, had Knight been planning this? Had he been working with Malc Hughes somehow? Knight had said there was evidence, and surely the men themselves would speak up if they were innocent, whatever Hughes had threatened them with. Could she trust him? Shea's words floated back into her head: *I don't think you know Jonathan Knight at all.*

She ran the hot tap again, wishing she could sleep in here, the water soothing her as she worried. Knight had said there would be no repercussions, but how could he know that? She was furious with him, angry that she had been dragged into a situation that she didn't understand and had no control over. She had worked hard, always done the right thing, followed the rules and played fair. She felt deceived, caught out and humiliated, and the worst of it was that none of this was her fault.

She hesitated, then climbed out of the bath, wrapped a towel around herself and padded into her bedroom. Picking up her phone, she selected his name.

'Catherine? Are you okay?' Knight's voice was tinny, as if he was far away.

'What did Malc Hughes whisper to you?' she demanded.

Knight hesitated for a couple of seconds. 'He said, "You can get that tattoo removed now."'

Catherine swallowed. 'And what did he mean?'

'I think he meant that we're even.'

'What did you do with the evidence bags?'

'Forget about it.'

She ended the call without saying goodbye, went back to the bathroom and immersed herself in the bubbles again.

Later still, as she climbed into bed, her phone beeped. A text: Ron Woffenden arrested tonight. Ten girls rescued, in hands of social services. Will keep in touch. Owen. Catherine set the phone on the bedside cabinet, tears welling in her eyes. The girls would be deported, back to whatever lives they had been trying to escape before. It wasn't a comforting thought. She turned over, hugged the spare pillow close and hoped for sleep.

54

The beer frothed as it escaped from the bottle and cascaded onto the worktop. Knight grabbed a cloth and soaked up the mess. Taking his drink through to the living room, he settled onto his battered brown leather settee and tried to relax. With the tang of Malc Hughes' aftershave still polluting the air, it wasn't easy.

He set his drink down on the floor and crossed to the log burner. It was late to set a fire, but it was necessary tonight. As the flames took hold, he sat back down and sipped his beer. His eyes were heavy, closing. He might just be able to sleep, if he could put the expression on Catherine's face and the tone of her voice out of his mind.

The flames were dying down when he woke again. He sat up, rubbed his aching neck then crossed to the log burner and opened the door. From his pocket he removed two photographs. He gave them one last glance before feeding them to the flames.

ACKNOWLEDGEMENTS

Once again, my agent Britt Pflüger of Hardy & Knox (hardyandknox.com) has been an invaluable source of advice and encouragement. Her professionalism is second to none and the book would be much poorer without her input and editing expertise. She also helped me with the book's description, a task I was really struggling with. Thank you Britt.

Thank you to my wife Tracy who has always believed in my work and given me so much support and encouragement. Thank you also to my son, Mum, Grandma, Paul and the rest of my family for their constant support.

My friends have again provided lots of encouragement and advice. Thank you all. Special thanks also to Kerry Eccles who read an early draft of the book and kindly provided some very useful feedback.

My thanks to Christa Holland of Paper and Sage Design (paperandsage.com) for another great cover.

Finally, last but not least, a huge thank you to everyone who bought and read *On Laughton Moor*. Special thanks to those people who took the time to contact me about it. It means a huge amount to receive an email from someone who has enjoyed your work and for me is a dream come true.

My website is lisahartley.co.uk and you can follow me on Twitter: @rainedonparade

Thank you for reading *Double Dealing*. Catherine Bishop and her colleagues will return soon.

21936778R00237

Printed in Poland
by Amazon Fulfillment
Poland Sp. z o.o., Wrocław